SHE WILLED HERSELF NOT TO MOVE AS HIS LIPS NIBBLED HERS, SENDING HER PULSE ON A ROLLER COASTER RIDE

This was trouble. But she never wanted it to end.

He drew away, his steely gaze holding hers. When he spoke, his voice was thick and husky. "In case you're wondering, that's what I want from you, Maggie," he said. "Now I want the truth about what you want from me. No pretty lies, just plain honesty."

Maggie fought back welling tears. This was the moment of truth—and the truth had just become cheap and ugly. "I want your father to be our new Santa," she said. "And I want you to reconcile with him so you can work together with the horses and sleigh."

The lines of his face had shifted and hardened. He opened the car door. "That's what I thought," he said. "Goodbye, Maggie."

JANET DAILEY

My Kind of Christmas

ZEBRA BOOKS
KENSINGTON PUBLISHING CORP.
http://www.kensingtonbooks.com

Chapter 1

Branding Iron, Texas, early November

Travis Morgan muttered a curse as he scraped the frost from the inside of his bedroom window. Last night's storm had started as rain. But sometime after midnight, a brutal cold front had swept in, freezing the rain wherever it struck.

Ice had covered the windmill with a frigid glaze, freezing the vanes and connections solidly in place. Wind howled around the corners of the old frame house, shaking the bare cottonwoods along the road and sending showers of ice to the ground. The windmill, however, wasn't moving.

With the cold spell expected to last the rest of the week, Travis reckoned there was nothing to do but climb to the platform of the windmill and free the apparatus.

Swearing under his breath, he layered on warm clothes, laced up his boots, and pulled on thick leather work gloves. Even after nearly a year on this run-down ranch, Travis didn't know much about windmills—or a lot of other things that country-raised folks took for granted. He'd grown up with his mother and stepfather in a mid-size Oklahoma town. As a man, he'd planned to build a future there—until a career with the Oklahoma State Highway Patrol had ended with a botched arrest and a charge of involuntary manslaughter.

Freed after serving three years, he'd discovered that the stigma of being an ex-con would follow him for the rest of his life. Unable to find decent work anywhere, he'd turned to the only refuge he had left.

This small Texas ranch had been in his mother's family for generations. He'd even lived here, in this house, for the first two years of his life, before his parents split up and his mother took him away from Branding Iron. Now that the other heirs had passed on, the long-abandoned place was his— every drought-ravaged, rock-strewn, snake-infested acre of it.

As he opened the door and stepped onto the rickety covered porch, a blast of cold wind hit him like a runaway freight train. He staggered backward. Maybe this wasn't such a good idea. But the storage tank was getting low. If he didn't get the windmill working, the house would soon be out of water.

The rusty bucket that held his tools sat next to the door. Whatever he chose to do the job would have to be small enough to tuck into his belt, freeing his hands to climb. After a moment's deliberation, Travis chose a claw hammer. With luck, a few well-placed blows would shatter the ice and fix the problem. If not, he'd be in trouble. But he would cross that bridge when he came to it.

The front steps were glassy. Bracing against the wind, he took them one at a time. The ground was bare of snow, but everything in sight—the fields, the trees, the sheds, and even his battered '99 Ford pickup—glittered with a patina of ice.

The windmill stood on the far side of the yard. Its height was about average for this part of the country. But right now, looking up from its base, it appeared as tall as a skyscraper. And every rung of the narrow ladder leading up one side was coated with ice.

This is insane! You're going to break your damn fool neck!

Closing his mind to the thought of danger, Travis placed a foot on the bottom rung and began to climb. The soles of his work boots held fine, as long as he placed each foot securely. His hands were another matter. Even through his thick gloves, the cold was numbing. His fingers could barely feel the rungs he was holding. By the time he got to the top, he would have no feeling in his hands at all. But now that he was more than two-thirds of the way up, it didn't make sense to quit.

Minutes later, he gained the platform and clung there, shivering and willing himself not to look down. He'd never been one for heights, but this had to be done. Fumbling under his coat, he managed to pull the hammer out of his belt. He could see where the rain had dripped and frozen in a solid lump, blocking the motion of the gears. He aimed at the spot, muttered a prayer disguised as an obscenity, and struck a sharp blow. The ice shattered, showering pieces over the platform. Slowly, then faster as the wind caught, the windmill began to turn—and Travis began to breathe again.

Thank God for small favors. Now all he had to do was get down.

Leading blindly with his feet was harder than he'd expected. More than once, his boot missed the rung, and he had to save himself by grabbing with his hands. But at least the job was done. At least he was on his way down.

He'd made it more than halfway when the sound of a motor caught his attention. A vehicle was coming down the narrow road that ran between the fence lines. Travis was used to seeing farm trucks out here. But this was no farm truck. Cruising along the road, moving a little too fast on the frozen surface, was a big, sleek, black Lincoln Town Car.

He kept easing his way down the ladder, stealing glances at the Lincoln as it came closer. Travis had an eye for cars. This model, which appeared to be in good condition, was about fifteen years old, the kind of vehicle a well-heeled senior citizen might own. Maybe the driver had taken a wrong turn and was lost. There was no other reason a car like that would be on this road.

He was about eight feet from the ground when the Lincoln hit an icy spot, spun in a half-circle, and slammed into Travis's gatepost.

Distracted for an instant, Travis let his foot slip the barest inch too far. His cold-numbed hands lost their grip. He slipped down several rungs and fell backward, landing on the hard ground with a force that felt like being hit by a ten-ton truck. For the moment, all he could do was lie there and close his eyes until the world stopped spinning. Nothing seemed to be broken. But when he got his breath back and his legs under him, some old codger was going to catch hell!

Maggie Delaney, the newly re-elected mayor of Branding Iron, had driven out to check on Abner Jenkins, whose farm was a few miles out of town. Earlier that morning, she'd called the old man to make sure he was prepared to play Santa in this year's Christmas parade. His landline phone had rung six times without an answer. Worried about the old man, she'd climbed into the big Lincoln that had been her late father's and gone to check on him. She'd found Abner's truck missing from the yard. His house, when she checked inside, had been empty.

After leaving a note on his door, she'd been about to turn around and drive back to town when an impulse had changed her mind. The recently paved road, which cut off the highway and ran past Abner's place, had been an icy mess. Two passing farm trucks had almost slid into her. Maybe it would be better to go forward, following the less-traveled part of the road where it looped through the back country and rejoined the highway a couple of miles to the south.

It had been a bad idea. The rest of the road was even icier. She was already late for her 10:00 meeting with the library board, and now her dad's beloved old Lincoln had slid, spun, and crashed into a metal gatepost, causing a startled man to fall off his windmill.

From the car, she could see him lying on the frozen ground. He didn't appear to be moving. Good Lord, what if she'd killed him?

She flung herself out of the car, her kitten-heeled boots barely finding purchase on the ice-encrusted ground. The car had pushed the gatepost to one side, freeing the gate to swing open in the wind. She hurried across the bare yard to where the man lay at the foot of the windmill, sprawled on his back.

Approaching, she could see the faint rise and fall of his chest beneath the old woolen peacoat he wore. His long legs, clad in faded jeans and worn-out work boots, were moving slightly. At least he appeared to be alive. But he'd taken a nasty fall. He could be badly injured.

Her gaze took him in. He was a stranger—tall and lean as a whip in his worn-out work clothes. Below the knit cap that covered his head and ears, the planes of his face were sharply chiseled, the closed eyes narrow and deeply set.

It was a striking face, handsome in a stubble-jawed, Clint Eastwood sort of way. But how could she be ogling the man at a time like this? She needed to be checking him for injuries and calling 911.

As she bent over him, his eyes opened—slate-colored eyes, their look so cold and piercing that she drew back with a little gasp. His lips tightened. He cleared his throat. "What the blazes did you think you were doing?" he muttered.

With effort, she found her voice. "I was trying to decide whether you need an ambulance. Are you hurt?"

He stirred, wincing as he sat up. "I'm fine. That's not what I meant. You were driving like a bat out of hell down that icy road. You're lucky you didn't break your fool neck—and mine."

"You sound like a cop."

His mouth tightened. "I hope that's a joke," he said.

She stood as he hauled himself to his feet. Maggie was a statuesque woman, almost five foot nine. He loomed over her by half a head.

"I was late for a meeting in town," she said. "I'm sorry for distracting you. And I'm sorry about your gatepost. My purse is in the car. I'd be happy to write you a check for the damage."

"Don't bother. I'll fix the damn thing myself." He turned away from her and walked over to the metal gatepost, which stood askew against the front bumper of the car. Maggie could tell he was in some pain.

What was he doing out here? As she recalled, this run-down ranch had been abandoned for several years, since the people who'd been leasing it moved away in the middle of the night. What was this ragged-looking stranger doing on the property? Was he some homeless derelict needing shelter from the cold? Or worse, a fugitive criminal, hiding out from the law?

Either way, it was clear that he didn't want her around. Maybe she should ask the sheriff to check him out. There was something raw and a little wild about the man. Something that whispered *danger*.

Her key was still in the ignition. If she was smart, she'd get back in the car, lock the doors, and pray that the engine would start.

Travis gripped the gatepost with his gloved hands and tried to pull it straight. It didn't budge. What the hell, everything else around here was broken, why not the gate? It wasn't like anybody was going to come in and rob him.

The car didn't look too badly damaged. Just a slight dent in the bumper. These old Lincolns were built like Sherman tanks. Come to think of it, the woman wasn't built too badly either. Tall and curvy, she was well dressed in a thigh-length tan trench coat over tailored slacks, cashmere gloves, and pricey-looking boots. A green silk scarf flowed around her neck. Its color matched her eyes and contrasted with her shoulder-length mahogany hair. She appeared to be in her mid-thirties. Probably married to some rich dentist or banker. All in all, she was the kind of woman he had no use for—spoiled, pushy, and wearing her upper-class status like a suit of armor.

She was shivering, her hair blowing around her face. He was cold, too. The sooner he got her out of here and on her way, the sooner he could go inside and make a fire in the old iron stove.

The driver's side door, which she'd left open, had blown shut. He opened it and held it against the wind. "Unless you're stuck, you shouldn't have any trouble driving," he said. "There's nothing for you to do here. Climb in, and get back onto the road."

She moved past him, slid her shapely rump into the driver's seat, and turned the key. The big Lincoln roared to life. Wheels spun on the ice as she geared down and backed away from the gate. It took some rocking back and forth, but she finally made it onto the road and shifted gears again. At least she knew how to drive a stick shift.

He gave her a parting wave. "Slow down," he yelled. But she gunned the engine as if she hadn't heard him. That, or she was just being contrary. She struck him as the type.

He watched the car until it disappeared from sight. It would serve the fool woman right if she slid off the road again. But it wasn't his job to worry about her safety. He wasn't a cop anymore.

By the time he'd checked the water storage tank and made sure no pipes were frozen, he was in serious pain. The hard fall hadn't broken any bones, but he ached in every joint and muscle. He knew, without checking, that there was nothing in the medicine cabinet except toothpaste, dental floss, Band-Aids, and a flattened tube of antibiotic salve. If he wanted to make it through the rest of the week, he would need to pick up some ibuprofen and maybe some good old-fashioned liniment. That would mean driving to town—a trip he made no more often than necessary.

Chiseling the ice off the front and rear windshields of the truck took almost half an hour. The forecast for last night had been rain. If he'd known the rain was going to freeze, he would have covered the vehicle with a tarp or parked it in the barn. Live and learn. He'd arrived here late last winter and managed to survive. But the season had been mild, with only one big storm. Something told him this winter would be different.

The truck started on the first try. Travis was a decent mechanic. Last summer he'd managed to get the abandoned tractor running and used the old tiller, rake, and other rusty attachments to raise two crops of hay. The barn was piled high with rectangular bales that were just light enough for a man to lift. When Travis had started up the old hay baler, he'd forced himself to forget that this machine had cost his father one of his legs. That had been thirty years ago, when Travis was a small boy. His father still lived in Branding Iron. But Travis had bitter memories of the man. Now he wanted nothing to do with him.

As he backed out of the gate, which swung loose from the damaged post, he asked himself one more time whether he could really make a go of this ranch. There was so much to be done, and so little in the way of resources to do it with. Maybe he'd be better off selling the land, pulling up stakes, and starting over somewhere new.

Selling the hay to neighboring farms and ranches had given him enough money to live on—but he was barely getting by. He needed more income from the ranch. But buying even a few calves to raise and sell would require money he didn't have, and no bank he'd ever talked to would grant a loan to an ex-convict.

He could look for a job. He hadn't tried in Branding Iron. But facing another string of rejections was more than his pride could handle. A man with his record couldn't be trusted to muck out a stable without stealing the horses.

Gloomy thoughts for a gloomy day. As he drove toward the highway, he made a mental shift to the memory of the woman who'd crashed into his gate that morning. She reminded him of somebody— some actress he'd seen on TV back in the day. He recalled little details, the way her dark red hair curled against her porcelain cheek; the way her emerald green scarf matched her eyes; and the cool, challenging look those eyes had given him. Classy and confident—those were the words that came to mind. Something told him the lady knew how to play hardball. But there was softness about her full lips and amply curved body. She hadn't introduced herself. But that was just as well. He certainly didn't plan on meeting her again—not even if she'd spun off down the road.

Coming up on his left was the home of his nearest neighbor. Jubal McFarland was in his front yard, clearing ice off the front walk. He waved as Travis drove past. Travis returned the greeting and drove on. Good people, the McFarlands. They'd invited him to dinner a couple of times, but knowing he couldn't reciprocate, Travis had made his excuses.

He could almost envy what Jubal had—a prosperous ranch, a loving wife, and two children who'd make any man proud. But Travis knew better than to dwell on what he'd never have. Any hope of such a life had vanished with the thump of a judge's gavel and the clang of a cell door.

Turning onto the highway, which had been salted to melt the ice, was a relief. As he passed Hank's Hardware on his right, Travis noticed a crew of workers unloading cut Christmas trees from a big flatbed truck and stacking them in the store's fenced side lot. Sweet racket, those trees. Hank had the only Christmas tree lot this side of Cottonwood Springs, and he charged top dollar for every one of them. Not that Travis cared. Damn sure, he wouldn't be buying a tree this year, or any other year—especially from Hank.

He pulled into the Shop Mart parking lot and climbed out of the truck. His muscles had stiffened on the ride to town. Even walking hurt like blazes. He grabbed some liniment and some over-the-counter pain pills off the shelves and checked out through the express line. On the way back to the truck, he wrenched the lid off the ibuprofen and swallowed two capsules dry.

The cold wind was bitter through his coat. His rumbling belly reminded him that he hadn't eaten since last night. By now, Buckaroo's Café would be open. A cup of good, hot coffee and a slice of their flaky apple pie would hit the spot. The money would be better saved for necessities, but there were times, like this morning, when he needed something extra.

Travis climbed into the truck and headed downtown. He was hungry, discouraged, and felt like three-day-old roadkill.

So why did he have this strange sense that something was about to happen—something he would never have expected?

Chapter 2

Buckaroo's, on Main Street, was the only restaurant in Branding Iron, except for the B and B, which just served breakfast. Tucked away between a barber shop and a small parking lot, it was mostly a burger and pizza place, but they served good coffee, and the pie, made and delivered by a woman in town, was first-rate.

The place had just opened when Travis walked in, but it was already filling up. The stools at the counter were occupied, as were the three booths. The only empty seat was in the corner, opposite an old man who lived at the far end of Travis's road. The two had met and talked a few times. Abner—that was the old duffer's name. Abner Jenkins.

"'Morning, Abner," Travis greeted him. "Mind if I sit here?"

"Suit yourself." The old man, usually amiable, didn't even look up as Travis slid into the booth.

He was gazing down at his fresh coffee like a death row inmate contemplating his last meal.

Travis had always believed in minding his own business. But something about the old fellow's downcast expression roused his concern. "You don't look so good, Abner," he said. "Is there anything I can do to help?"

Abner glanced up, as if noticing him for the first time. "Not unless you can take ten years off this old body. The doc's convinced my kids that I mustn't live alone on my farm. They've sold the place right out from under me. This week the new owners are movin' in, and I'm goin' to Denver to live with my daughter's family." A tear rolled down his plump, bewhiskered cheek.

"I'm sorry, Abner," Travis said. "But you never know. It might be nice having family around you." Travis paused to give his order for coffee and pie to the waitress. On second thought, he ordered a slice for Abner, too. The old fellow looked as if he could use it.

"Oh, it's not me I'm worried about," Abner said. "It's my two old horses and my dog, Bucket. I can't take 'em to the city with me, and the fancy new owners don't want 'em." Another tear plopped into his coffee. "The horses are old, and Bucket is goin' on eight years. I know what happens to animals nobody wants. Bucket will get put to sleep. Patch and Chip will get sold for dog food, or glue, or whatever the hell they do with horses these days. Those critters are like family to me. Just thinkin' about 'em makes me want to bawl like a baby."

The waitress brought Travis's coffee and two

servings of pie. Travis slid one toward Abner. "This one's for you," he said.

"Thanks, that's right neighborly of you." Abner picked at the pie with his fork but didn't seem to have much appetite.

"Can't you find somebody to take your animals?" Travis asked. "Surely with all the farms and ranches around here, somebody would want them."

"I put notices up in the post office and the library, but nobody's called me. The trouble with Patch and Chip is that they're draft horses. They're gentle, and I've trained 'em good, but folks don't want 'em for riding because they're so big. And everybody's got tractors these days. Folks don't need horses for work anymore.

"Bucket, now, he's a great dog, half border collie and smart as a whip. But people who've got dogs don't want another one. Or if they do, they want a puppy." Abner's sad eyes brightened as he looked at Travis. "Say, what about you?"

Travis choked on his coffee. He took a sip of water to cool his throat. He should've seen this coming before he walked right into it.

"I've been by your place," Abner said. "You've got a barn that's empty, except for the hay you're sellin'. It's even got a few stalls for horses. Patch and Chip would do fine there. And Bucket's a great watchdog."

"But I don't know anything about horses!" Travis protested.

"What's to know? You give 'em hay and water and muck out their stalls every few days. In good weather, you can turn 'em out to pasture. If it's money you're worried about, I'll have a little left over from sellin' my farm. I can give you a few hundred for their feed."

Travis felt as if he'd stepped into quicksand and was sinking deeper by the minute. "I just don't know . . . ," he muttered.

"Hey, what's a ranch with no animals on it?" Animated now, Abner shoveled in a bite of pie. "Tell you what. If you don't want to keep 'em, can I at least leave 'em with you for now? They'll have to be put down if I don't find a place before I leave tomorrow."

Travis sighed. "For now? How long is that?"

"Just long enough for you to find 'em another home. Somebody's bound to want 'em." Tears welled in the old man's eyes. "Please, you're my last hope. Those critters are like my kids. I can't just go off and leave 'em to die."

Travis emptied his coffee mug. "Well, I guess I could at least stop by your place and have a look at them."

"Why take time for that? I can bring 'em over to your place this afternoon and stick around to help get 'em settled in. It'll be no trouble at all."

Something told Travis the old man was afraid he'd change his mind once he saw the animals. But what the hell—even after three years in prison, where he'd seen the worst of humanity, he was still a sucker for a hard luck story.

"All right," he said. "Will you need any help getting them to my place?"

Abner shook his head. "It's only a couple of miles by the road. I can walk the horses over behind the truck, and Bucket can ride with me."

"Fine. I'll be waiting for you. Watch out for the ice."

"Don't worry. I'll be fine. And thanks. There's bound to be a heavenly reward for folks like you."

"Somehow I doubt that." Travis put cash on the table for the coffee and pie and left Abner to finish eating. Only as he walked outside, to a clearing sky, did it hit him what he'd just committed to. He swore under his breath as he walked to his truck.

Why hadn't he just said no? He ought to have his fool head examined!

The sun was already warming the day, melting the ice on roads and sidewalks to slush. At the far end of Main Street, he passed the complex of wings that housed the city and county offices, the library, the sheriff's department, and the jail. There in the parking lot, in the space clearly marked for the mayor, was the big, black Lincoln Town Car that had crashed into his gatepost that morning. At least the uppity redhead had made it safely back to town. But she didn't appear fussy about whose parking place she took. She couldn't be the mayor. Maybe she was the mayor's wife.

Not that he gave a damn either way. She was just one more annoyance in a day that had taken on more trouble than he wanted. There was nothing to do but forget her, go home, try to fix the gate, and get the barn ready for Abner's animals.

Maggie left her desk and, after a word to the receptionist, walked down the hallway to the wing that housed the sheriff's office. The morning had kept her busy, but she still had questions about the gruff stranger at the old abandoned ranch. Maybe the sheriff would have some answers. If not, she would need to make him aware of the situation.

Sheriff Ben Marsden rose to greet her. Superman handsome, he kept a framed photo of his wife, son, and baby daughter on proud display. He and Maggie had gone through school together and were old friends.

"Have a chair, Maggie. What's up?" he asked.

"Maybe you can tell me." She took the chair opposite the desk and related the morning's misadventure.

Ben listened, leaning back in his chair. "You say the man was angry. Did he threaten you in any way?"

"No . . . but he definitely made me nervous. When I offered him money for the gate, he wouldn't take it. And he chewed me out for driving too fast on the icy road."

A smile tugged at Ben's mouth. "That sounds about right," he said.

"You know him?" Maggie asked.

"Not well. But well enough to tell you he's no danger. His name's Travis Morgan. He inherited that old place from his mother's family. He's been living there about a year."

"A year? But I've never seen him before—and I make it my business to know people in town."

"He keeps to himself. I met him last winter when I drove by the place and noticed somebody was there. We talked for a few minutes. All he really wants is to be left in peace."

"After meeting him, I'd certainly go along with

that," Maggie said. "The man's about as friendly as a rattlesnake."

"There might be a reason for that," Ben said, "although I hope you'll keep this to yourself. After I met him, I did some routine checking, to make sure he was who he said he was. He's an ex-convict—did three years in Oklahoma for manslaughter."

"Oh." Maggie's skin prickled. She waited, hoping to learn more.

"It's an interesting story, what I know of it," Ben said. "He was a highway patrolman, pulled over a driver on suspicion of kidnapping. I don't know the details, but things got out of hand, and he ended up shooting an innocent, unarmed man. It was a case of mistaken identity, but he lost his career and did time for it."

"I take it he's still bitter."

"Most people would be. But there's more. It seems he's Hank Miller's son."

"I'd forgotten Hank had a son," Maggie said. "You and I were barely out of diapers when Hank lost his leg in that awful farm accident. I only remember because my parents talked about it later. Didn't Hank's wife leave him after that?"

"Right. And she took their little boy with her. When she remarried, Travis took his stepfather's name. Evidently, he doesn't think much of Hank. As far as I know, they haven't spoken in decades."

"That's a shame. Hank's a good man." Maggie rose, glancing at her watch. "I won't keep you. But thanks for filling me in. Believe me, if Travis Morgan wants to be left alone, I won't have a problem with that."

"You have a good day, Maggie."

"You too. Say hello to Jess and the kids for me."

Maggie walked back down the hall in the direction of the mayor's office. A full day of meetings and appointments lay ahead of her. She needed to focus on doing her job. But thoughts of Travis Morgan and what she'd learned about him kept crowding into her mind. She remembered the chiseled planes of his face and the look in his startling, slate-colored eyes as she bent over him.

He was a bitter man, an angry man, too proud to accept payment for his damaged gate. And yet he'd been enough of a gentleman to open the car door and hold it against the wind. And now that she knew he'd been a lawman, his warning not to speed on the icy road took on a new meaning. He'd been honestly concerned about her safety.

Forget him, she told herself. As long as she knew he had the legal right to be on the ranch, and that he wasn't a danger to her or anyone else, Travis Morgan was none of her concern.

Still, one memory haunted her. When she'd bent over him and he'd opened his eyes, in the instant before his gaze hardened, she'd glimpsed something wounded and vulnerable . . . something she couldn't forget.

Lost in thought, she didn't see the cocky figure coming toward her until she'd almost bumped into him. She gasped and took a step backward. Stanley Featherstone, the constable, who took care of minor violations in Branding Iron, was not a physically intimidating man. But something about him always made her uneasy. Maybe it was his way of edging into her personal space when they spoke. Like now.

"Hello, Maggie." He was so close that she could feel his warm breath. She took another step backward and found herself trapped against a wall.

"What is it, Stanley?" she asked, trying to be polite. After all, she had to work with him—in fact, she was his supervisor. He was good at his job, dutiful, thorough, and always on time. She could find no fault with the man. He just plain annoyed the living daylights out of her.

"I saw you coming out of the sheriff's office just now," he said. "I was wondering what you talked about."

"Nothing to concern you, Stanley. Everything's fine. Now, if you don't mind, I'm late for a meeting." She tried to step aside, but he seemed rooted to the floor.

"I left my weekly report on your desk. I was wondering when you wanted to go over it with me."

"I'm sure it's fine. If I have any questions, I'll call you in. Now I really do have to go."

This time he let her. She hurried away, taking deep breaths to calm herself. Stanley had asked her out more than once, but she'd kept to the ironclad excuse that she didn't date coworkers. At least he hadn't asked her again—a small bright spot in a day that had started out with a dinged bumper, a broken gate, and an encounter with a disturbingly attractive man.

In the barn, Travis had cleaned out two roomy box stalls for Abner's horses, lining the floors with straw, piling the feeders with hay, and filling two big plastic buckets with fresh water. Lord, he didn't know anything about horses—or even dogs, for that matter. Growing up, his stepfather, a fastidious, germ-phobic dentist, had been allergic to animal hair, so Travis had never even had a pet. How was he supposed to take care of a whole damned menagerie?

At least he wouldn't have to keep them forever. An online ad on some local site should be enough to find them new owners. But he was already sorry he'd walked into Buckaroo's that morning and even sorrier that he'd fallen for old Abner's hard luck story.

Wandering back outside, he gazed up the road, expecting to see Abner's old truck approaching with the horses tied behind and the dog riding along. He didn't have a doghouse or any dog food, but if Abner didn't provide any, the dog could sleep in the barn and eat table scraps—or maybe catch gophers. There were plenty of those around.

While he waited, he decided to fix the damaged gatepost. On inspection, the metal didn't appear to be bent, but it was leaning from its base. Travis fetched a shovel and began digging around it. The post was set solidly in concrete, but the big Lincoln's impact had loosened it in the ground and pushed it to one side. It was fixable. But digging around the lump of cement to straighten it would cost him some effort.

He was nearly finished with the job when he heard the growl of an engine and the snorting of horses. He watched the truck come into sight, moving slowly, with two immense gray horses tethered alongside. As the truck rumbled closer, he could see that it was towing something on a flatbed trailer—something big and bulky, covered with a canvas tarp.

"What the hell . . . ?" he muttered as the truck pulled up to the gate. But there was no time to wonder. Abner opened the door and climbed out of the cab. His round, whiskery face wore a grin.

"Well, here we are," he said.

"Yes . . . here you are." As Travis spoke, a scruffy-looking black and white dog jumped down from the cab, trotted over to him, and began sniffing his boots. Abner had said he was half Border Collie. The other half must've jumped over the fence.

"Looks like Bucket's checking you out," Abner said. "That's a good sign. He doesn't take to just anybody."

"Why do you call him Bucket?" Travis shifted uneasily as the curious dog sniffed his way up his leg.

Abner shrugged. "He had that name when I got him as a pup. Don't rightly know how he came by it, but it's the name he answers to. He's a right smart dog. You'll see."

"Listen up, Bucket." Travis scowled down at the dog. The dog looked up, tail wagging expectantly. "If we're going to get along, you'll need to know whose place this is and who's in charge here. Understand?"

Bucket gave a sharp little *woof!*

"Go on, now. Go chase a rabbit or something," Travis said.

The dog's tail went down. He trotted over to the newly straightened gatepost, sniffed at its base, and lifted his leg.

"See, he's markin' his territory," Abner said. "I

told you he was smart. I brought along a bag of food for him. I'll leave it on the porch."

"Fine," Travis said. "Now let's get those horses into the barn."

Abner had mentioned that the gray Percheron geldings were big. "Big" was a gross understatement. They were gargantuan—almost six feet at their massive shoulders, each one appearing to weigh in at nearly a ton. Their shod hooves were the size of small dinner plates.

They would probably eat him out of house and home, Travis reflected as he took one of the lead ropes and followed Abner cautiously toward the barn. For all their massive size, the huge horses were calm and easy to handle.

They were a splendid pair, with their dappled coats and stately bearing. A white patch on the face of one horse made it easy to tell them apart. That one would be Patch. The other was Chip.

"Where did you get these horses?" Travis asked the old man.

"Raised 'em myself from babies," Abner said. "That's why I couldn't stand the thought of leavin' 'em for the slaughterhouse. Now you see why."

"They're amazing," Travis said. "But I don't have a clue what I'm going to do with them."

"You'll figure somethin' out." They led the horses into the stalls with hay and water. Travis turned away while the old man said a tearful goodbye to his pets. Then they walked out of the shadowy barn, into the sunshine. Bucket was nowhere in sight.

"I've got a box in the truck with their grooming tools and some tack," Abner said. "I'll leave it here, along with some money for extra feed—I want you to take it. I know those horses eat a lot."

"All right, thanks." Travis swallowed his pride. After all, he was doing the old man a big favor.

"There's one more thing I need to leave," Abner said. "I guess I should've asked you first. But I know you've got some empty sheds out back, and I can't leave this to be hauled off for junk."

Travis followed the line of the old man's gaze to the canvas-covered object on the flatbed he'd towed behind the truck. It looked about the length of a compact car, only higher at one end. Maybe it was an antique. Travis might not know much about animals, but he did know cars. This one could be valuable.

"Let's have a look," he said.

Abner glanced at the sky, as if worried about the clouds drifting in from the west. "What do you say we haul it under shelter first? The flatbed goes with it. If you'll point me to an open shed and guide me, I can back it in with the truck."

"Wait a minute," Travis said. "Is this something you're coming back here for later? Am I storing it for you?"

Abner shook his head. "No—no, I'm giving it to you! I've got no more use for it."

Travis had the distinct feeling that Abner was trying to put something over on him. Whatever was under that tarp, the old man wanted to make sure it wouldn't be rejected and sent on its way.

But what did he have to lose by taking it? Travis reasoned. The worst it could turn out to be was a piece of junk that he'd have to haul away. And at least in that case the flatbed might come in handy.

"All right," he said. "Pull the truck in and follow me."

Beyond the barn was an open-fronted shed that would have once housed vehicles and farm equipment. It was wide and deep enough to accommodate Abner's mystery object with room to spare. Travis stood to one side, guiding with hand and voice signals, as Abner backed the flatbed up to the rear wall. "That's it . . . a little more . . . whoa!"

Grinning, Abner climbed out of the cab and walked back to unfasten the trailer hitch. Travis waited while he unhooked the clips that held the tarp in place. "Now you're going to see something special," the old man said.

Lifting the edges of the tarp with his hands, he swept it to one side with a flourish.

Travis's jaw dropped. Whatever he'd expected to see, it wasn't this.

On the flatbed, freshly painted in red and gold, stood a full-sized, old-fashioned sleigh.

Chapter 3

Travis stared at the sleigh. It was a stunning piece of work, beautifully detailed down to the polished brass trim and the gleaming runners. But what on earth was he supposed to do with it?

"Did you steal this from Santa Claus?" It was all he could think of to say.

Abner chuckled. "I built it myself, more than twenty years ago. It's been the star of Branding Iron's Christmas parade ever since. But in case you're wondering, no, I didn't need to steal anything from Santa Claus. I *am* Santa Claus."

Was the old man delusional? Travis's gaze took in the round, rosy face and twinkling blue eyes, the white stubble of a beard, his pudgy build. There was something Santa-like about Abner Jenkins. But Travis had never believed in fairy tales.

"Gotcha, didn't I?" Abner was laughing. "No need to worry. I don't fly through the sky delivering presents. But I've played Santa in the Christmas parade ever since I built the sleigh. It's a big event. The whole town looks forward to it." He studied Travis's skeptical expression. "You've never seen the parade?"

"I didn't bother to go last year. Before that I wasn't here." Travis didn't bother to add that he'd been in prison.

Inside the sleigh, there were two bench seats—a small, plain one, set low and forward, which Travis guessed was for the actual driver of the sleigh. The elevated rear seat, which appeared to have been salvaged from a high-end automobile, would be where Santa could sit and wave to the crowds. A step made it easier for an old man to get up and down.

Abner beckoned Travis closer. "Here. Take a look at this."

In the bed of the sleigh was a large, sturdy cardboard box. Opening the top, Abner lifted out a smaller box to reveal, beneath it, two sets of leather harness with collars, straps, buckles, and lines. The huge collars were trimmed with miniature brass bells. "For the reindeer," he joked.

Travis didn't have to be told that the old man's "reindeer" were the two massive Percherons munching hay in the barn. The whole picture was beginning to make sense. But Travis still felt as if he'd stepped into a surrealistic dream. And somehow, he couldn't seem to wake up.

"Patch and Chip have been pulling the sleigh for the past fourteen years," Abner said. "If there's no snow for the parade, the sleigh gets pulled on the flatbed," Abner said. "When there's enough snow for the runners . . ." Abner's eyes took on a faraway look. "That's when it's like magic. The sleigh almost seems to fly. Now take a look at this . . ." He unfolded the flaps on the smaller box. Inside was a red velvet Santa suit, complete with gloves, boots, a belt, a hat, and a fake beard.

"I've worn these in the parade every year." Abner dabbed at his eyes. "It makes me sad to think I've done it for the last time."

"Can't you stay for the parade, or come back?" Travis asked.

"My kids won't hear of it. They think being out in the cold might make me sick. So this gear is all yours now."

"Wait a minute!" Travis reeled as if he'd been punched. "You're not expecting *me* to play Santa Claus, are you?"

The old man surveyed Travis's lanky six-foot frame and shook his head. "You're too tall and skinny for the suit. You could always have it altered. But the important thing is that you have the Christmas spirit—that you really feel like Santa Claus."

Travis shook his head. "No way in hell am I going to put on that suit and play Santa," he said. "I'll keep the suit for now, but believe me, I'm never going to wear it."

Abner sighed. "Well, all right. If you don't mind keepin' it safe, I'll let Maggie know you've got it. Maybe she can find somebody else for the job."

"Maggie? Who's that?"

"Maggie Delaney, the mayor. Tall redhead. A

real looker, but too bossy for most men around here. Probably why she's an old maid. You'd remember her if you'd met her."

Something told Travis he already had. At least he knew why the big black Lincoln had been parked in the mayor's slot. So much for old-fashioned male bias. Maybe if she came by, he could talk the sexy mayor into taking the sleigh and the Santa gear off his hands. She might even know somebody who could take the horses.

Abner turned and ambled back toward the truck. "Well, I guess I'll be goin'. I'd say good-bye to old Bucket, but it looks like he's already off explorin' the new place. Give him a little extra attention, and he'll be fine. Thanks again. Sorry we didn't get to know each other better. You've been a true friend."

Travis accepted the old man's parting handshake. As he watched Abner drive out of the yard, a vague panic welled up inside him. At the start of the day, he'd had no worries except his own. Now he was solely responsible for the welfare of two horses the size of half-grown elephants and a mutt that seemed to have a mind all its own.

As the truck vanished toward the highway, he could hear the dog's muffled bark coming from the rear of the house. *Ignore it*, he told himself. He'd agreed to feed and shelter the dog he still thought of as Abner's. But he hadn't signed on to babysit the fool creature. Bucket could take care of himself.

The barking continued, growing louder and more intense. Maybe the damned dog was in some kind of trouble. It might not be a bad idea to check.

Cursing, Travis followed the noise around the house. From the far side of the back porch, he glimpsed flying dirt and heard excited yips.

A few more steps and he could see a black rump and plumed tail sticking out from under the porch. Some creature must've taken refuge under there, and Bucket was going after it, digging like a machine. For a moment, Travis was tempted to let him dig. But whatever was under the porch could be nasty—a badger, maybe, or even a rattlesnake looking for a warm place to den up. It was time to step in.

"Come on, Bucket, that's enough!" he said.

When Bucket didn't respond, Travis seized him by the hindquarters and pulled. Bucket resisted, digging in with his paws. He wasn't a big dog—forty pounds maybe—but he was stubborn and determined. Travis had to pull with all his strength. He was leaning back, tugging and cursing, when Bucket yelped and popped out of the hole. Travis lost his balance and stumbled backward, just in time to save himself.

From under the porch rose a foul, musky, nauseating cloud of stink. Travis choked and gagged. His eyes burned. The dog was rolling on the ground, rubbing his face and muzzle in the dirt. It was hard to tell if Bucket had gotten the full force of the skunk's blast, but hopefully he'd at least learned his lesson.

Now what?

Travis pulled a handkerchief out of his pocket

and carefully wiped his face and hands. Unless the skunk cleared out on its own, he'd have to shoot the animal and bury it. He'd probably have to bury his clothes, too, or burn them. Even then, he wouldn't be fit company in town for a week. And if the old wooden porch had soaked up the skunk spray, it would stink all winter. As for the fool dog . . .

Travis glared down at Bucket. Crouched with his tail between his legs, the dog gazed up at him. The look in his molasses-colored eyes would have melted granite.

Travis swore. The blasted dog would have to be bathed, but he couldn't do it in the house because of the stink, and it was too cold to do the job outside. He would have to set up a tub in the barn and haul warm water. Between the skunk, his clothes, and the dog, he would have his work cut out for the rest of the day—and that godawful smell would likely hang around for weeks.

So far, saying yes to Abner Jenkins had been one of the worst decisions of his life.

Maggie was reviewing tomorrow's agenda when the receptionist peeked around her office door. "You've got a visitor, Maggie," she said. "I know you wanted to get away early. Shall I tell him to come back?"

Maggie sighed. She'd been nursing a headache and had hoped for the chance to go home and lie down. But now that wasn't going to happen.

She glanced up at her father's framed photograph, which hung on the wall next to the American flag. Sam Delaney had been mayor of Branding

Iron for fifteen years. After he'd suffered a stroke, Maggie, who'd left her management job in Austin to come home and look after her widowed father, had shouldered the duties of his office. Last November, after his death, she'd been elected to serve in her own right.

But Sam's shoes weren't easy to fill. He'd been the consummate public servant, always cheerful and willing to help anyone who needed him, no matter who it was or how inconvenient the time might be.

Her eyes lingered on the affable square-jawed face. *All right, Dad, I know what you'd say. If somebody needs help, the mayor has no right to leave early.*

"It's Abner," the receptionist said.

"That's fine, Angela," Maggie replied. "Send him in."

Abner Jenkins walked through the door, his battered old cowboy hat in his hands. His expression would have suited a mourner at a funeral.

"Sit down, Abner." Maggie was genuinely glad to see the old man. His visit would save her the trouble of tracking him down later. "I went looking for you this morning when you didn't answer your phone. But you weren't home."

"You should've checked Buckaroo's. I was out of coffee at home, so I drove into town for a cup. Got me a free piece of pie in the bargain."

"Well, anyway, I'm glad to see you."

Abner remained standing, as if he didn't expect to stay long. "You might not be so glad when I tell you my news. My farm's sold. I'll be leavin' Branding Iron tomorrow to go and live with my daughter."

"Oh." Maggie took a breath, waiting for the

news to sink in. "I hope it'll be a happy move for you, being with family."

"Can't say it will be, but my kids didn't give me much choice."

"So you won't be here for the Christmas parade?" Maggie spoke the dreaded words. Abner had been playing Santa in the parade since she was a young girl. But he was getting old. She should have known this would happen.

"That's right, I won't be here. That's what I came to tell you. My neighbor down the road was kind enough to take the horses and sleigh, and the costume. I'm sure you can use 'em in the parade—in fact, he'd probably be glad for somebody to take 'em off his hands. But you'll have to find somebody else to play Santa."

"Your neighbor?" A memory tugged at her—angry slate gray eyes and a cold manner. Abner must be talking about a different neighbor, Maggie reasoned.

"Young feller," Abner said. "Moved into that old abandoned ranch last year. He keeps to himself, so you might not know him. But it was him treated me to pie this morning. And when I asked him to take my animals, even old Bucket, he said yes. He doesn't talk much, but you can tell his heart's in the right place."

Maggie remembered what Ben had told her about Travis Morgan. An embittered ex-convict didn't strike her as a candidate for playing Santa, even if he managed to fit the suit. But right now, he was all she had.

"Thank you for coming to tell me, Abner," she said. "Branding Iron is really going to miss you.

You've been a wonderful Santa and a great friend. I hope you'll leave me your daughter's contact information so we can keep in touch."

"Sure. I don't have the address with me, but I'll send you a note from Denver." He shuffled awkwardly. "Well, that's about it. I'll be goin' now."

Maggie came around the desk to shake his hand. She might have hugged the old man, but this was a professional meeting, and she didn't want to embarrass him. "Good luck, Abner," she said. "I hope this move works out well for you."

"Me too." He sighed and turned toward the door. "Good luck findin' a new Santa."

I'm going to need more than luck, Maggie thought as the door closed behind him. *If I can't find anybody for the parade, I could wind up wearing that blasted Santa suit and beard myself!*

She dismissed the thought of driving out to see Travis Morgan after work. He was probably still angry about the gate. And her headache was getting worse. She would go home, get some rest, and face him in the morning, when she was feeling up to the challenge.

And Travis Morgan would be a challenge. That much was certain.

The next morning, Maggie walked into the office at 9:00. After checking her messages, and without taking off her coat, she went outside to her car again and headed for the road to Travis's ranch.

The weather had cleared and warmed, melting the last traces of the ice storm. Cattle grazed in the pastures where the hay had been cut. Migrating geese rose in a cloud from a field of golden wheat stubble, then settled again to feed as she passed.

She could see the ranch ahead, with its unpainted wooden house, its sagging barn and sheds, and the rusty tractor parked out of the weather. Getting the place into shape was going to take time and more money than Travis appeared to have. Now that she knew his story and what he'd done as a favor to Abner, she was more sympathetic than before. But she could do little other than wish him luck.

As she pulled off the road and parked next to the gate, she noticed that the post had been straightened. The gate was closed, and the windmill was working.

No one was in sight, but the thread of smoke curling out of the chimney and the battered Ford pickup parked next to the house told her Travis must be there. Maggie unfastened the gate, stepped through, and fastened it again behind her—good manners in ranch country. "Hello?" she called. "Is anybody here?"

That was when a sharp, foul odor reached her nostrils. She grimaced. No need to guess what it was. Somebody—or something—had tangled with a skunk.

Just then, a black and white streak came rocketing around the house, headed straight for her. She'd made friends with Abner's dog over the years, and Bucket clearly recognized her. Tongue lolling, tail thumping, he flung himself against her legs with happy yips.

"Hello, old boy." She reached down, to pat him.

"How do you like your new—" The smell blasted her senses. "Oh, my stars!" she muttered.

"I bathed him—twice." Travis had come out onto the front porch.

"Well, it didn't work!" Maggie huffed, backing away from the dog. "What did you use on him?"

"Bath soap. All it did was make me smell almost as bad as he does. You might want to keep your distance, Mayor Maggie."

"At least I don't have to introduce myself," she said. "Have you recovered from your fall?"

"I'm sore as hell, but I've been worse. I'll live."

"I take it Abner told you to expect me," she said.

"I hope he told you there was no way I'd agree to play Santa Claus."

"He gave me that impression." She backed away from Bucket, who was still begging for attention. "Can't you call this dog off?"

"I can try. But he only minds when he wants to." Travis reached down and picked up a stick from the porch. "Look at this, Bucket—go get it!"

He flung the stick so far that it vanished from sight. The dog wheeled and raced after it. "Come on inside," Travis said. "That's the only place you'll be safe from him."

Maggie followed him inside. Even here there was a faint odor of skunk. But the place was clean and orderly, if sparsely furnished. The kitchen and living room were combined in one open space that was heated by an old-fashioned, wood-burning stove. Two unmatched armchairs, with a small table between them, faced the stove at a comfortable distance.

He motioned for her to sit, which she did. There was an air of quiet authority about him. But then he'd been a patrolman, Maggie reminded herself. She knew that prisoners tended to be rough on convicted cops. He couldn't have had an easy time of it in prison. She was looking at one very tough man.

"Coffee?" he asked. "I just made some."

"Sure, thanks. I take it black." She let him pour her some in a chipped mug. It was hot and good.

"Bath soap won't work on a dog that's been skunked," she said, breaking the silence. "What you need is tomato juice. You get a case of those big cheap cans and soak him in it. The juice neutralizes the spray. After that, you can bathe him with soap."

"Thanks. That's just one more thing I didn't know," he said. "Growing up, I never even had a dog, let alone horses. If you know anybody who wants Abner's animals, they'd be doing me a favor. I only took them because the old man was desperate. He said they'd be put down if he went off and left them for the new owners. I guess I was a soft touch. But, Lord, I don't know the first thing about taking care of them. It's like suddenly having children dropped off on your doorstep."

"I take it you've never had children." She gave him a teasing smile, which didn't seem to have much effect.

"Not a chance. At least I did something right."

"Your neighbors have animals. I'm sure they wouldn't mind giving you some help with them."

"Maybe." Stubborn pride showed in the set of his jaw. "But I don't know my neighbors all that well, and I don't like bothering them. I'll figure things out on my own."

He glanced at the cup she'd put down. The flames that glowed through the stove's mica panes reflected fiery glints in his eyes. "More coffee?"

"Thanks, but I've had enough." Maggie realized she'd lost track of her reason for coming here. She rose. "I need to get back to work. The parade is the Saturday before Christmas. Since you've got the sleigh and horses here, can I count on your help in getting the rig to town?"

He hesitated. Maggie could tell he didn't want to get involved. "I've never handled horses," he said. "You'll want to recruit somebody who knows what they're doing, especially with those big Percherons. They'll need an expert hand."

"I'll keep that in mind, but you could always help with the sleigh."

"Parades have never been my thing. I've already regretted saying yes to Abner. Don't expect me to say yes again."

"Well, let me know if you change your mind. Meanwhile, I'll be beating the bushes for somebody else to play Santa and man the sleigh." She started for the door.

"I'll walk you to your car," he said, taking her elbow. "That front step has a loose board I've been meaning to fix."

Maggie's pulse quickened at the light physical contact. He was only being a gentleman, she told herself. But the flush of heat made her feel like a hormonal sixteen-year-old. As his grip tightened going down the rickety wooden steps, her heart raced. How long had it been since the last time she was this close to an attractive man? Evidently too long. She was in a bad way.

At the bottom of the steps, she pulled a little away from him. "Thanks." Her voice came out slightly breathless. "I'll be fine from here."

"Okay. Be careful. And have a nice day, Mayor Maggie." As she fled to her car, he stood watching her, an amused smile on his lean, chiseled face.

Maggie willed herself not to look back as she drove away. That would be bad form, especially if he was still watching her. Clearly, Travis wanted no part of the Christmas parade. But she needed his help, and she hadn't given up on him—far from it, in fact. She hadn't made it to the middle management of a large company—or been elected mayor of a small town—without a talent for getting people to do what she wanted.

She was just starting on Travis Morgan. And she knew exactly what she was going to do first.

Chapter 4

Later that morning, when Travis opened the front door to go out and check the mail, he found a large cardboard carton on his porch.

What the devil . . . ? His first thought was that Abner had left him more orphaned animals—chickens, maybe. But when he nudged it with the toe of his boot, it was solid and heavy, the top glued shut as if it had come from a factory. There was no name on it, not even his.

Whipping out his pocketknife and opening the blade, he crouched beside the box and slit the flaps. The box was packed with layers of giant economy-sized cans, a dozen in all. Only when he lifted one can out of the box and saw the label did he realize what it was.

Tomato juice. Enough to give Bucket a good bath.

Travis managed to laugh and swear at the same

time. Only one person could have been responsible for this gift—sexy Mayor Maggie.

Had she lugged it up the steps herself or hired one of the baggers at Shop Mart to sneak up and deliver it? Either way, Maggie had to be behind it.

Travis didn't like accepting favors, even small ones. It made him feel obligated—which was probably just what Maggie wanted. She didn't strike him as a woman who'd do something for nothing. But short of storming into her office and returning the juice—a stupid idea, since he needed it—he had no choice except to be in her debt.

And Maggie, no doubt, would find a way to collect.

Surprisingly, he was looking forward to it.

Maggie had ordered the case of tomato juice from Shop Mart and promised one of the bag boys twenty dollars for delivering it. The money was waiting on the reception desk, to be picked up when he came by.

She would've enjoyed delivering it in person, just to see the look on Travis's face. But the rest of her morning had been busy. The most pressing concern had been Branding Iron's upcoming Christmas celebration. The holiday was more than six weeks away, but she was already feeling overwhelmed. So much to do—the Christmas lights wouldn't go up until the day after Thanksgiving, but before that, the strings would need to be tested and the burned-out bulbs replaced. The town Christmas tree had to be chosen, bought, and set up; the Cowboy Christmas Ball planned by a committee; the parade organized and planned, with floats, dancers, and the Branding Iron High School Marching Band.

And then there was the star of the parade— Santa Claus and his sleigh. Until yesterday, she'd assumed it would be Abner again. Now everything was up in the air.

Maggie had spent much of the morning making phone calls. She'd called every man she could think of who might make a good Santa Claus. Nobody was willing. And none of the farmers and ranchers she'd spoken with had been interested in adopting Abner's horses.

She'd give it a rest until tomorrow, she decided. Maybe someone new would come to mind. Or one of the people she'd already called would have a change of heart.

Meanwhile, there was the next item on her list—the Christmas trees. Slipping on her coat and grabbing her purse, she headed for her car.

Hank's Hardware, on the highway south of town, had the only Christmas tree lot this side of Cottonwood Springs. Hank Miller usually saved at least one extra-large tree for the city's outdoor display and another for the Christmas ball in the high school gym. But with businesses like Shop Mart as well as nearby smaller towns wanting nice, big trees, Maggie couldn't expect Hank to hold a tree he had a chance to sell. She'd learned to show up soon after the trees were unloaded, before the lot was even open to the public.

"Howdy, Maggie. I had a feeling you'd be coming around today." Hank greeted her with a smile. He was stocky, round-faced, and balding, with a paunch that overhung his belt by a couple of inches. It was hard to believe he was Travis's father—until she noticed his eyes. They were that same striking shade of gray.

"Come on out. I'll show you what I've set aside for you." He pulled on a pair of leather gloves and moved ahead of her, toward the side exit of the spacious hardware store. He walked with a noticeable limp. Everyone in Branding Iron who was old enough to remember knew the story of how he'd lost his leg in a horrific farm accident and had to wear an artificial limb. His wife had left him after the accident, taking their young son. That son had been Travis.

Now the two of them, who could do so much for each other, were estranged. What had happened between them, and how could it be mended?

"Take a look. What do you think?" Inside the wire-fenced compound of the Christmas tree lot, two large pines leaned against the side of the store. With a gloved hand, he grasped the trunk of the taller one and stood it up for Maggie's inspection. The tree was about eleven feet tall, full and bushy on all sides.

"That will be perfect for the town Christmas tree," Maggie said. "Now let's see the other one."

The second tree was about two feet shorter and equally pretty. "I can show you a few more if you want," Hank said.

"No, these will do nicely," Maggie said. "I'll pay you when we get back inside."

"Great. I'll put SOLD tags on them and store them in a safe place until you're ready to put them up. Since that'll be a few weeks off, I'll even set them in water for you."

"Thanks so much. I can always count on you, Hank."

"Anytime." He walked away to get the tags. Maggie waited by the tree, watching him. There was something about his rounded physique and slightly rolling gait, something about the set of his graying head on his shoulders that made her think of . . .

Santa Claus!

Something clicked in her mind. Why hadn't she thought of Hank sooner? He'd make a perfect Santa!

But would he do it—especially when his estranged son had the horses, costume, and sleigh? Maggie knew better than to come right out and ask him. It would be too easy for him to say no. She would need to take her time—not too much time, but enough to find his soft spots and give him a reason to take the job.

This was going to take some scheming.

She helped him tie the tags on the trees and walked with him back toward the store entrance. "I've met your son a couple of times," she said, trying to sound casual. "He seems like a good man."

A pained look flickered across Hank's face. "I imagine he is a good man. But if you talk to him again, don't mention my name. Travis doesn't want anything to do with me. And given our past history, I can't say I blame him." He gave her a warning glance as if expecting a question. "Don't ask me to talk about it, Maggie. It's best forgotten—except that Travis won't forget. He doesn't even come into the store. I'm guessing that if he needs anything, he drives to Cottonwood Springs."

"I'm sorry," Maggie said.

"Like I say, it's best forgotten." He opened the door for her, and they walked back into the store.

"Well, hello there!" Francine McFadden, co-owner of the local bed and breakfast and Hank's steady girlfriend, was waiting next to the counter. "What have you two been up to? Not trying to steal my guy, are you, Maggie?" It was a joke, and both women knew it.

Maggie shook her head. "No woman on earth could steal a man from you, Francine."

Francine beamed. She was a voluptuous woman in the bloom of early middle age. Fresh from the beauty salon, her hair was bleached and curled, her long, crimson nails and glamorous makeup done to full effect. She looked like a small-town Dolly Parton wannabe, overblown and overdone. But Maggie knew her to be all heart. It was impossible not to like her.

"Maggie's just been picking out the town Christmas trees." Hank took the town credit card Maggie handed him, ran it, and handed it back to her with the receipt.

"Hank always saves us the best trees," Maggie said. "I hope he knows how much we all appreciate him."

"I'll make sure he knows that," Francine teased. "Oh—speaking of Christmas, I heard a rumor at the beauty parlor. Is it true that Abner's leaving town?"

"I'm afraid that's true," Maggie said. "He's sold the farm, and he's going to live with his daughter."

"But that's terrible! What are we going to do for a Santa Claus?"

"I'm still looking for a volunteer. If you have any suggestions, let me know." Maggie studied the woman who was closer to Hank than any other person. Decades ago they'd almost married, before a dashing rodeo rider had swept Francine away, and Hank had married someone else. In recent years, they'd picked up the relationship again. Hank had supported Francine's recovery from alcoholism, and the two spent as much time together as possible.

If anybody could help her talk Hank into playing Santa, it would be Francine.

Francine had turned to Hank. "I just stopped by to make sure you were coming to dinner tonight, honey," she purred. "I've got the makings for chicken and dumplings, your favorite."

Hank grinned. "I'll be there with bells on."

With bells on. Maggie could only hope his words were prophetic.

"Say, Francine," she said, catching the woman's attention. "Do you have time to go to lunch with me? My treat. I've got to make some decisions about the Christmas celebration, and I could use your input."

"Why sure, honey," Francine said, "though I don't know how much help I'll be."

"Buckaroo's, then, in twenty minutes. I need to check in with the office first. I'll meet you there."

Francine was waiting when Maggie walked into Buckaroo's. She was saving the corner booth, where it was quieter and easier to talk. They ordered tuna melts and Diet Cokes, sipping their drinks while they waited for their sandwiches.

Francine turned to face Maggie in the booth. "Thanks for the treat, honey," she said. "But something tells me you've got more in mind than getting my take on the Christmas celebration."

"That depends." Maggie swirled the ice in her Coke. "I'm still looking for a Santa Claus, and I've found someone who'd be perfect. But I don't know if he'd be willing."

"It's Hank, right?"

Maggie nodded. "What do you think?"

"I think he'd look awesome with a red suit and a beard. But I don't know what to tell you, Maggie. Hank has always been self-conscious about his leg. You know, it's the reason he lost his family."

"But he'd be sitting in the sleigh the whole time. And a lot of the people wouldn't even know it was him—especially the kids. For them, he'd be the real Santa."

Francine looked thoughtful. "I know Hank loves kids. He's always been sorry that he doesn't have any little grandkids of his own. But even that might not be enough. He's going to need some powerful persuading."

"And you're the most persuasive person I know, Francine." Maggie grinned. "But there's another thing. Abner left his sleigh and his team with his neighbor—Hank's son, Travis. From what I understand, Travis and Hank aren't even on speaking terms."

"Now that could be a problem," Francine agreed.

"Have you met Travis?" Maggie asked.

"No, but I've seen him in Shop Mart. *Ooh la la!* What a man!" Francine batted her long, false eyelashes. "If I were twenty years younger . . . My goodness, girl, you're blushing!"

"Ignore it. It's a redhead thing." Maggie welcomed the arrival of their tuna melts, overflowing with grilled cheese. She took a few bites, giving her face time to cool. "Has Hank ever told you what happened between him and his son?"

"Not really. I know Hank started drinking after he lost his leg. It got so bad that his wife left him, took their little boy away, and remarried. Hank didn't have any contact with his son for years. That's all I know."

"But surely that wouldn't have caused so much bitterness between them," Maggie said. "Something else must've happened—something bad enough to tear them apart."

Francine wiped a dab of cheese off her chin. "Maybe so, honey. But Hank's never said a word about it, not even to me."

"Travis would be glad to have somebody else take the animals and the sleigh. He didn't want them in the first place, but Abner was afraid the horses and dog would be put down when he left them."

"It sounds like Travis has a good heart." Francine gave her a teasing wink. "And it sounds like you've gotten to know him pretty well."

"Not that well. Believe me, he's not all that easy to know." Maggie felt the hated blush creep into her cheeks again. It was humiliating. Thirty-two-year-old mayors didn't blush.

Francine, who never missed a thing, finished

her sandwich and leaned back in the booth. "This is how I see it, honey. We've both got guys we like, and we both want the same things for them. We want the two of them to settle the past and be family again."

"And to team up for the parade," Maggie added. "As long as they're not speaking to each other, that isn't going to happen."

"Right," Francine said. "I don't know how we're going to manage it. I just know that we'll have a better chance if we work together. What do you say we think about it for a day or two and then check in, say, before the weekend?"

"If this is going to happen, it's got to happen fast," Maggie said. "Otherwise, I'll be wearing that Santa suit myself."

"And with that hair of yours, red isn't your color. You're more of an autumn," Francine joked. "So do we have a deal?"

"We do." Maggie put a bill on the table and rose. "I have to go now, but I'm in, and I'll get back to you. Thanks for your help, Francine."

"My pleasure, honey. And good luck."

The two women fist-bumped. Then Maggie hurried out to her car. Having Francine as her co-conspirator could make a difference. But they were dealing with two stubborn men. There were plenty of pitfalls. And there was always the chance that their meddling would only make matters worse.

But if they succeeded, it could mean a win for two good men, for the town of Branding Iron, and for the spirit of Christmas.

* * *

Travis had used eleven cans of tomato juice to bathe the dog and saved the last one for himself. The clothes he'd been wearing were buried, and the skunk had departed when he'd left a radio playing punk rock on the porch. That godawful smell would probably linger for weeks, but at least it was no longer knock-you-flat overpowering.

Meanwhile, he couldn't forget to take care of the horses. He'd given them fresh hay and water and shoveled steaming heaps of manure out of their bedding straw. At least it would help fertilize the spring hay crop. But the huge Percherons had nothing to do but stand in their stalls. While the weather was mild, they needed to be outside for fresh air and exercise.

The ranch had no corral. But the hay pasture, which covered several acres, was fenced all around with rusty barbed wire. He'd seen horses in neighboring fields, so he guessed the Percherons would be safe there. But the distance from the barn to the pasture gate was about fifty yards. Could he lead them that far without spooking them? And could he catch them again when it was time to put them back into the barn? As long as they were calm and docile, that shouldn't be a problem. But if anything went wrong, he was no match for an out-of-control one-ton horse. All he could do was get the hell out of the way.

Truth be told, they made him damned nervous.

The next morning, he decided to give it a try. He remembered how Abner had clipped the lead ropes to their nylon halters, which they were still wearing. The big animals had plodded along without resistance. The first time would be the hardest, he reminded himself. With luck, nothing would go wrong. After that, it would be easier.

As he walked out to open the pasture gate, Bucket stuck to Travis's heels. The dog seemed to follow him everywhere he went, always keeping a little behind, almost as if he were herding his new master. Bucket still smelled faintly of skunk, but after multiple baths, his black and white coat was like fluffy silk. He was a handsome animal, and he seemed to know it. He carried his plumed tail like a banner, letting the long hairs flutter in the breeze.

Returning to the barn, Travis steeled his resolve and opened the first box stall. The horse—Patch, the one with the white spot—snorted softly but stood still as Travis clipped the lead rope to the metal ring on the halter. Bucket sat at the entrance to the stall, ears perked, tongue lolling.

Travis moved toward the open gate of the stall, tugging gently on the lead. With a low nicker, Patch responded, following him out of the barn and across the yard. Bucket trailed behind, staying just clear of the massive hooves.

By the time he'd put the second horse in the pasture and closed the gate, Travis was feeling more confident. The big Percherons were docile and well trained. *He* was the one who needed training—how to handle them, how to give them commands, how to groom and care for them, how to put them in harness . . .

But what was he thinking? Lord, he'd never wanted a horse, let alone two. He didn't even like horses. There had to be somebody—maybe in Cottonwood Springs or one of the other towns, who would have a use for them. He could run an ad—but what if the person who replied was just after horseflesh to sell to a slaughterhouse for dog food?

Damn! He was getting soft in the head! He was as sentimental as Abner!

Pausing, he turned and watched the two horses amble into the open field, stopping to nibble at the alfalfa that had sprouted after the fall harvest. The sky was clear, the wind brisk. They should be fine until tonight, he told himself.

Bucket nudged his hand and wagged his tail, wanting attention. Travis reached down and scratched his satiny head. Maybe the dog was lonesome for Abner. Dogs did get lonesome for their owners—at least the ones in books and movies did.

"What am I supposed to do with you, you old rascal?" He glanced down at Bucket, who wagged his tail. "So far, you've done nothing but get skunk-sprayed, gobble up food, and follow me around like a shadow. Abner said you were a good watchdog, but there's nothing around here worth stealing. How are you supposed to earn your keep?"

Bucket gave a little *yip*. Travis shook his head. "Okay, I guess we'll just have to figure it out as we go along."

But Bucket was the least of his worries. If he couldn't get rid of the horses, at least he needed to learn to manage them. Horses were complicated animals. An old friend of his, who'd made it big as a rodeo star, had owned a book on horse care that was as thick as his fist.

An old friend!

Maybe that was the answer. He and Conner

Branch had been best friends in high school, and they'd never really lost touch. Conner had even written him a few letters while he was doing time. Travis hadn't contacted Conner since he'd been released and moved to Branding Iron, but he still had Conner's old number on his phone. If anybody knew about horses, Conner did.

The number might not be good anymore. But it was worth a try.

Still standing in the yard, with Bucket at his feet, he took his phone out of his pocket, scrolled to the old number, and made the call.

Conner answered on the second ring.

"Hey, Travis!" He sounded happy. "What's up? I heard you were out, but then I lost track of you. I was afraid it might be for good."

"Sorry." Just hearing his old friend's voice raised Travis's spirits. "I should've called. I'm back on the old family ranch in Branding Iron. The place is all mine now. I'm trying to make it work but, man, it's a struggle. Nothing but beans and blisters. How about you? Still earning those fancy buckles and dazzling the women?"

There was a silent pause on the other end of the phone. "You haven't heard?"

"I'm sorry, what?"

"It was in the papers, but it's been a while."

"I can't remember the last time I read a newspaper. What are you talking about?"

"I'm finished, Travis. Got stomped by a bull in the Vegas finals. Bastard broke my hip and shattered my leg. Spent months in traction and rehab. I can walk okay, but it hurts like hell to sit a horse, and I'll never compete again."

A memory flashed through Travis's mind—a young Conner on a bronc in the junior rodeo championships, a cocky grin on his face. Rodeo had been Conner's whole life.

"Oh, Lord, I'm sorry," Travis said. "What rotten luck. Are you doing all right?"

Conner's chuckle was laced with irony. "I don't mean to dump on you, old friend, but you might as well hear the rest of the story. No insurance for bull riding. So my medical bills cost me damn near everything I had. Lost my big house. Had to sell my horses, and cars, and even auction off my buckles and trophies. Hell, my girlfriend left me, too, and took the dog—just like in those good old country songs. I'm living in this cheap rental in Waco while I figure out the rest of my life."

"Come live here, with me!" As soon as Travis spoke, he knew the words were right and true. "There's plenty of room in this old house, and Lord knows I could use the help. I don't know squat about running a ranch or taking care of these animals that got dumped on me. I couldn't pay you. But you'd get a free roof over your head, and we could be partners in whatever we decide to do."

"Partners? You're kidding!"

"I'm absolutely serious. I called you because I need advice about the horses. But having you here to help out would be the best thing I could wish for. Will you at least think about it?"

Conner laughed. "I don't have to. I'm in. I can be there in the next few days."

"You'd better be sure. Before you make up your mind, let me send you a photo of the house."

Travis strode toward the front corner of the house, snapped a photo from the best angle, and sent it. The three-bedroom frame home might have been a nice place fifty years ago. But it had long since fallen into neglect. The structure was sound, the shingled roof still holding against the rain and snow. But the rest was about as homey as an old miner's shack.

There was silence on the phone while Conner studied the photo.

"Well, what do you think?" Travis asked.

"One question. Has it got indoor plumbing?"

"If you don't mind rusty pipes."

"And cockroaches? I hate cockroaches."

"Haven't seen a one. If there ever were any, they must've all frozen to death."

"Then I'm in. I'll see you in about three days."

"Need any help? Can you drive all right?"

"I can manage, thanks. Just tell me how to get there."

Travis ended the call with a new lightness of spirit. He'd done his best to go it alone out here, but the past year had been hellishly lonesome and hard. Having a capable friend, who needed to be here for his own reasons, could make all the difference. Maybe together, they could find a way to make this broken-down ranch pay.

He found himself whistling as he set about getting a room ready for his friend, clearing out items that could be hauled away or stored elsewhere, scrubbing the floor and washing the single window. He was going to need a bed, a chair, and some kind of bureau with drawers, as well as curtains, bedding, and a rug. If he couldn't find some furniture in the want ads, the thrift store in Cottonwood Springs should have most of what he needed. What he couldn't find there, he would have to buy at Shop Mart, along with a fresh supply of groceries.

Luckily, he'd sold a truckload of hay last week, so he had some cash. He'd planned to make it last, but he wanted his friend to be comfortable. Conner had made good money as a rodeo star. He'd lived like a millionaire—a big house with stables out back, fancy cars and fancy women. Travis could only hope he wouldn't mind the shabby room that was the best he had to offer.

By the time he'd cleaned the room and rearranged the house, the sun was low in the sky, and the air had taken on a biting chill. Patch and Chip were still in the field. It might be all right to leave them outside for the night—wild horses, after all, lived outdoors all the time. But what if something went wrong—a storm, an accident, or even some predator? He couldn't take that chance. He needed to get the big Percherons back into the barn.

But Abner hadn't told him how to do that.

Would he have to catch them on foot? Would they come if he whistled? Would they know their food was in the barn and come back on their own? Travis felt like a fool—but if he didn't get them in soon, he'd be chasing them in the dark.

He took time to put fresh hay and water in their stalls. Then, leaving the stall gates open as well as the barn door, he looped the two lead ropes over his arm and walked out to the fenced hayfield, opened the gate, and stepped inside.

The horses were about a hundred yards out, standing close together. Would they let him approach, or would they spook and run if he went close? He was about to shut the gate behind him when a black and white streak rocketed past him, headed straight for the horses.

"Bucket! Come back here, you fool dog!" he shouted. But Bucket ignored him. Circling the horses, he darted in close, yapping and nipping at their heels, then darting out again. In a moment, he had them moving together toward the gate.

Travis watched in drop-jawed amazement as the dog herded the giant horses through the gate, across the yard, and into the barn. Chip and Patch seemed to know the drill. They ambled along together, making no move to resist Bucket's barks and nips.

When they were in their stalls, Travis closed and latched the gates. Bucket sat at his feet, grinning, as if to say, *See, I showed you something, didn't I?*

Travis scratched the dog's ears. "I'll be damned," he muttered. "I don't just have one new partner. I've got two!"

Chapter 5

By the next afternoon, Travis had found the furniture he needed, including a nearly new mattress set and a rug, at a Branding Iron moving sale. He paid the seller, loaded the pieces in the back of the pickup, and tied them down.

Driving away, he checked off one more item on his mental list of things to do before Conner arrived. He'd been lucky to find all the furniture in one place, and at a bargain price. But he still needed bedding and maybe a few extra towels, since Conner had implied that he wasn't bringing much. He wanted to lay in some groceries, too. He could find everything he needed at Shop Mart—hopefully, some of it on sale.

Travis had wondered, in passing, what Conner was living on. The money from the hay sales wouldn't be enough to support two people. But he dismissed the worry. Conner was a proud man—too proud to be a freeloader. He would find a way to pull his own weight.

He pulled into the crowded parking lot at Shop Mart and found an empty space. Only as he was climbing out of the truck did he notice that he was parked next to a familiar black Lincoln Town Car.

All thoughts of his errand fled. For the past couple of days, he'd been too busy to dwell on sexy Mayor Maggie. But she hadn't been far from his mind. Now, gazing across the sea of parked vehicles, he caught a glimpse of her coming out of the store with a tall paper bag in her arms. She didn't appear to have seen him, but she was moving steadily in his direction, toward her car. She was wearing jeans, a black motorcycle jacket, and the green scarf he liked. Her mahogany hair fluttered loose in the breeze.

Damn, but she was beautiful. And way out of his league. But at least he could thank her for the tomato juice and maybe offer to buy her coffee. The worst she could do was say no.

Leaning against the side of his truck, he took a shameless pleasure in watching her walk toward him.

Maggie was two rows away from her car when she caught sight of Travis, leaning against the side of his truck. When he tipped his hat and grinned, she knew he'd been waiting for her. The hormone surge was like homemade fudge boiling over on a hot stove. Heaven help her, the man was a convicted felon—bad news for any respectable woman. But the chemistry was all too real.

As she reached her car, he stepped forward and took the bag from her hands. "Here, I'll hold this while you open your trunk," he said.

"Thanks," she said, finding her keys and clicking open the lock. "It's not heavy, but it's nice to have an extra hand. You can put it right there, next to the spare tire."

He put the bag down and closed the trunk lid. "I was hoping to run into you," he said. "I wanted to thank you for the tomato juice."

"Did it work?"

"About as well as anything could. At least Bucket smells better. As for me . . ." He pulled up his sleeve and offered her his wrist. She sniffed deeply. His cool skin smelled of bargain brand soap, but the skunk aroma, faint but unmistakable, was not entirely gone.

"I won't be going on any hot dates for a while." His grin deepened a dimple in his cheek. "But I was hoping you'd at least let me treat you to Buckaroo's coffee and pie."

A prudent woman would have made her excuses, thanked him, and driven away, Maggie told herself. Travis Morgan was heartbreak on the hoof. But she had an agenda, and this was the perfect opening to carry it out. Learning about Travis's past, and his relationship with his father, could provide the key to healing the rift between them and giving her town its Christmas Santa.

"Thanks, I'd enjoy that." She glanced at his loaded pickup. "We can take my car. Nobody will bother your truck here. What are you doing with all that?"

"Upgrading my house. A friend is coming to stay with me. He's going to need a bedroom."

"Well, I hope I get to meet him." This was a new development. Dared she hope the newcomer would help her solve her problem?

"Let's go." She offered him the keys. "Want to drive?"

"Sure. It's been a while since I've driven one of these babies." He walked around the car to let her in the passenger side, then returned to slide into the driver's seat and turn the key in the ignition. The powerful engine purred to life.

"Runs smooth for an older car," he commented as they headed out of the parking lot. "I can tell it's had good care."

"This was my father's car," Maggie said. "It was his baby. I try to keep it up the way he'd have wanted me to."

"Are you sure he wouldn't mind me driving it?"

"Don't worry. I'm sure a man with your experience can drive anything on the road."

"My experience?" He glanced at her, his eyes narrowed. "What are you talking about?"

Maggie could have bitten her tongue, but it was too late to take back what she'd just said. Now her only recourse was honesty. "I know about your having been a patrolman," she said. "And I know you went to prison."

His jaw tightened, but he kept driving toward Main Street. "How did you find out?"

"I asked the sheriff. He told me. As mayor, it's my business to know about the people in this town."

"Is it, Mayor Maggie?" The question was laced with irony.

"Don't worry, I haven't told anybody, and I don't intend to." Maggie's voice betrayed her unease. This was not going the way she'd hoped.

"Did the sheriff tell you what happened?"

"A little, but I had the impression he didn't know the whole story."

"He knows."

Maggie didn't answer. There was nothing she could say that would ease the situation.

Travis stopped outside the restaurant but made no move to get out of the car. "Well, are you waiting for me to tell you?" he asked.

"Only if you want to."

He exhaled, gazing through the windshield at the faded leaves that blew along the sidewalk. The wind had picked up, blowing a bank of heavy clouds across the sun.

"It was after midnight, and I was working," he said. "We'd gotten an alert earlier about a kidnapping—a twelve-year-old girl. Her friend said she'd been grabbed by a stranger in the mall parking lot and thrown into the trunk of a dark blue Toyota Camry. We had a partial on the plate—the first three digits. The friend hadn't been sure about the rest.

"I was wrapping up a long shift, headed home on the freeway, dog tired, when a car passed me going twenty miles over the speed limit. Blue Camry, the plate matched what we'd been told. I turned on my lights and siren and pulled it over. The driver looked about twenty, like maybe a college kid. He seemed nervous. I took his license and registration, and then I asked him to open the trunk latch. He started the car and took off.

"All I could think of was that little girl, locked in the trunk and headed for God knows what kind of hell. I drew my pistol and fired through the back window. The car skidded off the road, into a ditch. He was dead by the time I got to him, shot through the head. When I opened the trunk, there was nothing in it but some OxyContin and a couple bags of weed."

"And the little girl?" Maggie asked.

"She showed up safe. It turned out she and her friend had made up the whole kidnapping thing." Travis shook his head. "The boy's family had money and influence. They made sure I paid for my mistake. Three years for manslaughter, and I'll never work in law enforcement again."

"That's awful," Maggie said. "So unfair. I'm sorry."

"I'm sorry, too. I ended an innocent life, and I'll always wonder what I could have done differently. But it's in the past and can't be changed. So what do you say we put it aside and go have that coffee and pie?"

"Sure." Maggie waited while he came around to help her out of the car. Life wasn't fair, she thought. All Travis had meant to do was save a child. Instead, his action had ended in tragedy—and a burden of guilt he would carry for the rest of his life. She was just beginning to discover the kind of man he was.

* * *

By now it was mid-afternoon. The Saturday lunch crowd had gone, leaving Buckaroo's more or less quiet. They took a booth, and Travis gave the waitress their order. He couldn't even remember the last time he'd taken a beautiful woman out to eat—not that this was any kind of date. But it wouldn't hurt to pretend a little.

Telling Maggie about his past hadn't been easy. But he was glad she knew and seemed to understand what had happened. At least she'd know he wasn't holding back. And she wouldn't have to get the story from someone else.

But why should it matter? he reminded himself. He knew why she was spending time with him. She wanted his help with the Christmas parade. But that was her problem, not his. Apart from a case of giant economy-sized tomato juice, he didn't owe Mayor Maggie a blasted thing.

"You said your friend was coming." She sipped the coffee the waitress had brought her. "I don't suppose he has a round belly and a white beard?"

Travis had to smile. "If I remember right, Conner's even skinnier than I am. He's been a champion bronc and bull rider—made the national finals five times and won twice. Took second in the all-around competition a few years ago. But I just found out he's been injured and needs a place to go, so I invited him here. Figured I could use his help, especially with the horses. He's driving in from Waco, could be here as soon as tomorrow. And he'll be tired. That's why I'm trying to get his room ready."

"Could you use some help?"

"From *you?*" His eyebrows shot up.

"I may not be as strong as you," she said, taking a dainty forkful of pie. "But I can help balance the heavy things and carry in the light things, like drawers. It could save you some time."

He frowned, studying the way her windblown hair curled around her face and how the loosely buttoned collar of her denim shirt revealed the barest shadow of cleavage. Why would she offer to help him with a heavy job that didn't strike him as women's work? He already knew the answer to that question. But that didn't mean he was going to turn her down.

"Sure, thanks," he said. "I'll need to pick up some sheets and blankets at Shop Mart on the way."

"No need. I've got a box of spare bedding I was planning to donate. My house isn't far. We can stop by and pick it up when I take you back to your truck."

"Thanks." He hesitated. "Are you sure you've got time for this?"

"It's Saturday. I was just going to run an errand or two and hang around the house. I'd rather make myself useful. Thanks for the coffee and pie, by the way. It's not very often I get treated by a man."

"I find that hard to believe, Mayor Maggie," he said. "I can imagine men lining up around the block just to buy you coffee."

She laughed. "Then you don't know Branding Iron—or me. My age qualifies me as an old maid around here."

That was what Abner had called her. He'd said

she was too bossy for most men. If that was true, Travis thought, it didn't say much for the male population of Branding Iron. Maggie Delaney was a goddess.

They left Buckaroo's, and Maggie drove to her house—a cozy-looking brick bungalow with a deep, covered front porch. It reminded Travis of the house he'd grown up in after his mother remarried.

Hank had a smaller house. Travis had driven by it once. That one time was enough for him.

"Do you need help with the box?" he asked her as she pulled into the driveway and stopped.

"It's not heavy. I'll be back in a jiffy." She climbed out of the car, darted into the house, and appeared minutes later with a hefty-looking cardboard box, which she slid onto the backseat. He should have insisted on helping her, Travis thought. But something told him Maggie wasn't accustomed to being helped.

She drove him back to the Shop Mart and let him off at his truck. "I'll see you at your place," she said.

"It still smells like skunk out there," he warned.

"I grew up in Branding Iron. I can deal with that." She gave him a cheerful wave as she drove away.

When Travis arrived home, he saw that she'd made it there ahead of him and propped the gate open for the truck. Maggie was on the front porch, with Bucket at her side. Travis pulled in, parked by the house, and got out of the truck to close the gate.

By now the sky was dark with clouds. Wind whistled through the ancient cottonwoods that lined the road. A storm front was moving in. Would it be chilly enough to bring the season's first snowfall?

Travis mounted the porch where she was waiting. "Hang around with that dog and you'll have to bury your clothes when you get home," he said.

She grinned. "Too late for that now. We're already pals. Come on, let's get that truck emptied before the weather hits."

"Right." As mayor, Maggie was clearly accustomed to calling the shots, Travis observed. No wonder some men found her off-putting. But he, for one, enjoyed a woman with backbone. He tossed her the leather work gloves he kept in the truck. "Put these on," he said.

She hesitated. "They'll be too big."

"Put them on—unless you'd rather get splinters."

She slipped the gloves on her hands. "All right, let's get to work," she said.

With Bucket trailing them back and forth, they hauled the pieces into the house. Maggie carried the bureau drawers and the nightstand in by herself. But it took both of them to lug and balance the rug and the ends of the wooden bed frame and wrestle the full-size mattress and box spring through the door and down the hall.

Travis had to admit Maggie was a lot of help. She was strong for a woman, and she didn't stand around waiting to be told what to do. It took them maybe fifteen minutes to get everything out of the truck and in the house, and another fifteen minutes to put everything together in the bedroom. When the mattress finally lay over the box spring on the bed, she fell backward across it with a little *whoosh* and lay there, laughing. "Now that was work!" she said.

As he looked down at her, with her cheeks flushed and her hair falling in glorious tangles, it was all Travis could do to keep from flinging himself down beside her and taking her in his arms. Not a good idea, he told himself. Either Maggie would slap his face, or she wouldn't, which could mean serious trouble for them both.

For a few more seconds, he feasted his eyes on the sight of her. Then after announcing that he was going to get the box from her car, he turned and strode outside. Safe on the porch, he took a breath.

Was the woman aware of her effect on him? He would bet good money she was. Maggie hadn't gotten to be mayor by being a shrinking violet. She was an expert at getting what she wanted.

He knew what she was up to—playing up to him, helping him with Conner's room, flirting with him in her maddeningly subtle way. But it wasn't going to work. He wanted nothing to do with the Christmas parade, especially if she expected him to play Santa.

Maggie sat up, pulled down her jacket, and brushed back her hair. She'd come out here hoping that Travis would open up about his father. Understanding what had driven a wedge between them could be the first step in getting father and son back together. But so far all she'd done was haul furniture.

Maybe she was wasting her time. Not that she hadn't enjoyed herself. Travis was the most attractive man she'd met in a long time, and the way he treated her made her feel—as the old Carol King song put it—like a natural woman. But she'd come here on business, and that business was getting nowhere.

She heard the front door open and close, then the sound of footsteps as he came down the hall with the box of bedding.

"I can make the bed for you," she offered as he walked into the room and set the box on the bed. "There's a mattress pad in the bottom of the box. It needs to go on first."

"I know how to make a bed, Maggie," he said. "You've been a lot of help, and I'm grateful, but you must have better things to do than hang around here."

The words felt like a cold slap in the face, but Maggie chose not to react. "Fine," she said. "Just one more thing. I'd like to look at the sleigh and the other things Abner left. I need to make sure everything is there and nothing needs to be replaced. Then I'll be on my way."

"Sure. Come on. But it's getting cold out there. You won't want to spend much time."

He led her through the kitchen and out the back door to the open shed. Bucket, who'd been waiting on the porch, tagged along after them.

Maggie could see the covered sleigh, mounted on the flatbed. She stepped back while Travis pulled the tarp to one side. "It looks fine," she said. "I'm always amazed by this sleigh. Abner put so much love into building it. And he loved being

Santa for the kids. When he was dressed up in that red suit and beard, it was like he was the real thing."

"Too bad he had to leave," Travis said. "I know you won't have an easy time replacing him."

"Actually, I have someone in mind." Maggie spoke cautiously, knowing she couldn't push him too far. "I think he'd be perfect, but I haven't asked him yet. I don't know if he'd be willing."

She held her breath, waiting for him to ask who it was. But at that moment, Bucket, who'd followed them into the shed, jumped into the sleigh and onto the seat. He wagged his tail and gave a little *yip*, as if to say, *Let's go!*

"Maybe Bucket could do the job," Travis joked. "All he needs is a red suit and a beard."

"Bucket always rode on the seat with Abner," Maggie said. "He even wore a red Santa hat. The kids loved him. Look at him now. He knows right where he belongs."

With Bucket supervising from the seat, Maggie inspected the boxes that contained the harness gear and the Santa costume. "Everything seems to be here," she said. "We've got all we need except our Santa." She glanced at Travis, wondering whether he'd be open to her mentioning his father. His stone-faced expression told her to wait. "Where are the horses?" she asked.

"They're out in the hay pasture. So far they've done all right. But Conner is the horseman. He'll know how to take care of them. Meanwhile, our resident horse handler is right here." He gave Bucket a nod. "Come on, I'll show you."

They covered the sleigh again and left the shed

with Bucket trotting at their heels. Fine, powdery snowflakes were blowing on the wind. Maggie felt their cold sting against her cheek as they walked out to the wire fence that surrounded the pasture. She could see the big Percherons in the middle of the field, standing close together as if to shield each other from the weather.

"Time to get them in." Travis glanced down at Bucket. "What do you say, boy?"

Bucket gave a *yip* and ran to the gate. Travis lifted the latch and swung it back. The dog raced through and made straight for the horses.

Maggie knew what she was about to see. Border collies were born herders, and Abner had trained his dog well. What surprised and delighted her was seeing Travis's pleasure as Bucket did his job and brought the horses in. It was the first time she'd seen genuine happiness on his face.

Hallelujah, there's hope for the man yet!

They stepped out of the way as the huge horses trotted through the gate with Bucket at their heels. When they were safely in their stalls, Travis closed the gates and rewarded the dog with a bowl of kibble.

"Does he sleep in the barn?" Maggie asked him as they walked outside, into the blowing snow.

"He's got a bed in the straw. So far, he seems to like it fine." Travis closed the barn door.

"Abner used to let him sleep in the house. Don't be surprised if he charms his way in as it gets colder."

"He won't be doing that until that skunk smell goes away. Come on." His hand cupped her elbow, firmly guiding her. "I'll walk you to your car."

Snow swirled around them as they walked to the

front gate. The flakes were fine and weightless, leaving the barest skim of white on the ground. Neither of them spoke. It was as if they'd run out of things to say. Whatever she'd come to accomplish here, she'd failed. The wall Travis had raised against her was as solid as ever.

He walked her around to the driver's side door. Maggie was shivering beneath her leather jacket. Travis put his hand on the latch, then hesitated. One hand moved upward to cup her jaw. Leaning down, he let his mouth touch hers in a light, lingering kiss that sent electric jolts through her body. She willed herself not to move as his lips nibbled hers, sending her pulse on a roller coaster ride. This was trouble. But she never wanted it to end.

He drew away, his steely gaze holding hers. When he spoke, his voice was thick and husky. "In case you're wondering, that's what I want from you, Maggie," he said. "Now I want the truth about what you want from me. No pretty lies, just plain honesty."

Maggie fought back welling tears. This was the moment of truth—and the truth had just become cheap and ugly. "I want your father to be our new Santa," she said. "And I want you to reconcile with him so you can work together with the horses and sleigh."

The lines of his face had shifted and hardened. He opened the car door. "That's what I thought," he said. "Goodbye, Maggie."

Chapter 6

Maggie drove home through a blur of snow and unshed tears. What could she have done differently? Lied about her motives? Slapped Travis's face? Begged his forgiveness?

Nothing would have made any difference. He'd backed her into a corner, stripped her emotions bare, and left her with no choice except to tell the truth. She'd deserved what had happened. But his abruptness, after that soul-searing kiss, had left her raw inside.

It wasn't just the way he'd dismissed her. It was the way he'd made her feel—like a lying, scheming manipulator. The sting was even worse because it was pretty much true. She couldn't blame him if he never spoke to her again.

At the house, she pulled into the garage, took her purse and the sack of groceries she'd bought out of the car, and carried them inside. As she was putting the milk and cottage cheese in the fridge, the dam broke. A tear trickled down her cheek, then another and another. Blast it, she was crying—crying over a man she scarcely knew, a man who meant nothing to her.

The last time she'd cried over a man was eleven years ago, when her fiancé had broken their engagement two weeks before the wedding, with the invitations sent, the venue reserved, the cake ordered, and dozens of gifts to be returned. After cleaning up that mess, she'd sworn off serious relationships and focused on her career. It had been a wise move. She was independent, successful, and financially solid. But she was alone, and at thirty-two, she was facing the reality that she might never have a family of her own.

Never mind, Maggie told herself. She had a town to run. And wallowing in self-pity wasn't going to get her a Santa Claus.

She wiped her eyes, blew her nose, and sat down at her computer to check her e-mail. Maybe she could advertise for a Santa in the *Cottonwood Springs Gazette*. But Abner had always played Santa for the fun and honor of it. A new applicant would expect to be paid, and there was no money allocated in the city budget for a Santa. She had to find someone who would do the job for free.

She had nearly finished her e-mails when her phone rang. "Hi, honey!" The cheerful voice on the other end was Francine's. "How's it going? Any luck with that hot-looking man of yours?"

Maggie hesitated, struggling with her emotions.

"That bad, huh?" Francine spoke into the silence.

"Oh, Francine! I've made such a mess of things!" Trying to pull herself together, Maggie told her story. "I don't know if he'll ever speak to me again!"

"Oh, I wouldn't say that," Francine said. "He's just going to need a little time, that's all."

"I don't have time. I need to make plans for the parade."

"Is that all this is about? The parade?" Francine clicked her tongue. "If you believe that, honey, I've got some beachfront property in Kansas you can buy cheap. You've fallen big-time for the man, haven't you?"

"It doesn't make any difference. I still have a job to do." Maggie took a deep breath and changed the subject. "How about you? Any luck with Hank?"

Francine sighed. "We're still friends. But I've hit a wall. I had him thinking about playing Santa. But when he found out who had the sleigh and horses, he shut it right down. I don't know what happened between him and his son, but it must've been pretty heart-wrenching."

"You say he might play Santa?"

"He was hemming and hawing at first. But he says that as long as Travis doesn't want anything to do with him, he's not interested. But don't worry, honey. Things will work out. You'll see."

"I wish I had your confidence," Maggie said. "Maybe what we need is a go-between, somebody who isn't emotionally involved."

"Now there's a thought," Francine said. "Got anybody in mind?"

"Not a soul. And even if I did have somebody, I don't know whether it would do any good. Right now, I'm out of options. All I want is to make myself a sandwich and crash in front of the TV."

"Then do that, girl. You've been working too hard. Get some rest. Things will look brighter in the morning."

Good luck with that, Maggie thought as she thanked Francine and ended the call. None of her problems were going to solve themselves overnight. Tomorrow morning, Travis and his father would still be enemies. Travis would still be angry with her. And Branding Iron would still be without a Santa Claus.

For the space of a long breath, she stood by the kitchen window, watching the fine snowflakes pepper the glass. Then she turned to the sink and began soaping Bucket's lingering skunk smell off her hands.

Sunday was cold and gloomy. But by Monday morning, the storm had moved on, leaving the land with a dusting of white that would melt in the midmorning sun. A flock of blackbirds had settled in a bare cottonwood. They rose in a cloud as a tan Jeep rumbled down the road, towing a small, closed trailer. At the sound, Travis glanced up from cleaning the horse stalls. His spirits brightened. Conner had arrived.

He walked out of the barn as the Jeep pulled up to the house and stopped. Conner, dressed in jeans and a fringed leather jacket, opened the door and eased his way to the ground.

He looked older and wearier than Travis re-

membered. Lines were etched beneath his startling blue eyes. But the close-clipped blond hair
and wiry build were the same. Most champion rid-
ers were small men. Conner wasn't much over five
foot nine, but he'd always had a steely confidence
about him. The girls who'd swarmed around him
in high school had liked comparing him to Steve
McQueen.

"Travis! I'll be damned!" A grin lit his face as he
moved forward, limping slightly on a stiffened
right leg. "You're lookin' good, man! Sorry you
can't say the same for me."

They shook hands and buddy-hugged. "I'm just
glad you're here," Travis said. "Come on in. I'll
make you some eggs and coffee. Then we'll get
you unloaded. Or if you just want to crash, your
room's ready."

"Coffee and eggs sounds fine. I drove all night,
but I'm too wired to sleep. Besides, I'm anxious to
get a look at the place."

"Not much to look at," Travis said. "You can see
the house and barn from here. The horses are out
in the field. And here's the rest of the crew."

At the sound of a visitor, Bucket had come rac-
ing around the house. Too well-trained to jump on
Conner, he circled his boots, wagging and looking
up at him.

"Hello, boy." Conner scratched the scruffy mutt's
ears, then drew back. "Good Lord, he stinks!"

Travis chuckled. "You think he's bad now, you
should've smelled him a couple days ago. His
name's Bucket. I wasn't keen on having him at
first, but he's turned out to be a pretty good horse
wrangler."

"Well, if you don't mind, I'll make friends with him after he airs out a little. Let me grab a few things, and I'll meet you in the house."

"What's in the trailer?" Travis asked.

Conner grinned. "That's my new horse. Come on, I'll show you."

Intrigued, Travis followed his friend around the trailer. Conner hadn't said anything about bringing a horse, only that he couldn't ride anymore.

Conner unlocked the back of the trailer and flung open the doors. "Here she is! What d'you think?"

Travis stared at the four-seat, four-wheeler ATV. He burst out laughing. "That's some horse!" he said.

"Thanks. Traded most of my gun collection for it. I was looking for a two-seater, but I was running out of time, and the price was right. Figured it might come in handy out here."

"That it will, especially since neither of us can ride worth a dang. Come on in and wash up. You can get settled while I fix us some breakfast."

Fifteen minutes later, Travis had bacon, scrambled eggs, toast, and coffee ready in the kitchen. Conner came in wearing a clean sweatshirt, his face and hair glistening with water. He took a seat at the table while Travis dished up the food and poured the coffee.

"So tell me about this place," Conner said. "I drove through Branding Iron on my way here. Can't say much for what I saw. What does a broken-down cowboy do for a good time around here?"

"Not much," Travis said, refilling his mug. "There's

a redneck bar called Rowdy's Roost on the far end of town—good place to go if you're looking for a fight. There's a one-feature movie theater that shows family stuff, a hamburger joint, and a bed and breakfast. Oh—and the whole town seems to make a big fuss over Christmas. If you need more excitement than that, Cottonwood Springs, half an hour up the highway, has a mall and a megaplex."

"Whoopee." Conner poured ketchup on his eggs. "How about the women? Any lookers?"

"A few. But most of them are married, and you don't want to tangle with their husbands." This wasn't going quite the way Travis had hoped. He'd wanted a partner to help him make the ranch pay. But so far, Conner only seemed interested in having a good time.

"How about you?" Conner asked. "You've been here almost a year. Have you found yourself a woman yet?"

The memory flooded Travis's senses—Maggie's sweet, trembling lips pressed against his, the nearness of her lush body tempting him to go further . . .

He forced it away. "I thought I had once," he said, "but it turned out she was just using me."

Conner grinned and shook his head. "There are worse things than being used by a pretty lady, my friend. What happened?"

"It doesn't matter. It's over."

"That bad, huh?"

Travis scrambled to change the subject. "Looks like we're about finished here. Do you want to see the ranch, or do you need to catch up on your sleep?"

"That strong coffee of yours perked me right up. I'll be good for hours. So how big is this ranch?"

"Not that big. Only about four hundred acres. I raised a couple crops of hay last year, but most of the land is unused. I figure we could do with some stock—cattle or sheep. Hell, maybe even alpacas. They seem to be the new thing."

"What we choose would depend on pasture—the soil, the graze, the terrain, the access to water, even fences. Since we can't put grazing stock out till spring, we've got plenty of time to think about it."

"Especially since we can't afford to buy stock," Travis added. "Even with the ranch as security, the bank won't lend money to an ex-convict."

"Or a broken-down rodeo cowboy with a bankruptcy in his recent past," Conner said. "We need to figure out a way to make money. You say you inherited the ranch free and clear. Is there any part of it you could sell?"

"Maybe. I hadn't thought of that. But who'd want to buy land out here? Far as I know, beyond what's been cultivated, there's nothing but rocks, weeds, and vermin."

"Far as you know? You mean you haven't seen it all?"

"Not all the way to the west boundary. It's been as much as I could do to plow and harvest the hay-fields. And there aren't any roads, or even trails, going out that way. If I tear up my truck out there or get stuck in a wash, I'm in trouble."

"So do we even know where the boundaries are, and who owns the land next to them?" Conner's interest was piqued, just as Travis had hoped. "Hell, what if we strike oil or find a gold mine out there?"

"Don't bet on it, friend." Travis shook his head. "I found an old aerial map with survey lines drawn in when I moved into the house. It's tacked to the wall, just this side of the front door. You can take a look while I clear away our breakfast."

Travis hurried to put the leftovers in the fridge and load the antiquated dishwasher. Then he joined Conner, who was studying the old map.

"When was this made?" Conner asked.

"There's no date on it, but I'm guessing it's at least ten years old. A couple from somewhere back east leased the place for a few years back then. Hippie types, the family lawyer called them. From what he told me, they had an option to buy it on contract, but they had some legal trouble and couldn't make the payments. They gave up and left."

"I can see the house and barn and the road," Conner said, peering at the map. "And I can see where the property line runs right up against that line of hills to the west. I'm guessing it might be government land beyond that. And then, on the north, it butts against your neighbor's property."

"Jubal McFarland. Nice family. He raises organic, grass-fed beef, and he builds good fences."

"Was it Mark Twain who said that good fences make good neighbors?"

"No, it was Robert Frost. But he was right."

"Well, keep in mind that good fences cost money, and you've got a lot of property," Conner said. "So what do you say we do some exploring? It's a nice day, even with that chilly breeze. And my four-wheeler can go anywhere."

Outside, they wheeled the ATV out of the trailer,

donned helmets, and climbed into the seats. Conner was about to start the engine when Bucket came tearing around the house, leaped into the ATV, and settled onto one of the rear seats.

"Oh, no!" Conner protested. "That stinky mutt isn't coming along."

"Hey, he's behind us. He'll be downwind the whole time," Travis said. "And look at him. How could you say no to that face?"

"You've gone soft in the head over that mutt!" Conner started the engine. It caught with a deafening roar.

"Lordy, I hope the neighbors don't complain," Travis said. But Conner, he realized, couldn't hear him over the engine noise. There wouldn't be much conversation on this ride, but Conner had studied the map, and he seemed to know the way. He was headed along the boundary of the property toward the west end at the base of the hills, a part of the ranch Travis had never seen. Last winter, after his arrival, it had been all he could do to get the house livable and stay warm. With the coming of spring, the hay crop had kept him too busy for exploring.

The rugged vehicle seemed to eat up the terrain, its knobby, oversized tires bounding over rocks and shooting through hollows. Conner had been right. The big ATV could go anywhere—especially with Conner driving it like he was on a blasted bucking bull.

He touched his friend's shoulder. "Slow down, damn it!" he shouted. Conner only grinned. Travis glanced back at the dog. Bucket was balanced on the rear seat, eyes half closed, tongue lolling like he was in heaven. Travis hung on and tried to relax. Maybe he'd been a highway patrolman too long and seen too many bad accidents.

They were moving into a line of low, scrub-dotted hills that stretched like a ripple from north to south across the Texas plain. Travis had been aware that the hills ran along the west edge of his property. He'd watched the sun set over them almost every night. But only now did it sink in that this wild section of land—this small piece of the earth—was really his.

Motor roaring, the ATV climbed a low ridge. At the top, the machine came to a sudden, silent stop with Conner staring down into the hollow below. "What the hell is that?" he muttered.

Travis was staring, too. Below the ridge, covering a piece of ground that Travis estimated at a little over an acre, a patch of dark, vibrant green stood out against the faded autumn landscape.

"Have you got somebody growing weed up here?" Conner wondered out loud.

"Nobody who could get away with it." Travis shaded his eyes against the bright sunlight. "No, it's trees. A whole damned forest!"

"Let's check it out." The engine roared as Conner started the ATV and gunned it down the hill. They stopped at the edge of the trees. Bucket jumped to the ground, trotted over to a spruce, and lifted his leg on the trunk. A blue jay scolded raucously from a branch.

"This is unbelievable," Conner muttered as they wandered among the closely spaced evergreens. "It's like coming across an alien spaceship in the middle of nowhere."

"There's got to be some explanation." Travis studied the lushly green pines and firs, their uniform height—averaging about eight feet. There were no old trees here, although there were a few small trees mixed in with the larger ones, as if they might have sprouted from seed. An undergrowth of yellowed grass and weeds covered the ground, hiding the pattern that became clear only after a few minutes of walking.

Travis swore in disbelief. "This isn't a forest," he said. "It's a Christmas tree farm!"

"You're kidding!" Conner said.

"Look around! The trees are growing in rows, and they all look to be about the same age. Somebody must have planted them."

"But who? They didn't just fall out of the sky!"

"The ranch was leased to those people about ten years ago. They were here for about five years before they went broke and left. They could've planted the trees, thinking they could sell them when they got big enough. But when they moved away, all they could do was leave them to grow."

"But why plant them clear out here?" Conner demanded. "Why not closer to the house?"

"It's higher here, cooler nights and summers for the trees. And maybe—" Travis paused as a faint sound reached his ears. "Come on." He strode ahead, with Conner and Bucket following close behind.

The spring was little more than a trickle, flowing out of a rocky outcrop. The shallow trench dug from the foot of the rock was all but eroded away, the black plastic hoses leading from the trench cracked with age and buried by grass and weeds.

"The young trees would've needed water," Travis said. "But by the time the people left, the roots would've been deep enough to get it out of the ground."

Conner was silent, his forehead creased in thought. Suddenly he burst out laughing—laughing so hard that he had to bend over and clutch his sides.

"What is it?" Travis stared at him, wondering if his friend had lost his mind.

Conner took a deep breath, bringing himself partway under control. "I just figured it out, Travis," he said. "Those folks weren't just growing Christmas trees. The trees were camouflage and cover for the real crop. In between those trees, they were growing illegal weed!"

"And when they moved, they harvested the crop, hauled it off, and left the trees!" Travis shook his head. It was a crazy idea, but it made perfect sense. He should have figured it out himself.

"Are you thinking what I'm thinking?" Conner asked.

"Uh-huh." Travis smiled. "You said something about finding a gold mine out here. I think maybe we just found one."

By midday, they had explored the stand of trees and estimated their number at around two thousand. They had also discovered an overgrown dirt road winding down from the trees to the hayfields—easier than the route they'd taken over open ground. They were in high spirits as they parked the ATV in the shed next to the covered sleigh.

"We owe ourselves a celebration," Conner said. "Since you made breakfast, what do you say you let me buy you a late lunch at that place in town you mentioned."

"Sure," Travis said. "We've got a lot to talk about." And they did. The trees they wanted to sell would need to be shaped and groomed. They'd need tools, a way to haul the trees, a place to set up their business, and probably a business license. They were facing a mountain of work—starting now.

Since Conner's Jeep was still hitched to the trailer, they took Travis's pickup into town. They'd meant to leave Bucket behind, but as the truck pulled out of the gate, Bucket took a flying leap and landed in the truck bed. When Conner glanced back through the rear windshield, the perky, black and white face was looking back at him.

"Well, at least nobody will bother the truck," Conner said. "Folks will be able to smell that dog halfway down the block."

Travis chuckled. It had occurred to him to wonder whether Bucket would be all right in the truck. But half the pickups he'd seen in Branding Iron had dogs riding in the back. Also, he'd scrubbed Bucket's collar, with the license attached, and put it back around the dog's neck, so if he did jump out, people would know he wasn't a stray.

Travis knew he worried too much. But it was a lifelong habit he couldn't seem to shake. He worried about his friends; he worried about strangers;

he even worried about fool dogs. It couldn't be helped.

Sometimes he even worried about Mayor Maggie and her search for a Santa. But given who she had in mind for the job, he could only wish her luck. The one person he didn't worry about was Hank Miller.

"So I guess this is our competition coming up." Conner's voice broke into his thoughts. Just ahead, on the right-hand side of the highway, he could see Hank's Hardware and its outside lot already half full of Christmas trees. A truck loaded with flattened trees was backing up to the gate to unload more. Hank, in khakis and a fleece jacket, stood outside giving directions.

"He's got a great location and plenty of trees to choose from," Conner said.

"Yeah," Travis agreed. "He's got the only tree lot this side of Cottonwood Springs, and he makes a killing every year. But look at the trees coming off that truck. It's probably been a week, at least, since they were cut. Then they're flattened in shipment and have to stand until the boughs spread out again. By then they're already half dried, and they've lost most of their scent. By the time somebody gets them home, they're starting to shed needles."

"I get your drift," Conner said. "We can offer folks fresh-cut trees. All we have to do is get set up and put the word out."

"Easier said than done." Travis turned onto Main Street and headed for Buckaroo's. "The season's about to start. If we're going to do this, we'll need to work fast and work smart."

"Gotcha. We can make some plans while we eat." Conner glanced back at the Christmas tree lot, which was behind them now. "I'm guessing that fellow won't be too happy when we start cutting into his profits."

"I don't give a damn about him and his profits," Travis said. "We have as much right to sell trees as that self-serving sonofabitch does."

"Whoa!" Conner frowned at him. "Is there something going on here that I need to know about?"

Travis turned onto Main Street and headed for Buckaroo's. "You'll find out sooner or later, so it might as well be now. That man's my father."

Maggie was returning from an errand at the high school when she drove past Buckaroo's and saw Travis's truck in the parking lot with the dog in the back.

Torn between hard bravery and easy cowardice, she pulled her car to the curb. Painful as her last parting from Travis had been, she had a job to do. Part of that job was keeping communication open with the owner of the sleigh and horses.

With a sigh, she climbed out of the car. Bucket had spotted her. He was yipping and wagging his tail. Fearing he might jump out of the truck bed, she walked over to greet him.

"Hi, boy!" She scratched his silky head. He still smelled of skunk, but nothing like before. "What are you doing out here?"

Bucket wagged his tail and licked her hand.

"You stay and watch the truck, okay? If you're still here when I come back, I'll stop by. Stay, now."

Bucket looked forlorn, but didn't try to follow her. As she walked toward the door of Buckaroo's, she felt a knot of tension in the pit of her stomach. Would Travis be friendly or hostile? Never mind. Whatever he felt toward her, she was braced. She was not about to let him humiliate her again.

Chapter 7

Maggie took a deep breath and opened the door to the café. It was a small place and not crowded after the lunch rush. There was no way Travis wouldn't see her come in. But would he greet her or pretend not to notice she was there?

The familiar smells of frying food and the murmur of cooking and conversation washed over her as she walked in. The aging sound system was playing an old Hank Williams song. She saw Travis right away. He was sitting in the corner booth, deep in conversation with a wiry, blond stranger. That must be Conner, the friend he'd said was coming to stay with him.

They had beers but no food yet, and they seemed intent on talking. Travis had a pen and appeared to be jotting notes on a paper napkin.

She almost turned around and left. But then she mustered her courage and walked over to their table. Both men looked up as she cleared her throat.

"Hello, gentlemen. Please don't get up," she said.

"Hello, Maggie." *What do you think you're doing here?* Travis's expression seemed to say.

"I won't keep you," she said. "I just need a moment. It's business."

Sure it is. It's always business with you. His look made her feel about two feet tall.

"Well, you can sit down, at least!" Conner grinned and scooted over to make room for her next to him. "Join us. We've ordered an extra-large combo pizza. There'll be more than enough for everybody. We can make a party of it!"

Travis looked pained. "Maggie, this is my friend and partner, Conner Branch. Conner, it's my pleasure to present the honorable Mayor Maggie Delaney." His voice dripped sarcasm.

"Pleased to meet you, ma'am." Conner was a blue-eyed charmer. "Come on, sit down. What'll you have to drink?"

Maggie hesitated, about to decline. But this friendly, handsome cowboy was a potential ally. She couldn't afford to turn him down. She sat, giving him a smile. "Thanks. I'll just have a small Coke."

"Coming up!" He caught the waitress's attention—which hadn't wandered far from him—and gave her the order before turning back to Maggie. "You're really the mayor?"

"I am," Maggie said. "My father was mayor of Branding Iron for years. When he got sick, I came home to take care of him. After he passed away, I was elected in his place."

"You said you had some business, Maggie." Travis looked dour.

"Yes. I'll get right to it," she said. "Since you won't be playing Santa, there's no reason for you to keep the costume. I hope you won't mind my coming by to pick it up. That way I can get it cleaned and ready for the next Santa—whoever that might be."

"Feel free. The box is still in the sleigh. Anything else?"

"Well, maybe. I did some checking. If you don't want to store the sleigh, there's room for it in the city equipment shed. We'd just need to tow it into town on the flatbed. Unfortunately, you're still stuck with the horses. Nobody I've talked to is willing to take them."

Travis shrugged. "Whatever. If you've got room for the sleigh, you might as well—"

"Wait!" Conner shot forward in his seat, almost spilling his beer. "We've got a sleigh?"

"I mentioned it on the phone," Travis said. "It's in the shed, next to where we parked your ATV."

"Who owns the sleigh, Maggie? The city?"

"No," Maggie said. "Abner built it years ago. It was his."

"So now it belongs to Travis, right?"

"I suppose so." Maggie could imagine wheels turning inside Conner's head.

"So, if you don't mind, we'll keep it for now. All right, Travis?"

"Fine."

"But we can still use it in the parade?" Maggie asked.

"I suppose so," Travis said. "As long as the city picks it up."

"And brings it back right after the parade," Conner added.

Just then the waitress, a plain-looking girl who looked barely old enough to be out of high school, appeared with their pizza and Maggie's Coke. When Conner thanked her with a smile and a wink, her thin face flushed a becoming pink. The man was a natural-born flirt, Maggie observed. Heaven help the female population of Branding Iron if he stuck around.

But she was immune, she realized. Her eyes were only for the sad, angry ex-cop.

The men fell to eating. Maggie chose the smallest slice of pizza and nibbled on it while she sipped her Coke. Just then a family walked in—two parents, a little girl, and a boy who appeared to be about twelve. Maggie didn't recognize them, but she surmised they must not be local. If they were, the children would be in school at this hour. Maybe they were traveling.

They had just seated themselves when the boy started staring in their direction. Suddenly he jumped out of his chair and, before his parents could stop him, raced over to where Maggie, Travis, and Conner were sitting.

"You're Conner Branch, aren't you?" His eyes were wide with wonder, his young face split in a wide grin. "I've seen you on TV. You're the best bull rider ever! I want to be just like you!"

Conner gave him a friendly smile. "Then I hope you don't get hurt like me," he said.

"I know. I saw you get hurt. I cried when they said you'd never ride again."

"I cried, too." Conner reached past Maggie and laid a hand on the boy's shoulder. "I'm right pleased to meet you, son. What's your name?"

"Jamie. Jamie Foster. Can I please have your autograph?"

"Sure. My pleasure." Conner took a fresh napkin from the dispenser, lifted the pen from Travis's hand, and scrawled a brief message and a signature on the napkin.

"Wow! Thanks! I'll keep this forever!" The boy took the napkin and scampered back to his family. Conner gave them a smile, tipped an invisible hat, and turned his attention back to his lunch companions.

"Heavens, we've got a celebrity in town," Maggie joked. "I'm sorry I never saw you ride."

"What you've got is a washed-up has-been struggling to become something else," Conner said. "But as long as you're here, Maggie, I have a question for you. How do we go about getting a business license?"

"The county clerk's office should be able to help you with that," Maggie said. "What kind of business do you have in mind?"

Conner grinned. "You're never going to believe this, but we've found a—"

"Actually, we're keeping it under wraps for a while," Travis said, cutting him off. "You'll find out soon enough, but for now, it's a secret project." He glanced at his friend. "Right, Conner?"

"Uh, yeah. Right." Conner gave Maggie an awkward smile. "So don't even ask."

Maggie took her cue. "Well, I need to get back to the office," she said, rising. "Is it still all right for me to come and get the Santa costume?"

"Anytime," Travis said. "If nobody's home, just take the box."

"Will do. Thanks for sharing your lunch." Maggie made her exit. Walking back to her car, she saw that Bucket was still in the truck bed. She stopped long enough to scratch his ears and tell him he was a good boy. Then she got in her car and headed back to work.

Something was up with Travis and Conner—something that Travis, at least, didn't want her to know about. She couldn't help being curious. But Travis had made it clear that it was none of her business. For now, she had little choice except to respect his wishes.

"So she's the one!" Conner chuckled as the door closed behind Maggie. "I don't know about you, but a woman like that could use me any damned way she wanted to."

"What makes you think she's the one?" Travis growled.

"Are you kidding? The way the two of you were looking every which way but at each other—polite strangers don't behave like that." Conner finished his beer. "Man, she's a goddess. Do you know who she reminds me of?"

"I can hardly wait to find out."

"Did you ever see the TV show *Mad Men*? That gorgeous redhead? Christina Hendricks—that's the actress who played her. Do you know who I mean?"

Travis did. But he wasn't ready to admit it. "I didn't watch much TV in prison," he said.

"Your Maggie's even got the same figure."

"Cut it out, Conner. And she's not *my* Maggie."

"Oh? You could've fooled me. I'd have hit on her myself, but I got the feeling she only had eyes for you."

"I said cut it out. We're not in high school anymore."

"Oh, all right." Conner fished in his wallet for some bills, which he laid on the table. "But why did you stop me when I started to tell her about the trees? I thought we'd want the whole town to know. And who better to spread the word than the mayor?"

"It's a little early to spread the word. We need to be sure we can do this. And we need to have our plan in place." Travis rose, stuffed the napkin with their notes into his pocket, and stepped away from the booth. "Besides, Maggie's good friends with Hank. We don't want her sharing our plans with him."

"You mean your father? The man who owns the hardware store?"

"That's right." He led the way to the door and walked outside. "He's had a monopoly on the Christmas tree business for years. If he finds out we'll be competing with him, there's no telling what he might do to stop us."

"Like what?" Limping, Conner still managed to keep pace with him.

"Maybe call a lawyer and find some petty excuse to shut us down. Maybe spread some ugly stories, or even pay somebody to sabotage the trees."

"Wow. You really don't think much of that guy, do you? What happened between you two anyway?"

Travis shook his head. "That's a story for another time. What do you say we drop by the city and county building and pick up the application for our business license? We can fill out the forms when we get home."

They had reached the truck, where Bucket greeted them with wags and yips. Travis gave him the sliver of pizza he'd saved. The dog wolfed it down.

"You're spoiling that mutt," Conner said.

"Makes more sense than spoiling a woman. At least dogs don't have a hidden agenda." Travis climbed into the cab and waited for Conner to walk around and get in on the passenger side.

"Man, you must've really been burned," Conner said. "When did you figure out Maggie was using you?"

"When I laid it on the line and she told me the truth." Travis started the truck and pulled out of the parking space. "She wanted me to mend fences with Hank so he'd agree to play Santa Claus in the Christmas parade, with me handling the sleigh."

"Given what you've told me, I'd guess that was a deal-breaker. Too bad."

"She was playing up to me, helping me unload

furniture—all a waste of her precious time," Travis said. "Even if I was willing to work with Hank, there's no way I could manage those big horses, especially in a crowd of people. I don't know the first thing about it."

"I can hitch and drive a team," Conner said. "I did it on my grandpa's farm when I was a kid. Maybe I ought to call Maggie and volunteer."

"Think about it," Travis said. "By Christmas week, if all goes well, we'll be cutting into Hank's profits big-time. He won't want anything to do with either of us."

"*If* Hank's the one who ends up playing Santa. Hey, *you* could do it. Just put a couple of red pillows in that red suit. It would be great for business. And think how happy it would make Maggie."

Travis gave him a scowl. "No comment. If you want to talk, let's talk about something else."

They drove down Main Street in silence before Conner took his cue and changed the subject. "Say, if we're going to apply for a license, we'll need a name for our business. Have you got any ideas?"

"Not off the top of my head," Travis said. "We need something about Christmas trees. And some way for folks to know that they'll be buying them fresh from the ranch, not from a lot in town . . ."

"Then how about Christmas Tree Ranch?" Conner suggested.

"Christmas Tree Ranch . . ." Travis repeated the name in his mind. "Christmas Tree Ranch. That's perfect."

"Hot damn!" Conner grinned. "We're really doing this! And we're already on our way!"

* * *

Maggie glanced out of her window in time to see Travis's pickup, with Bucket in the back, pulling up to the county wing of the building that housed the clerk's office. It appeared that Travis and Conner were on their way to apply for a business license.

She understood why Travis had kept Conner from sharing their plans. She'd crushed his male ego the last time they'd met, and Travis was not a forgiving man. His rebuff had stung her. Even so, she couldn't help being curious. Conner had started to say that they'd found something on the ranch when Travis cut him off. And then, when Travis had agreed to let the city take the sleigh, it was Conner who had stopped him.

What was going on?

Maggie tried to tell herself it was none of her business. But whatever affected Branding Iron's Christmas celebration *was* her business. As mayor, anything that went wrong would be her responsibility.

She could pay a visit to the county clerk's office later and sneak a look at the application. But snooping was beneath the dignity of her office. The only honest way to learn what the two men were up to would be to win back Travis's trust. And that wasn't going to be easy.

It was time to get some good, old-fashioned advice.

She busied herself with other things until Travis's truck had left the parking lot. Then, knowing better than to use her office line, she took her cell phone out of her purse and called Francine's number.

"Hello, honey." Hearing Francine's voice was like sinking into a cushiony pillow. "How is Operation Santa Claus coming along?"

Maggie had to smile at the name Francine had given their secret mission. "I may have had a breakthrough," she said. "But I'll need to play my hand very carefully. Otherwise, I might make things worse. Before I tell you about it, is there anything new on your end?"

"Not really new. I talked with Hank again. What he really wants is to make peace with his son. If—and it's a very big *if*—they could put the past behind them and at least be civil to each other, he says he'd be willing to put on that red suit and climb into that sleigh."

Maggie sighed. "Well, at least that's a good start. But I'm just beginning to learn how stubborn Travis can be."

"So what about you, honey? Any progress?"

Maggie related everything that had happened at Buckaroo's that afternoon. "Conner's very likable," she said. "I think having him around will be good for Travis. But when I offered to take the sleigh off their hands, Conner wouldn't hear of it. They're planning something, but they don't want to let me in on the secret."

"So what's next?" Francine asked.

"I'm not sure. Maybe I should just back off and leave them alone. But we do need the sleigh and horses for the parade. That makes it my business to find out what's going on."

"And it gives you a good excuse to snoop," Francine teased.

"Travis said I could come by and pick up the box with the Santa costume in it. I thought I might go tonight. But I want to make sure the situation doesn't just go from bad to worse. How do you think I should handle it?"

"Honey, you're dealing with a couple of healthy, red-blooded males," Francine said. "I have just two words of advice for you."

"Two words?"

Francine chuckled. "Bring food."

Travis and Conner stood by the gate, watching as Bucket rounded up the horses and herded them toward the barn. With the setting sun, the air had taken on a chill. A dry wind rustled the yellow grass along the fence.

"I've got to hand it to that dog of yours. He really knows his stuff," Conner said. "And the horses look good. They're old, but I can tell they've had decent care."

"They seem pretty calm," Travis said. "I haven't had any trouble leading them, but I've never tried hitching them up or driving them. I wouldn't know where to start."

"Nothing to it," Conner said. "After a few lessons, I'll have you driving like a mule skinner."

"You still haven't told me why you wanted to keep the sleigh," Travis said as they walked behind the dog and horses to close the stalls.

"In the summer, when I was growing up, my grandpa used to hire out his old hay wagon and team for nighttime hayrides," Conner said. "Church groups, family groups, whatever, they all had a great time, and it paid pretty well. Grandpa could play the guitar and sing, and he'd have me drive the team. Afterward, there'd be hot chocolate or, if they wanted to pay extra, a barbecue."

"I see where you're going with this," Travis said. "We could do sleigh rides. We've got horses and a sleigh. All we need is snow."

"What are the chances of that?" Conner asked.

"Around here, it's a toss-up. Some years we get plenty of snow. Other years we barely get a flake or two."

"Then we'll just have to trust our luck, won't we?"

Travis paused to think. "I've got an old hay wagon. I used it last summer—pulled it with the tractor. We could always do winter hayrides. But it wouldn't be as much fun as a sleigh."

"We've got time to figure that out. First, we need to decide how to sell the trees."

The two of them walked back toward the house, with Bucket trailing behind. They'd spent much of the afternoon at the kitchen table, talking, taking notes, and filling in parts of their business license application. Neither of them had thought of supper. Now they were getting hungry.

"We could whip up some more bacon and eggs," Travis said. "Maybe an omelet this time. I was planning to stop by Shop Mart on the way home, but then we got talking about the business and it didn't happen."

"Well, that'll have to do, I guess." Conner opened the back door. "You know I'm not counting on you to handle all the cooking and shopping. We need to work out a plan so I can do my fair share."

"One more plan." Travis shook his head. "Hell, I've got plans running out of my ears, and you haven't slept since you got here. Maybe we should just make peanut butter sandwiches and call it a night."

Travis was about to follow Conner inside when he happened to glance toward the road. Through the gathering dusk, he could see headlights approaching. A moment later he heard the smooth purr of the old Lincoln's motor.

"Maggie's here." He passed the word to Conner through the back door. "Gather up that paperwork and get it out of sight. I'll stall her outside."

"Roger!" Conner responded.

As Maggie pulled up to the front gate, Travis was there to open it for her. As she pulled in and climbed out of the car, Bucket came tearing around the house to greet her. She fended the dog off, laughing.

"I only wish you were that happy to see me." Her humor sounded forced.

"If you've come for the box, I can get it and load it in your car," Travis said.

The wind stirred her hair and fluttered the scarf around her neck. *Damn it, but she was beautiful.*

"Actually, I brought something," she said. "Call it a welcome to Branding Iron gift for Conner, if you like. It's chicken enchiladas, still warm. The dish is on the other side of the car, on the floor. And I brought a salad with brownies and ice cream for dessert. If you want to get the box for me, I'll carry the food into the house."

"Sure." Travis walked around the car and opened the passenger door for her. The foil-covered dish, a lidded bowl, and a paper grocery sack were on the floor. The savory aroma wafting from the dish made Travis's mouth water.

She picked them up, doing her best to balance everything between her hands and her arms, but clearly struggling.

"Here." He took the bowl and the sack from her and headed for the porch. "Come on inside. We can get the box later."

So far, so good. Maggie followed Travis inside the house, carrying the warm casserole dish by its handles. Francine had given her excellent advice—including the admonition to bring the hot food in a nice ceramic dish, big enough for leftovers, that would need to be returned.

Conner's face lit in a grin as she walked in the door. "Wow! That smells heavenly! Is it for us?"

Maggie gave him her most gracious smile. "Well, you did buy my lunch. And I wanted to give you a proper welcome to Branding Iron. I hope you'll invite me to join you."

"Hell yes—excuse me, ma'am. You're just in time for supper. Have a seat." He pulled out a mismatched chair. Maggie set the enchilada dish on the table, hung her jacket on the back of the chair, and sat down. Conner pulled three clean plates from the dishwasher, along with a handful of cutlery, and began hurriedly setting the table.

Travis, quiet as usual, set the salad bowl on the

table, put the ice cream in the fridge, and set the bakery box of brownies on the counter.

"Napkins?" Maggie asked.

Travis tore three paper towels off a roll on the counter and tossed them onto the table. "Best thing we've got, I'm afraid," he muttered.

"No need to apologize. My father used to do the same thing," Maggie said.

Conner lifted the foil off the enchiladas. "Hot damn, but these do look good!" He took a fork and scooped two onto his plate. "And you made a lot. Does that mean we get leftovers?"

"That's the idea."

"This was a thoughtful thing to do. Thank you, Maggie." As he held the dish for Maggie to serve herself, Travis spoke the words like lines from a movie. Was he thinking she'd come to manipulate him again? Was he right?

Knowing this wasn't the time to pry for information, she turned her attention to Conner, asking him about his growing-up years and how he became a champion bull rider. Conner was easy to talk to. He was as open and friendly as Travis was guarded. Prison could make that difference in a man, she reasoned.

"Travis and I went to high school together back in Oklahoma," he told her. "He was a town boy, football and track hero. I was one of the farm kids. Even then, all I cared about was rodeo. But we hit it off somehow and became friends. We've kept in touch ever since. When I got hurt and was down on my luck, he invited me to come here."

"Believe me, it wasn't all one-sided." Travis

cleaned up the last bite on his plate. "I needed his help. When I called him, I didn't even know he'd been hurt."

"So this has worked out for both of you."

"Yes, but we need a way to make some money off this ranch," Conner said. "We're hoping we've found it."

A stern glance from Travis stopped him from saying more. Maggie knew better than to press for answers. She was here on a goodwill mission, nothing more, she told herself.

But when she looked at Travis, she couldn't help wondering what had really brought her here tonight.

"How about some dessert? No, stay put. I'll get it." She rose, gathered up the dinner plates, and carried them to the counter. Finding saucers, she put a brownie and a scoop of vanilla bean ice cream on each one.

Conner took a bite of brownie. "Mmmm! Did you make these, too? If you say yes, I'm proposing here and now!"

Maggie laughed. "Sorry. The brownies came from Shop Mart's bakery department. If you want to hang on to that proposal, I'll get you the phone number of the cook. Maybe she's single."

"You've treated us like kings tonight, Maggie," Travis said. "When we're finished here, I'll volunteer Conner to clean up while I walk you outside to get that box out of the sleigh. Okay, Conner?"

"Sure, if I can push myself away from the table. Did you mean we could keep those leftover enchiladas, Maggie?"

"You bet. The salad, too. Just cover the dishes and put them in the fridge. I'll pick them up later."

"No need. I'll drop them off at your office on my next trip to town." Travis pushed his chair out and stood. "Ready to go outside, Maggie?"

"I guess." She let him help her with her jacket. The brush of his hands on her shoulders sent a tingle of awareness through her body.

Bucket was waiting on the porch when they went outside. He tagged along as they walked back around the house to the open shed. The night was chilly, with stars emerging from among drifting clouds. Travis had brought a flashlight. It made a pale circle on the ground as they walked slowly, side by side.

"Thanks for the meal, Maggie," Travis said. "Whatever you had in mind, it was a nice gesture."

"But you still don't trust me. Not even after I was honest with you. Is that what you're trying to tell me?"

"It's not that I don't trust you. It's that you're wasting your time. I washed my hands of my father years ago, and nothing's going to change that."

"That's too bad. I have it on good authority that if you'd go to him and settle the past, he'd consider playing Santa in the Christmas parade."

His jaw tightened. "Is that damned Christmas parade the only thing that matters to you, Maggie? Is that why you came here tonight, with all that food and fake sweetness?"

"It wasn't fake! I care about all the people in this town—and not just because it's my job. The old folks, the parents, the kids—even outsiders like you and Conner—they all matter to me. I want Branding Iron to be a happy place—especially at Christmastime."

"Conner might be willing to drive the sleigh. He can already handle a team, and I know he wouldn't mind doing it. But Hank might have issues with Conner, too, for reasons you aren't aware of. Your best bet would be to find a different Santa Claus."

"Can't you at least talk to Hank? If you could settle your differences—"

"I'm sorry, Maggie, but that's not going to happen, especially now."

They'd paused outside the shed. "I know Hank's been through a lot, but he's a good man," Maggie said. "I can't imagine what he could've done to make you so set against him."

He turned to face her in the darkness. "Are you asking me to tell you?"

"I'd like to understand, at least."

"Listen, then," he said. "But if you don't like what you hear, don't say I didn't warn you."

Chapter 8

As he spoke, trailing the words out slowly, Travis kept walking, past the shed and out into the yard. Maggie matched her steps to his, following the beam of his flashlight.

"You know how my father—Hank—lost his leg, don't you?"

"Most people around here do. It must've been an awful accident. Do you remember it at all?"

"Not really. I wasn't much more than a baby then. I don't even remember living in this house. But this ranch is where it happened. I guess my parents were doing okay before. But their marriage couldn't survive the accident. I can imagine what it did to their love life, and to other things, like his ability to work. According to my mother, he started drinking to kill the pain. After that, she said, he was drunk most of the time, and when he got drunk, he got mean. She told me how he'd hit her and call her foul names and how afraid she was that he might hurt me, too. When she couldn't take it anymore, she took me and left Branding Iron for good. Not long after that, she married my stepfather, and they settled in Oklahoma, where I grew up."

His long, silent pause made her wonder whether the story was finished. "Is that all?" she asked.

"Not quite." His voice had taken on a flat, bitter tone. "My stepfather, who adopted me, was a decent man. He tried to raise me right. But he was pretty strict, and like a lot of teenagers, I was a smart-ass kid. We argued a lot.

"When I was about sixteen, after one big blowup, I decided I was going to run away and find my *real* father. My mother had painted him pretty black over the years. She'd made sure I understood what a mean, worthless, drunken bum he was. But I found myself thinking, how bad could he be? Maybe if I showed up, he'd even let me live with him.

"I knew he was still in Branding Iron, so one night I filled my backpack, snuck out of the house, and caught my first ride with a trucker. By the end of the second day, using my thumb and my wits, I'd made it to Branding Iron.

"I went into a pool hall—the place is gone now—and asked where I could find Hank Miller. Somebody who knew him gave me directions to a broken-down trailer on a vacant lot by the old railroad yard. It was night when I found the place. There was a junk car parked outside, and I could see what looked like lantern light through the window. By then I was shaking, but I forced myself to knock on the door. My father opened it."

Travis paused by the wire fence that surrounded the hayfield. He took a slow breath, his jaw clenching tight with the memory.

"What happened?" Maggie asked when he didn't speak.

"About what you'd think. The man in the doorway was foul-mouthed, filthy, and so drunk he could barely stand. When I told him who I was, he cursed me—called my mother a bitch and worse. 'Get the hell out of here, boy!' he said. 'Forget you ever saw me! If you come back here again, I'll call the police!' "

"I'm sorry." Maggie could think of nothing else to say.

"My mother was right. He was a mean, worthless, drunken bum. After he shoved me off the step and slammed the door, I cried myself to sleep in an alley behind a Dumpster. The next morning, I lit out for home and swore I'd never speak to him again."

Maggie laid a hand on his sleeve. "That was a long time ago. Hank's a different person now. He went to AA and sobered up, got a job at the feed store, and arranged to buy the place when the owner retired. Over the years, he's added the hardware business and earned the respect of the whole town. And he's one of the kindest men I know."

"I'm a different person, too, Maggie. I know what it's like to hit bottom and struggle back from nothing. I'm not entirely hard-hearted, but there are things you don't know—things I'm not at liberty to tell you. Later, when you know, you'll understand. But for now—"

"Oh, stop making excuses!" She wheeled away from him. "Why do things have to be so complicated between good people?"

"And why does your whole life have to revolve around your job and that damned Christmas parade?"

He tossed the flashlight to the ground, caught her hand, and spun her back toward him. His arms crushed her close. His gaze burned through the darkness between them. When he kissed her, it was not like the first time, but fierce, rough, his mouth taking full possession of hers. Maggie's response blazed. She melted against him with a low moan, loving the taste and feel of him, loving the luscious sensations that swirled through her body as the kiss went on and on.

He had to know what he was doing to her, and that she wanted him as much as he wanted her. From somewhere in the back of her mind, a cautious voice whispered that this wasn't a good idea. Right now, she didn't care.

He drew back, just far enough to talk. "Damn it, Maggie, why can't we just keep this, you and me, apart from all the other craziness? Why can't we just stop asking questions and enjoy this while it lasts?"

While it lasts . . .

Those words were enough to sober her. She'd been carried away by Travis's kiss and the thrill of being in his arms. But she wasn't a *while it lasts* kind of woman. For her, it had to be all or nothing.

Years ago, she'd let herself say yes to a man who

wasn't fully ready to commit. That broken engagement had left her determined not to make the same mistake again.

Gently, she untangled herself from his embrace. "Maybe we need to give this a rest for now," she said. "What do you say we get that box and put it in my car?"

It was as if his face had assumed a mask—the one he wore with strangers. "Message received and copied," he said, picking up the flashlight and turning back toward the shed. Maggie had to stretch her legs to keep up with his long strides. Bucket frisked ahead of them, his white markings a beacon in the dark.

Handing her the flashlight, he raised the edge of the tarp that covered the sleigh and lifted out the box. "Got it," he said. "Let's go."

"Why didn't Conner want to give up the sleigh?" she asked against her better judgment.

"You'll have to ask Conner about that." He waited while she opened the door of her Lincoln. Then he slid the box onto the rear seat. "You're welcome to come back in. I know he'd like to thank you for the meal."

"No need for that. It was my pleasure. Here's your flashlight." They were behaving like polite strangers, speaking as if that blistering kiss had never happened. Maggie kept up the pretense as she closed the rear door and walked around the car to the driver's side. Whatever she'd hoped to accomplish here tonight, she'd failed.

"Good night, Travis," she said. "Thank you for telling me about your father. I wish I could change things between the two of you, but I know better than to try. Only you can do that. I won't trouble you again."

She slid into the driver's seat. When she started the car and turned on the light, she saw that he'd stepped away and called Bucket to him, to make sure the dog stayed clear of the wheels.

He stayed where he was, watching her, as she backed out of the gate and onto the road. Pausing to change gears, she gave him a casual wave, as if to say *no hard feelings*. He gave her a nod and a tip of an invisible hat before she pressed the gas pedal too hard and roared away.

She wasn't going to cry this time, Maggie told herself. She'd done all she could. Now it was time to walk away and leave Travis to pursue his own agenda. Unless Hank was willing to play Santa with Conner driving the sleigh, she would give up on that idea and look elsewhere. There was always another solution—that was what her father used to tell her. Somehow she would find it.

As for Travis, she wouldn't expect to see him again. The next time he came into town, he would likely leave her dishes on the front porch of her house, or maybe with the receptionist at work. But he wouldn't stop in to say hello.

And she could handle that, Maggie told herself. After all, she was a big girl. And big girls didn't cry. Wasn't that what the old song said?

Conner looked up from loading the dishwasher as Travis came back into the house. "Hey man, you were out there so long, I was hoping you'd gotten lucky. But you're looking more like your grandma's been arrested by the Border Patrol. What happened?"

"You don't want to know," Travis growled. "And I don't want to talk about it."

Conner shook his head. "I take it things didn't go well with your sexy lady mayor. Too bad. She's not only gorgeous, she's one hell of a good cook."

"I said I didn't want to talk about it. And since you like her so much, feel free to go after her yourself. If you'd offer to cozy up to my father and drive that sleigh in the parade, she'd probably be yours for life."

Conner added detergent to the dishwasher, closed the door, and started the cycle. "So that's what this is about."

"It's not what I want it to be about. But she won't let it go. I'm done. She's all yours."

"I doubt she'd have me. I've seen the way that woman looks at you." Conner stifled a yawn. "Besides, once we get our Christmas tree business going, your father won't want anything to do with either one of us." He glanced at the box of paperwork he'd hastily stowed on top of the fridge. "So, shall we take up where we left off when lovely Maggie showed up?"

Travis shook his head. "You're running on caffeine and adrenaline. Get some sleep, or you'll be worthless tomorrow."

Conner yawned again. "Sounds like a plan. Thanks for the welcome, friend. I mean it. You've saved my life, and I'm not going to let you down."

"Go on, before you get all mushy on me. You can have dibs on the bathroom. I'll be awake for a while."

"Thanks. I mean it."

"Get some rest. I'll wake you in time for chores."

After Conner had vanished down the hall, Travis walked out onto the front porch and stood at the rail. In the sky, the waxing moon drifted behind a thin veil of clouds. The ancient cottonwoods that lined the road stood bare against the sky. A dry wind rattled their branches and stung Travis's face where he stood. No storm tomorrow. Good, he thought. He and Conner would have enough to do without battling bad weather.

The business license application would need to be completed and turned in as soon as possible. But once it was in the hands of the county office, their plans would no longer be a secret. In a small town like Branding Iron, news traveled fast. It wouldn't take long for word to reach Maggie, or even Hank.

Then what?

Maybe they should hold off a little longer, until their plans were in place. Lord, so many decisions.

Christmas Tree Ranch.

He liked the name—the sound of it, the way it rolled off the tongue, whispering of snow and sleigh bells and the scent of fresh pine. In prison, Christmas had been just another day. In his years as a patrolman, he'd always volunteered for work that day, giving the officers with families a chance to be home. This would be his first real Christmas since his boyhood.

Not that it would be a traditional Christmas, with family opening presents around a decorated tree. That was something he might never have. But he had come to this ranch a year ago with nothing.

If he could celebrate this Christmas with a successful business venture behind him, cash in his pocket, food on the table, and a friend to share it, he would call life good.

As for the rest . . . Travis gazed down the road where Maggie's Lincoln had long since vanished. He had never shared that early experience with his father. But something about Maggie's warmth had prompted him to tell her, and to take her in his arms. The woman was as sensual as she was smart and classy. Her response to his kiss had shown him that much. But for anything more than a few cheap thrills, she was out of his league. The sooner he accepted that and moved on, the better off he'd be.

Something pressed against his leg. Bucket had come onto the porch. Was it for company, Travis wondered, or just warmth? He reached down and rubbed the dog's silky ears. The nights were getting cold, and the skunk smell had all but faded from his coat.

Turning his back on the night, he walked to the front door and opened it. "Come on, boy," he said, glancing back at the dog. "It's all right."

The dog followed him into the house, glancing around as if to make sure he was allowed. In the back of the closet, Travis found an old blanket he'd used in his truck. Folding it to make soft layers, he placed it in a warm corner of the kitchen, near the stove. "Behave yourself, and it's yours," he said, giving the animal a stern look.

Bucket walked over to the blanket, sniffed it, made a circle with his body, and closed his eyes.

Travis turned off the light and went to bed.

* * *

With Thanksgiving just around the corner, the business application had been turned in and granted with surprising speed. So far there'd been no reaction from Maggie or Hank. But once the signs they planned to make went up along the highway, there were bound to be some fireworks. They would have to be ready.

They'd also spent a grueling day clearing the old road that led from the ranch to the tree site, filling in potholes, digging out clumps of sage and prickly pear, and rolling away rocks. By the time it was done, they were sore, blistered, and filthy, but the rough road was now wide and solid enough to support the pickup.

In Cottonwood Springs, they'd found a shop that sold secondhand tools and bought a heavy-duty, gasoline-powered chain saw, as well as two smaller power saws, and some hand-pruning tools for trimming the trees. Another shop had a good deal on a two-wheeled cart that was light enough to be towed behind the ATV. Conner had splurged, paying five dollars for an old-style TV that worked in the shop, even though Travis had told him there was no cable service at the ranch. Never mind, Travis had told himself. If fiddling with the TV would keep Conner amused at night, what was the harm?

At Travis's suggestion, they'd stopped by a Christmas tree lot in Cottonwood Springs to check prices. Even trucked-in trees were expensive. For fresh-cut trees, they could charge even more. But how much would people be willing to pay, especially in Branding Iron? One more decision to make.

They loaded up and headed for home with their purchases in the back of Travis's pickup. The afternoon was gray and cold. Wind battered the side of the truck as they drove south, down the highway to Branding Iron.

"Let's pray for blue skies and sunshine tomorrow," Conner said. "Trimming trees in this weather will be a bitch."

"We'll do what we have to," Travis said. "The other night I did some research on your laptop. Tree trimming is usually done a lot earlier, while the young trees are still growing, not when they're big enough to sell. We'll have to keep the trimming to a minimum—just lop off the limbs that spoil the natural shape. If we trim too much, our trees will look butchered—like a bad haircut."

Conner rested the boot of his good right leg on the dash. "This is getting damned scary," he said. "We've got to open for business by next weekend, or by December first at the latest. And there's so much yet to do—have you thought about it?"

"I haven't thought of much else," Travis said. "We'll need to buy lights for the house and yard and put them up. We'll need stands for the trees, or at least some kind of rack to lean them against. We'll need twine so folks can tie the trees to their cars. And most people will want to pay with credit cards. We'll need a way to run them. I don't know the first thing about that, do you?"

Conner shrugged. "I guess we'll just have to figure it out, or find somebody to ask. We'll need Christmas music, too, and some kind of speaker to play it on, even if it's just an old boom box." He exhaled. "Lordy, what if we've bitten off more than we can chew? What if we do all this work and spend all this money, and all we end up with is a yard full of dead Christmas trees? What if everybody just goes to Hank's because that's what they're used to?"

"That's not a question I wanted to hear," Travis said. "But it's worth asking. We need to offer them something they can't get at Hank's—or anywhere else. We need a reason for them to come to us."

Conner stared out the window for a few minutes. Then he lowered his boot from the dash. "This might be a crazy idea, but I'll run it by you. I was thinking about those hayrides my grandpa used to give, singing songs and having cocoa after. What if we had a nice little campfire in the front yard, with hot chocolate and roasted marshmallows for people who come?"

"I like that," Travis said. "And I just thought of something else. We could have some cut trees in the yard, but if folks wanted the full experience, we could take them on the road to where the trees are. They could choose their own tree, and we could cut it down and haul it back with them on the trailer."

"Yeah!" Conner's voice was charged with excitement. "We could use the ATV as a backup. But if it snows—*really* snows—we could use the sleigh. Imagine that! Horses, sleigh bells, snow, and Christmas trees! Too bad we let Maggie take that Santa suit."

Travis still felt a twinge at the mention of Maggie's name. "It sounds like a grand idea," he said. "But we'd have to charge extra to make it worth our time. And Branding Iron isn't a wealthy town. I don't know how many families would spend the money, especially if they're already cash-strapped from buying presents."

"So we advertise in Cottonwood Springs," Conner said. "There are plenty of folks there who could afford it and would drive half an hour to give their kids the experience. And we could hold a drawing in Branding Iron, with free rides as prizes. Another thing—once we get busy, we won't be able to handle the operation by ourselves. If we hire a few high school kids to help out, we'll get their families coming, and the word will spread. This is going to come together and work! It's got to."

Travis nodded his agreement as they came into Branding Iron. He envied Conner's enthusiasm—but then, Conner was a man whose idea of making a living was climbing onto a murderous, half-ton animal and trusting that it wouldn't kill him. Even the fact that his last ride had crushed his body and ended his career had done little to dampen Conner's sunny spirit.

Comparing Conner's background with his own was like comparing day and night. In his work as a patrolman, things were expected to go wrong. It had been his job to keep them from happening if he could, and to deal with them if he couldn't. And in prison . . .

But those three years were a closed door. He was a free man now, and he never wanted to think about them again.

They drove through Branding Iron, passing Hank's Hardware on the way out of town. The lights strung in the Christmas tree lot glowed in the twilight, where a few families were already checking out the trees. The scene only served to remind Travis of how far behind they'd already fallen in getting their own trees ready.

They pulled into the yard and unloaded their purchases in the shed. Bucket, who'd been waiting on the porch, trotted down to greet them, then barked and ran to the pasture gate as if to remind them that it was time to bring the horses into the barn.

"I'll go with him and handle the gates," Conner said. "You look dead on your feet."

Did he look that bad? Until Conner's remark, he hadn't realized how tired he was. He climbed the front steps, went into the house, and hung his coat on the rack. In the fridge, he found a cold beer and popped the tab. At least they'd filled up on burgers and shakes before leaving Cottonwood Springs. Nobody would feel like cooking tonight.

Setting the beer on the table, he pulled his wallet out of his hip pocket and found the receipts for their day's purchases, including gas for the truck. After smoothing them out, he opened the file drawer in his desk and slipped them into a folder. The business was going to need some kind of bookkeeping system, especially after the money started coming in—*if* the money started coming in.

Money had been a worry ever since starting this venture. The trees were free. But everything else— the licensing fee, the tools, the trailer, the coming publicity, the endless small things they needed— they all added up. He and Conner had almost maxed out their credit cards, and they were just getting started. They would need a small miracle to keep them afloat until the trees were sold. But tonight he was too tired to think about it.

Maggie's clean casserole dish and salad bowl sat on the counter. The leftover food she'd brought was long gone. Travis had put off returning the dishes—partly because he'd been so busy and partly because of the awkwardness. Should he deliver them to her porch, or maybe her office, and leave without seeing her, or was he man enough to face up to the stunning redhead who'd returned his kiss and walked away?

He glanced at his watch. It was early enough for a trip back to town. Maybe it was time he faced the music and returned Maggie's dishes. If she wasn't home, he could leave them on her covered porch. If she was, especially if she had company, he would thank her politely and go.

Decision made, he put on his coat, picked up his keys and the dishes, and went outside to tell Conner he was leaving.

Conner, with Bucket at his heels, was coming out of the barn, where they'd just put the horses away. When he saw the dishes in Travis's hands, he grinned. "So you're finally going to take those back. I've been waiting for that."

"I'm just returning them; that's all. It's not like I'm going to stay and visit."

"Sure," Conner teased. "Don't worry. I'll take care of Bucket. And if you're not back by bedtime, I won't call nine one one."

Travis climbed into his truck without answering. He knew Conner was only having fun. But sometimes his jokes could be annoying as hell. Maybe because, deep down, Travis wished they had some basis in truth. Maggie had gotten to him as few women ever had. But he wasn't into rejection, thank you. He would leave the dishes at her house, wish the lady a good night, and head for home.

The night was getting darker, the wind stronger. Clouds raced across the face of the moon. Travis kept both hands on the wheel. He had felt nothing at the house, but now, as he drove, a strange premonition crept over him—a sense that something unforeseen was about to happen.

Chapter 9

By the time Travis pulled up in front of Maggie's house, a fine sleet was peppering the windshield of the truck. Shadowed by the deep porch, the front window glowed with lamplight.

Picking up the dishes, he climbed out of the cab and strode up the front walk. The wind tore at his jacket as he mounted the steps. Maggie wouldn't be expecting visitors on a night like this. He didn't want to startle her or make her uncomfortable in any way. But his pulse quickened at the prospect of seeing her again.

Don't be an idiot, he told himself as he pressed a finger to her doorbell. *Just give her the damned dishes and leave.*

He heard a stirring from the other side of the door and the metallic *snik* of the dead bolt sliding back. The door opened a few inches, then wider as she recognized him.

"Come in, Travis." She was dressed in black leggings and a baggy gray sweatshirt that had slipped off one shoulder, showing a lacy pink bra strap. "Here, let me take those." She reached for the dishes in his hands. "I hope you didn't drive all the way here in this weather just to return them."

"No," Travis lied. "I just thought I'd drop them off on my way home. Sorry to be so long in getting them back to you."

"No problem. If I'd needed them, I'd have taken them with me when I left your place. Take off your coat while I put these things away. There's a coatrack behind the door." Barefoot, she pattered into the kitchen. Travis hesitated, then took off his coat. He hadn't meant to stay. But she'd clearly invited him. And her living room was so cozy and inviting that he couldn't make himself leave.

An overstuffed sofa faced the fireplace, where a cheery blaze crackled on the brick hearth. There were soft cushions, an abundance of green plants, and a wall of shelves filled with well-worn books. The aroma of freshly baked cookies that wafted from the kitchen made his mouth water.

Maggie reappeared with a tray of cookies and milk. "You're in luck," she said. "I had to bake chocolate chip cookies for a work party tomorrow. There are plenty left over, and they're still warm."

"I can't stay long," he said. "I need to get home before the weather gets worse."

"I won't keep you," she said. "But I can't send you away hungry when we've got warm cookies." She put the tray on the coffee table and moved the cushions to clear a space for him. "Have a seat," she said. "And help yourself."

Travis sat and took one cookie, then a second. The cookies and cold milk were delicious, but it was Maggie who stunned him. Warm and rumpled, she looked so tantalizing that it was all he could do to keep his hands off her. He swore silently. This wasn't why he'd come. And he'd be damned if he was going to let her do that maddening hot and cold number on him again.

But, so help him, there were worse things to do on a blustery night than sit in front of a warm fire, sharing cookies and milk with a gorgeous, sexy woman.

Maggie hadn't expected anybody to show up on her door-step tonight, especially Travis. But now that he was here, she realized how much she'd wanted to see him again.

Her eager gaze took him in—the way his damp hair, in need of a trim, curled over his forehead, the lean, chiseled face and earnest gray eyes. The man was heartbreak on a bun. But she'd learned that being alone and thinking about him all the time was no picnic either. She'd memorized the moment when he'd kissed her, his strong arms crushing her close, his lips like cool velvet on her mouth, the taste of him, the feel of him . . .

Had he come here for a reason, or was he just, as he'd said, stopping by to return her dishes?

"How's your search for Santa coming along?" he asked, as if just making conversation.

"Are you about to volunteer?" she asked.

"Not on your life. I was just wondering, that's all."

"Too bad." Maggie broke a cookie and dipped half in her milk. "I would have taken you up on it. The Santa suit was so old that it fell apart at the dry cleaner's, so we'll have to rent a new one. But so far there's nobody to fill it."

And that was literally true. Carrie Mae, who worked in the county clerk's office, had slipped her the news that Travis and Conner had applied for a license to sell Christmas trees. Once Hank found out that they were going into competition with him, there was no way he would play Santa—especially since his competitors owned the sleigh and horses.

For Maggie, the situation was turning into one massive headache.

"So what's the backup plan?" he asked. "Do you have one?"

"Not a good one. But the parade's got to have a Santa. So if I have to, I'll wear the suit myself."

His eyes twinkled. "I'd pay good money to see that."

"Maybe so. But the kids would know the difference. They deserve better. They deserve a real Santa in a real sleigh, like they've always had. But I know better than to ask Hank again. Even if he says yes, he's bound to change his mind when he finds out about the trees—"

She stopped herself, realizing she'd just admitted to knowing his plan. "Sorry," she said.

"Did you snoop?" He raised an eyebrow, half amused.

"No, for what it's worth. I was fighting temptation and winning. Then somebody in the county office told me. Hank's bound to be livid about your competing with him."

"This is America. Competition is allowed. If he chooses to be mad, that's his problem."

"And mine," Maggie said. "I can't blame you and Conner for taking advantage of an opportunity. But you've just changed Christmas for the whole town."

"Maybe it'll be a good change. We've got some great plans in the works." He gazed at Maggie's downcast face. "I guess I'd better go." He stood, brushing the crumbs off his jeans. "Thanks for the cookies and milk. Are you going to tell anybody about the trees?"

"I've known for days, but I haven't told a soul, and I don't intend to. That's your business." She rose to see him out. Heaven knows, it wasn't what she wanted. But things had become awkward, and she could think of no excuse to keep him there.

"Thanks for understanding," he said. "At least you know why it wouldn't have done any good for me to square things with Hank."

"Yes, I know."

He was reaching for his coat. She checked the impulse to fling herself into his arms and beg him not to leave. Twice he'd taken her in his arms and kissed her. Twice he'd met the wall of her fear— the fear of being hurt again. Travis was a proud man. He would not risk a third rejection.

Please don't go! The words rushed to her lips, but something held them back. She stood silent and helpless as he shrugged on his coat. "Good night,

Maggie, and good luck," he said, and opened the front door.

A fierce gust of hail-laden wind ripped the door-knob out of his hand, slamming the door inward against the wall, and shoving Travis backward so hard that he almost lost his balance.

Righting himself, he wrestled the door closed. Maggie rushed forward to help him hold it while he fastened the latch. As it clicked into place, she stood between him and the door. "You can't go out there now," she said.

"Is that an invitation, Maggie?" His expression was unreadable.

"You know storms like this don't last long. It won't hurt you to wait till the worst of it passes." She was talking too fast, the words coming in bursts.

There was a flicker of hesitation. Then, as if making up his mind, he stripped his arms out of the coat and let it drop to the floor. Turning toward Maggie, he laid his hands on her shoulders and held her at arms' length. His slate gray eyes drilled into hers.

"No more games, Maggie," he said. "Is it yes or no?"

A quiver passed through her body. "Yes . . ." Her hands slid up his chest as she whispered her reply. "And no more games."

His kiss stole her breath and sent heat spiraling through her body. Pulse throbbing, she pulled him down to her, deepening the contact, teasing him with her tongue. He responded with a growl of need, his body pressing hers, his hands moving up her bare back to find the clasp of her bra.

Then, abruptly, he stopped and eased her gently away from him. "I think we're headed for trouble, Maggie," he muttered in a husky voice. "There will be better times for this."

Maggie nodded and forced herself to take slow breaths. Travis was right. With so many things unsettled between them, falling into bed too soon would only create more complications. If this was meant to be, they'd have all the time in the world later on.

The storm was still howling outside. Wind rattled the windows. Hail hammered the panes like buckshot. Moving away from her, Travis picked up the remote and switched on the small TV that stood next to the fireplace. "I hope you don't mind," he said. "Maybe we can get some news about the storm."

He found a local news channel, lowered himself to the sofa, and laid an arm along the back. "Come here," he said, with a nod to the empty space beside him.

As the weather update came on the screen, Maggie settled against him with a contented sigh, her head resting in the hollow of his shoulder. It felt right, being with him like this, as if they'd been close forever. She tried to pay attention, but in the warm room, nestled against the man who made her feel happy, relaxed, and exquisitely comfortable, sleep crept up on her. She stifled a yawn and felt his arm tighten around her.

The drone of the TV announcer's voice faded as her eyelids drooped, grew heavy, and finally closed.

*   *   *

Travis stirred and opened his eyes. The lamp was on in the room, but the fire had burned down to coals. Aside from the TV, broadcasting an infomercial, the night was eerily still.

He could no longer hear the storm.

When he tried to move, he discovered that his left arm was numb and weighted in place. Maggie was nestled in the curve of it, still fast asleep.

Lord, what time is it? Blinking himself awake, he focused his gaze on the mantel clock above the fireplace. It was 1:15 AM.

He sat up straight and shifted his arm. Maggie opened her eyes, looking muzzy and adorable. "Hullo," she murmured.

He bent his head and kissed the tip of her nose. "Wake up, sleepyhead," he said. "It's after one in the morning. I've got to get out of here before your neighbors start gossiping."

"Is it still storming?" She pushed herself up and brushed her tousled hair back from her face.

"I haven't looked, but I can't hear it anymore. Whatever the weather's like out there, I need to get going."

She rose unsteadily to her feet. "Let me make you some coffee."

"We'd better not take the time." Travis picked up his coat, then paused to take her in his arms. "Things are bound to be crazy until after the holidays. If you don't hear from me—"

"I know." She touched his cheek. "I won't take it personally. And things will be pretty crazy for me, too. We might have to put you and me off until after Christmas."

"In that case, I'd like to reserve you for New

Year's Eve, if you're free. We can dress up and go out on the town—"

"Or stay right here and snuggle," she said. "I think I might like that even better."

"Your choice. Got to go now." He kissed her quick and hard, tearing himself away before temptation could keep him there any longer. Spending the rest of the night with her would be heaven. But it wasn't going to happen now.

He pulled on his coat and stepped out onto the porch, closing the door behind him. The air was cold and still, the sky clear. But the hailstorm had left a thin layer of white on the ground. The roads would be slippery going home. At least he had decent tires, and there shouldn't be much traffic at this hour.

The surrounding houses were all dark. Good. The last thing he wanted was to have some nosy neighborhood gossip causing trouble for Maggie. Nobody would believe how chaste their evening had been. Hell, Conner would have a field day with it. But he would just have to grin and bear his friend's teasing.

He had to brush the hail off the truck, but once he was inside, it started right up. The road was like an ice rink, but as a patrolman, he'd driven under all sorts of conditions. Getting home shouldn't be a problem.

Gearing down, he kept his speed at a steady twenty miles an hour. Progress was slow, but it was better than sliding off the road and getting stuck.

He remembered his premonition on the way here, the feeling that something was about to happen. If that "something" had meant finally getting on solid ground with Maggie, he would never complain again. That smart, sexy woman could be the best thing that had ever happened to him. Now, if he could just make his business plans work out, he'd be on top of the world.

Along Main Street, the lights gleamed on the icy white surface of the road. There was no traffic at this hour, but he stopped at the red lights anyway. Old habits died hard, even when a stop meant easing to a halt by tapping the brake to avoid a skid, then rolling forward until he gained enough traction to pick up speed again.

Ahead, he could see the last stoplight, where Main Street intersected with the highway. After that, the going would be easier—and he was in luck. This light was green. He pressed the gas pedal, just enough to give him a little more speed. He would barely make it.

The light turned yellow as he passed under the signal. He was just easing into the left turn when a pair of high-beam headlights almost blinded him. In the same instant, a huge, dark shape hurtled out of the darkness and slammed into the right side of the pickup, crumpling it inward like an empty soda can.

Anchored in place by his seat belt, Travis was flung to one side by the impact, but in the seconds it took for the shock to wear off, he realized he wasn't hurt. However, from the way the far side of the truck was stove in, he would guess that the old Ford was totaled.

His trooper instincts kicked in. Somebody was in the other vehicle—somebody who might be injured and need help.

The frame had bent around the driver's side door, but Travis managed to kick it open. Jumping to the ground, he ran around to the other side of the truck. That was when he saw what had hit him.

Even in the dark, it wasn't hard to recognize the hulking outline of a black Hummer h1 Alpha.

The big off-road vehicle was built like a tank. The heavy grille bar on the front end, which had crushed the pickup, had protected the Hummer, which wasn't likely even scratched.

But right now, that wasn't his concern.

Sprinting to the driver's side of the Hummer, Travis flung the door open. The man in the driver's seat was rubbing his head, looking confused.

"Are you all right?" Travis demanded.

"I . . . think so."

"Is anybody else in the vehicle?"

"No. Just me. You sound like a cop. Are you?"

"Nope. Here, let me help you out. You might have trouble standing." Travis offered an arm to balance the man as he slid off the seat and dropped to the ground. Standing in the faint glow of the street light, he was a little taller than Travis, close to him in age, with rumpled dark hair. A small gash on his forehead was oozing blood. Travis offered him a clean handkerchief to press on the wound.

"What the hell happened?" He glanced around, a confused expression on his face.

"You were in an accident." Travis's brain had clicked into the detachment mode that had enabled him to survive as a highway trooper. It was still sinking in that this man's driving had destroyed his truck and, except for some lucky timing, could have killed him.

"Accident?" He blinked as if trying to rouse himself.

"Your vehicle ran a red light and hit my truck," Travis said. "Take a look."

"What?" He turned around and saw the damage, which seemed to shock him to his senses. He turned slowly back to face Travis. "Oh, hell, I'm sorry," he muttered. "I remember now. I saw the light and slammed on the brakes, but I couldn't stop. I slid right into you. Must've hit my head. Don't worry, I've got insurance. I can get you my card—"

"Thanks." Travis was still in cop mode. "Don't you know better than to hit the brakes on an icy road? That'll send you into a skid every time. And you need to put that Hummer in four-wheel drive. I know they've got it."

"Sorry. I'm from Phoenix. We don't have slick roads there."

"Phoenix?" Travis shook his head. "That explains a lot. If you'd been going any faster, we might not be talking right now."

The stranger frowned and fumbled for his wallet. "I'll get you my insurance information. But first, I've got one question."

"What's that?"

His bewildered gaze swept from the hail-slicked ground to the traffic signal, which continued to change. "Where in hell's name am I?"

"You don't know?"

"I haven't got the foggiest idea."

"This is Branding Iron, Texas. Does that ring a bell?"

He shook his head. "Never heard of it. I was headed for Fort Worth. Must've taken a wrong turn somewhere." He surveyed the wreck again. "Shouldn't we call the police or something?"

"In this town, a policeman would just have to get up in the middle of the night and give you a ticket. Nobody's badly hurt, and you've offered your insurance information. If you'll give it to me and help me push my truck off the road, I'll make a call and report the accident in the morning."

"Thanks." He slipped two cards out of his wallet and handed them to Travis. One was a policy card from a well-known insurance company. The other was a business card. "Keep them. I've got extras," he said.

Travis held the business card up to the light and managed to read most of it.

DR. J. T. RUSHFORD, DVM
1642 PALO VERDE DRIVE, PHOENIX, AZ

"DVM? So you're a veterinarian?" Travis asked.

"That's right. Most folks just call me Rush." He extended a hand.

"Travis Morgan." Travis accepted the handshake. The stranger seemed like a decent sort, but all he really wanted was to have his truck back and drive home. Unfortunately, he knew that the old Ford was done for. He would never drive it again.

"So what's a vet from Arizona doing clear out here in the middle of the night?" he asked.

"That's a long story," Rush said. "Let's get your

truck out of the road. Then, if you'll allow me to drive you home, I'll tell it to you."

The truck was too badly damaged to drive, but with Travis steering and the Hummer pushing from behind, they managed to get it onto the shoulder of the highway. Travis blocked the wheels, scrawled a note, and tucked it under the windshield wiper. He could've called Conner to come and get him, but as long as Rush was willing to drive him home, it made sense to take him up on the offer. Besides, he was interested in hearing the man's story.

The cab of the Hummer was a study in functional luxury, with leather seats and a dash that looked like the cockpit of an airplane. Some technical updates, like Bluetooth and a GPS, had likely been added after 2006, the last manufacturing date for this model. Travis buckled himself in and gave directions. "Five miles south down the highway and then you turn left. I'll tell you where. But not too fast. That surface is still slick."

"Got it," Rush pulled back onto the road. "I still say you sound like a cop."

"I used to be. Long story. But right now, I'm more interested in how an Arizona vet wound up in the Texas boondocks. Wasn't your GPS working?"

"Damn thing hasn't worked right in days. Whoever that woman's voice belongs to, I think she's mad at me. But then, I haven't had great luck with women lately."

"You promised me a story," Travis said.

"So I did. And a sad tale it is. The moral is, never marry a girl with a rich daddy—especially a rich daddy who buys her whatever her greedy little heart desires, including a million-dollar house."

"And that's what got you lost in Texas?"

"I'm getting to that." Rush switched the headlights on high beam. They lit up the road for half a mile. "I wanted to be the one to support her and our baby girl. But after four years, she decided that being married to a guy who was always working wasn't much fun. She found some idiot with a trust fund, kicked me out, and moved him in. Since the house was in her name and we had a prenuptial, she was within her rights to do that. I'd have shrugged it off, except for our daughter and the fact that my veterinary practice was on the property, attached to the house. She put her daddy's lawyers to work, and I was toast. I was lucky to keep my equipment. I've got it with me now, loaded in the back."

Forty yards ahead, two deer bounded into the headlights. Rush's foot jerked to the brake pedal. "Easy, now." Travis cautioned him. "Just light taps, like I told you, or you'll skid and spin off the road."

Rush did as he was told. The lumbering vehicle slowed and shuddered to a stop, the engine dying, as two more deer came leaping out of the trees and crossed the road, one so close that its haunch brushed the grille. Rush sank back in the seat with a *whoosh* of breath. "Thanks. One accident's enough for tonight."

"You still haven't told me how you ended up in Texas," Travis said.

"Well, here goes." Rush started the engine again and moved ahead at a crawl. "I didn't have the money to buy or even lease property to set up a new practice in Phoenix. But I came across an ad in a professional journal. A clinic in Fort Worth had a vacancy and was looking for a third vet. I contacted them, and they offered me the job. By then, I was living in a motel with my equipment in storage. I was happy to take whatever I could get. I loaded up and headed out.

"I was less than a day away when I got a text from them. The clinic had been sold, and the new owners didn't need me."

"Rotten luck," Travis said.

"My sentiments exactly," said Rush. "I figured that since I'd come this far, I might as well go and meet the new owners. Maybe I could talk them into hiring me. By then, it was getting dark, and a storm was blowing in, but I figured I could drive all night and make Fort Worth by morning. You know the rest."

"Sorry about that," Travis said. "The road to my ranch is just ahead on your left. You'll need to slow down to make the turn."

Rush slowed the Hummer expertly and eased into the turn. At least the man was a fast learner. "You've got a ranch?" he asked. "What kind of stock do you run? Cattle? Angus, maybe?"

Travis had to laugh. "Right now, our stock consists of two old horses and a dog that still smells like the skunk he tried to catch. The King Ranch it isn't. But if you need a place to sleep for the rest of the night, my friend, I have a beat-up couch that comes with pretty good coffee in the morning." When Rush hesitated, Travis added, "You'd be crazy to keep going tonight. You're lost and so tired that you're liable to fall asleep at the wheel and run off the road."

He did sound like a cop, even to himself, Travis thought.

"You'd put me up, even after I totaled your truck?" Rush asked.

"Don't remind me."

"If that's a yes, I'll take you up on it—as long as I'm not putting you out."

"Believe me, you're not." Travis said. "But to get back to your story, there's one thing I'm still wondering about. You said you had a daughter."

"I do. She's three. Her name's Claire. I try not to think about her too much."

"What happened?"

Rush's jaw tightened. "That," he said, "is a story for another time."

Chapter 10

The porch light was on when they drove in through the gate. "Welcome to Christmas Tree Ranch," Travis said. "You can pull up next to the house."

"Christmas Tree Ranch?" Rush switched off the engine, climbed out of the cab, and looked around. "I guess I'll have to take your word for it," was all he said.

From inside the door, Bucket raised an alarm of furious barking. "It's all right, boy," Travis shushed him. "Everything's fine."

The barking ceased, but a light had come on in the back bedroom. Travis hadn't meant to wake Conner, but what was done was done. As he opened the front door, Bucket came out to inspect the newcomer, sniffing Rush's jeans and boots before showing his approval by wagging his tail. Rush scratched the dog's ears before following Travis into the house. "I see what you mean about the skunk smell," he said. "I could use a bathroom. Then point me to the couch, and I'll be fine."

Just then Conner came stumbling out of the hall. Dressed in the worn thermals he wore to bed on cold nights, he looked sleepy and none too pleased.

"What the hell, Travis?" he muttered. "I was hoping you'd gotten lucky and decided to spend the night. Did Maggie throw you out?"

"Not quite the way you're thinking. But it doesn't matter. I brought an overnight guest."

Rush stepped forward, hand extended. "J. T. Rushford. You can call me Rush," he said. "I'm afraid I totaled your friend's truck."

"No kidding?" Taking a moment to remember his manners, Conner accepted the handshake. "Conner Branch. Pleased to meet you, uh, I guess."

"Well, at least I've got good insurance. I . . . Wait!" Rush stared at Conner in sudden recognition. "Conner Branch! I saw you ride in Phoenix, when I was filling in as a rodeo vet. You were amazing! Damned sorry about your accident."

"Yeah, me, too." Conner yawned, then brightened. "You're a vet?"

"Yes, for what it's worth. Mostly large animals, but I can treat the occasional cat or French poodle."

"Well, as long as you'll be around in the morning, maybe you can take a look at one of our horses. I noticed he was favoring one leg when he came into the barn tonight."

"Sure," Rush said. "It's the least I can do."

"The nearest vet is in Cottonwood Springs, and

we don't have any way to haul the horse there, let alone the money to pay."

"No problem. I'll check both horses for you while I'm here."

"I'm sorry we can't offer you a real bed," Travis said. "We have a spare bedroom, but it's full of stuff, and there's no furniture."

"The couch will be fine." Rush glanced down the hall. "Bathroom?"

"Down there and to your right."

Conner gazed after Rush as he disappeared. "That guy totaled your truck, and you invited him to spend the night?"

"It was an accident. He couldn't stop on the slick road. He said his insurance would pay, and he drove me here. What else was I supposed to do, slug him?"

"I might've done that if it had been me. It'll take some time to replace your truck—and it's time we don't have. But he seems like a decent sort. I'll give him that much." Conner glanced at Bucket, who was curled on his blanket by the stove, fast asleep. "Now there's somebody who's got the right idea. Morning will be here before you know it. I'm going back to bed."

After Conner had wandered back down the hall, Travis got a pillow from his bedroom and a spare quilt, which he laid over the back of the couch for Rush. He remembered his earlier feeling that something was about to happen. For better or worse, he'd been right. But would tonight's accident be a passing event, or had his whole life taken a subtle turn?

Never mind. He would think things through tomorrow, when his mind was clear. For now, he was dead on his feet. He would go to bed and hope to drift off with the delicious memory of holding Maggie in his arms.

Travis woke at dawn to the smell of coffee—surprising, since he was usually the first one up. He rolled out of bed, pulled on his work clothes, and, still sleepy, lumbered down the hall to the kitchen.

He found Rush sitting at the table, enjoying a fresh cup and checking the messages on his phone. "I hope you don't mind," he said. "I found everything I needed to make coffee, so I went ahead. Help yourself. Hope it's not too strong."

"Thanks, I like it strong." Travis filled a mug and sat down across from him.

"I called my insurance company," he said. "They're on the East Coast, so I figured they'd have somebody in the claims department. I still need to give them your information and get verification of the damage, but once they have it, you should be getting a check within the next few days."

"Thanks, I'm going to need it." Travis sipped the hot, black brew. "Sorry about the accommodations. Did you get any sleep?"

"Slept like a log until the dog nudged me awake about half an hour ago. He wanted out, so I opened the door for him. I hope that was all right."

"Fine. Bucket knows his way around. So, will you be heading out this morning?"

"Not right away. I told Conner I'd check the horses. And I don't want to leave till everything's squared away with your truck and the insurance company."

"I appreciate that. There's a map of Texas in my truck. If you can get your hands on it, it's yours."

"Morning, y'all." Conner, dressed for chores but still looking sleepy, meandered into the kitchen. "Coffee smells good." He poured himself a cup. "Ready to check the horses?" he asked Rush.

"Soon as we've finished here," Rush said. "If I need any gear, I've got it in the truck, but I'll take a look first. After that . . ." He trailed off, sipping his coffee. "After that, I wouldn't mind seeing why you call this place Christmas Tree Ranch when there's not a Christmas tree in sight."

After they'd finished the coffee, the three men went outside. Usually they'd have let Bucket herd the horses to the pasture while they cleaned the stalls. But this morning Conner led Patch into the yard for Rush's inspection.

Rush studied the big Percheron's gait for a moment. It was easy to see that Patch was limping slightly, favoring his right foreleg.

"I don't see any sign of an injury," Rush said. "But something's clearly hurting him. I'm betting it's just a rock. Will he stand still and lift his foot?"

"He should," Conner said. "I haven't tried it with him, but these old horses are well trained."

Rush strode to the Hummer, opened the back, and rummaged in a leather case. He came back with what looked like a small metal rod with a rubber handle and a V-shaped prong on the end. "This is a hoof pick," he explained. "You should get one and keep it handy for the next time this happens."

Conner would know all this. But Travis appreciated Rush's taking time to explain what he was doing. Horses were complicated animals, surprisingly fragile in their own way.

While Conner soothed the horse, Rush stood against Patch's right shoulder, shifted his weight inward, and lifted the huge hoof to expose the underside. Seeing that Travis was watching, he pointed to a small, sharp rock, lodged against the center part of the hoof. "This area is called the frog," he said. "It's pretty tender. Even a little rock like this one can cause pain." Using the hoof pick, he worked out the rock, tossed it away, and set Patch's hoof down.

Rush took time to check and clean the other hooves. Then he ran his hands down the horse's back and legs and checked his mouth. "Sound as a dollar," he said. "You can turn him loose."

Conner released his hold on Patch's halter. No longer limping, the big horse allowed Bucket to herd him through the open pasture gate while Conner went to fetch the other horse.

While Rush was checking Chip and cleaning his hooves, Travis decided to voice an idea that had come to him. True, he hadn't taken time to weigh the wisdom of it or share it with Conner. But it felt right, and his instincts told him that Conner would agree. Besides, this might be his only chance to speak.

"I've been thinking about something, Rush," he said. "Hear me out and take this for what it's worth. Branding Iron needs a vet, and you need a job. Why not stay here?"

Rush glanced up with a surprised expression. "Here? But there's no clinic."

"Sure there is," said Travis, nodding toward the Hummer. "You could run a mobile clinic out of your vehicle and go where you're needed. Nobody wants to haul a sick horse or cow to the vet, let alone a whole herd. Believe me, you'd have all the business you could handle. Later on, when you were ready, you could build your clinic right here, on our property. Meanwhile, until you're ready for fancier digs, we could clear out the spare bedroom for you."

"That's a crazy idea." Rush finished cleaning Chip's hooves and straightened, meeting Travis's gaze.

"Think about it," Conner said, breaking into the conversation. "Travis has a great idea. You'd be building your own business and doing a service to the community."

"But you'd need to be paid for the room and for the use of your property," Rush protested. "Right now, I can't even pay rent."

"We could work that out, maybe even with some kind of partnership," Travis said. "Just don't say no yet. Give it some thought. Check out Fort Worth if you need to. We'll be here."

Rush shook his head in disbelief. "But you don't even know me."

"And you don't know us," Conner said. "We're just a couple of crazy fools with a dream. When you're done checking that horse, we'll show it to you."

* * *

Half an hour later, they were seated in the ATV with Conner driving and the cart loaded with tools hitched on behind. Last night's hail and wind were gone. The weather was sunny but cold.

The road Travis and Conner had worked so hard to clear was still bumpy in spots. But with a good snowfall, it would do for the sleigh and horses. Travis looked up at the blue sky and murmured a silent prayer for December storms.

"Whatever you're about to show me, you're being damned mysterious about it," Rush joked. "I hope it's not something illegal?"

Conner laughed. "Wait and see."

They came up over the last low rise, and there were the trees, like a carpet of festive green spreading over the hollow.

"Now you know why we call it Christmas Tree Ranch," Conner said. "All we need to do now is get these babies ready to sell. Today we start trimming."

"And that's what these tools are for?" Rush glanced back at the loaded cart.

"Right," Travis said. "But don't worry, we're not planning to put you to work. We'll unhitch the cart and leave Conner to start trimming while I take you back. Then I'll need to go into town to get my truck out of the way. There's only one garage in Branding Iron, but the man who owns it is as good as gold. I hope your insurance company will take his word on the estimate."

"I'll go with you to make sure they do," Rush said.

They left Conner with the tools to start on the

trees, and Travis drove the ATV back to the house.
They'd be taking Conner's Jeep into town and
leaving the loaded Hummer behind the house,
where Rush had moved it. "Give me a minute to
make a call," he told Rush. "My lady lives in town.
If she sees that wrecked truck with no sign of me,
she'll be worried."

The words *my lady* tasted sweet in his mouth—
still strange and new, but after last night, somehow
fitting.

"So you've got a lady, have you?"

"I do. She's the mayor." Travis placed the call,
and Maggie picked up.

"Hi."

He guessed from the crispness in her voice that
she was already at work.

"What's up?"

"I just didn't want to worry you." He told her
briefly what had happened. "I wanted to get word
to you before you saw the truck," he said.

"Thanks. I didn't see it, but if I had, I'd have
been calling the police and the hospital in a panic."

"It's nice to know you care that much."

"You know I do." There was a pause. "Somebody
just walked in. Gotta go."

She ended the call, leaving Travis a trifle let
down. But this was Maggie, he reminded himself.
If he wanted to keep her, he would have to get
used to sharing her with the whole town.

After driving into Branding Iron, Travis and
Rush contacted Silas Parker, who owned the garage.
Silas, a master mechanic who'd been in business
twenty-five years, was able to give the insurance
company a reliable estimate of the truck's value

and a description of the damage. Before the wreck was towed away, Travis cleaned out the glove box and rescued the road map of Texas, which he gave to Rush.

"Maybe now you won't get lost again," he joked as they climbed back into the Jeep.

"Who knows? Maybe I was supposed to get lost." Rush tucked the map into his expensive-looking lambskin jacket. "It's almost noon. Can I treat you to lunch before we head back?"

"It's tempting, but I need to get back and spell Conner on trimming those trees." Travis started up the Jeep and headed out of town. "Think about the offer we made you. We're starting from scratch this year, but given time and work, this ranch could be a nice place, with plenty of room for your clinic."

"I will think about it," Rush said. "But money-wise, I'm scraping bottom. What I need right now is a steady paycheck. I've got to at least try my luck in Fort Worth. That, or look somewhere else."

"Well, keep us in mind. The door's open, for now at least."

Travis let Rush out by the Hummer, shook his hand, and stood with Bucket, watching him drive away. Then, shifting his thoughts, he went into the house, made a few sandwiches to share with Conner for lunch, packed them up with some cold sodas, and set out on the ATV with the dog riding in back.

They were shooting for Thanksgiving weekend to start selling trees. With just days left, the task of trimming, cutting, putting up signs, running an ad in the Cottonwood Springs paper, and setting up their display would keep them busy almost around the clock. They'd be lucky to find time for sleep. Even his relationship with Maggie would have to be put on hold.

They had one chance to make their plan succeed. The days ahead would be do or die.

By the end of that first day, Travis and Conner were sore, scratched, and exhausted. Trimming seven- and eight-foot trees, making them look good, and doing it efficiently was harder than they'd ever imagined it could be. They'd worked until the daylight was gone, then loaded up the cart and headed back to the house.

The horses were waiting at the pasture gate. After turning Patch and Chip into the barn, the two men stumbled into the house to gulp down milk and warmed-over pizza from the fridge. They'd planned to work on their advertising plan, but they were too tired to think. It was all they could do to shower and fall into bed.

Lying in the darkness, Travis found himself too wired to sleep. What if they'd bitten off more than they could chew? What if they gave this project their all and still couldn't be ready in time to sell their trees?

Time wasn't the only problem. They were also running out of cash, and they had yet to buy what they needed for their display. Hell, they could barely afford to keep food on the table and the lights on in the house.

They needed help, or a damned miracle.

Even thinking about Maggie wasn't enough to settle him for sleep. He wanted to pursue what was between them. But Maggie was a classy woman who deserved the best a man could offer her—and he had nothing. How could he ask her to wait, when he couldn't even afford a cheeseburger date at Buckaroo's?

After what seemed like hours of tossing and turning, he finally drifted off. He was deep in slumber when Bucket's barking and a rap on the front door jerked him awake. He sat up and glanced at the bedside clock. It was 3:15 AM.

"What the hell . . ." Swearing, he staggered to his feet. There was no sign of life from Conner's room but, as he'd already learned, when Conner was tired, he could sleep through an earthquake.

The house was dark. He cursed as he stubbed his bare toe on the coatrack. Bucket had stopped barking. His tail thumped as Travis turned on the porch light and opened the door.

Rush stood in the circle of light, looking dead on his feet. "Sorry to wake you," he said. "I got halfway to Fort Worth and changed my mind about your offer. If you'll still have me, I'm in."

Travis managed a grin of relief. "You know where to find the couch and the bathroom," he said. "We'll talk in the morning."

On the day before Thanksgiving, the city offices closed at noon. Maggie was just about to leave work when her cell phone rang. The caller was Francine. Maggie sank back into her chair to take the call.

"Hi, honey. Just wanted to wish you a happy holiday and see if you'd made any progress."

"On the Santa search?" Maggie sighed. "No luck. Do you think Hank would do it if we rented a fancy convertible to use instead of the sleigh? He could sit up on the back and wave at the kids from there, with someone in the seat throwing candy. It wouldn't be as good as the sleigh and horses, but it would be better than nothing."

"I could ask him, honey, but I don't think it would do any good. Hank's a stubborn man, and he's dug in his heels. He wants a reunion with his son—or at least a face-to-face chance to apologize. Hank told me what happened between them. It wasn't pretty, but it was a long time ago. He's a different man now. He'd like a chance to prove it."

Maggie thought about the secret she knew—Travis's plan to sell Christmas trees. She hadn't shared that secret with anyone, especially Francine. But two days from now, Christmas Tree Ranch would be open for business. There was no way Hank was going to be happy about that.

"It's not going to happen, Francine," she said. "In fact, unless something changes, things are only going to get worse. I can't tell you why, but you'll find out soon enough."

"Well, all right." Francine sounded mildly piqued. Maggie knew she liked to be up on all the goings-on around town. But Travis and his partners were planning to open with a bang on the day after Thanksgiving. Nothing could be allowed to spoil the surprise.

She decided to change the subject. "I guess you'll be having Thanksgiving dinner with your daughter's family, won't you?"

"That's right, honey. Turkey and all the trimmings. Then I get to spend time with my little grand-daughter. Hank's coming, too. How about you, honey?"

Maggie hadn't even thought about Thanksgiving dinner. Travis, who'd kept her updated with occasional phone calls, would be too busy to join her, and she had no family. "I could use a rest," she said. "Maybe I'll just sleep in, eat popcorn, and watch movies."

"Oh, honey, that's no good. Come have dinner with us. There's always room for another place at the table."

"That's awfully nice of you, but I'll figure something out. I'll be fine."

"Well, all right," Francine said. "But we can't give up on Operation Santa Claus. Keep me posted, honey, and I'll do the same for you."

Maggie thanked her and ended the call. Maybe Francine was right. Maybe there were better things to do on Thanksgiving Day than sleep in and watch movies. Even if Travis was too busy to come to her house, he and his friends would need to eat. She could fix a meal and take it to them at the ranch.

Still at her desk, she took time to jot down a list of things she'd need. Then she picked up her coat and purse, closed her office, and, sidestepping a lurking Stanley Featherstone on the way out, headed for her car and drove to Shop Mart.

The big box store was packed with pre-Thanksgiving shoppers. Maggie navigated her cart through jammed aisles, smiling at people she knew and apologizing when she blocked some shopper's way. Locating everything she needed took a long time. She found herself, at last, in front of the bakery department.

She knew better than to wear herself out making pies and rolls from scratch. With so little time left, it made more sense to buy them.

She was looking through the glass counter at the pies on display when a familiar voice greeted her. "Hi, Miss Maggie."

"Katy?" She spotted the petite, blond girl behind the counter. Silas and Connie Parker's daughter, who had Down syndrome, was a favorite in Branding Iron. She'd always lived at home with her parents, but now that she was twenty-two years old, she was showing an independent streak.

"I didn't know you had a job, Katy," Maggie said. "That's great!"

"I've been working here a month," Katy said. "Right now, I'm just helping people, but I'm learning to bake." She leaned across the counter, her pretty blue eyes sparkling. "Guess what? I've got a boyfriend. He's right over there."

Maggie followed the direction of her gaze. At one of the registers, a young man was bagging groceries. Noticing their attention, he gave them a grin. He, too, had Down syndrome.

"His name is Daniel," Katy said. "We talk a lot. Sometimes he holds my hand. It's nice."

It did sound nice, Maggie thought. Katy deserved some romance in her young life. But she couldn't help wondering how much Katy's protective parents knew about the relationship, and how they viewed it.

Other customers were waiting, so Katy couldn't continue to visit. Maggie chose a dozen fresh dinner rolls and two pies from the dwindling supply in the bakery and took them, along with her other purchases, to the checkout stand with the shortest line. Daniel, who was bagging groceries, gave her a quiet smile. He was a nice-looking young man, short and heavyset, with dark hair and gentle brown eyes. His family must be new in Branding Iron. Otherwise, she would surely have noticed him earlier.

Thinking back, Maggie remembered that Katy had been home-schooled by her mother. In this small Texas town, she'd had little chance to meet other young people like herself. No wonder she was so drawn to Daniel. Maggie could only hope the budding romance would turn out to be a good thing.

She spent too much time worrying about people—at least that was what she'd been told. She was the town mayor, not the town mother. But she couldn't help being concerned about Katy and Daniel, their parents, and all the families in Branding Iron. She wanted them to be safe and happy and have what they needed. And she wanted the town's Christmas celebration to leave everyone in a festive mood.

So far that wasn't working out so well.

"Can I help you outside?" The soft voice at her shoulder was Daniel's. He gave her a shy smile. Ordinarily, Maggie would have carted her own groceries outside and loaded them in the car, but she wanted to know more about the boy who'd captured Katy's innocent young heart.

"That would be nice, thank you," she said. "My car's on the far side of the lot."

She walked beside him, taking her time as he pushed the cart. He was no taller than her shoulder, his dark hair carefully brushed to one side. Beneath the red Shop Mart apron, his clothes were neat and clean.

"I haven't seen you before today," Maggie said. "Is your family new in town?"

"We just moved here. My dad teaches sixth grade at the school. My mom is a writer. This is my first job." Daniel guided the cart carefully along the crowded lanes of the parking lot.

"You seem to be doing fine." Maggie made a mental note to look for his family and introduce herself. It was surprising she hadn't met them earlier. She could only assume they were private people who kept to themselves.

"I saw you talking to Katy," Daniel said. "Are you her friend?"

"The whole town is Katy's friend," Maggie said. "Everybody who knows her loves her."

"I love her, too."

Just like that. His simple honesty caused Maggie's throat to catch. Why couldn't more men be that sure and straightforward?

"She's the prettiest, nicest girl I've ever met," Daniel said.

"How many girls like Katy have you met?" Maggie knew she was prying, but for Katy's sake, she needed to know. "Have you had other girlfriends?"

He gave her a sharp glance. "We lived in St. Louis. I went to a special school. There were lots of kids with Down syndrome. Lots of girls. But not any like Katy. Not any that I loved."

Maggie had to smile. Score one for Daniel. She

had underestimated the young man. "Have you met her parents?" she asked.

"I've seen her mother in the store. But I haven't met them. I'm kind of nervous. What if they don't like me?"

"I understand," Maggie said. "Silas and Connie are some of the nicest people I know. But they're very protective of Katy. If it helps, I'll put in a good word for you."

"Thanks." He gave her a grin as they reached her car.

Maggie clicked the trunk, and he loaded the grocery bags.

"It's nice to have somebody on our side."

On our side? Was she really on their side? Maggie asked herself as she drove away. Heavens to Betsy, didn't she have enough on her plate without taking sides in what could turn out to be a Romeo and Juliet romance? Why couldn't she learn to mind her own business?

At home, she put the fresh turkey in the fridge and set about organizing the rest of her supplies for tomorrow. Maggie hadn't cooked a Thanksgiving dinner since her father had passed away. She was looking forward to doing it again.

She'd almost finished sorting her supplies and setting out the pots and pans she'd need tomorrow morning when her phone rang. Her pulse did a little skip-hop when she saw the name on the caller ID.

"Hi." Travis's voice triggered a ripple of pleasure. They hadn't seen each other since the night of the storm, but they'd kept in touch by phone. Their separation had only sharpened Maggie's hunger to be in his arms again. Against her better judgment, she had fallen hard for the man. Past hurts had taught her to brace for the letdown that was sure to come. But for now, she was on top of the roller coaster, hooked on the sweet high of anticipation, too happy to let go and back away to a safe place.

"How's it going?" she asked, trying to sound cool when all she really wanted was to throw down the phone and drive out to find him.

"Crazy. Everything's got to be ready by Friday morning, and there's still a lot of last-minute stuff to do. We're running our legs off. We won't even have time to sleep."

"Well, at least you'll need to eat. That's why I'm bringing Thanksgiving dinner to your place tomorrow. I'll do everything. All you three will have to do is show up at the table."

There was silence on the other end of the call. Maggie's heart sank. "Did I say something wrong?" she asked.

He sighed. "I know you mean well, Maggie, but we won't have time to sit down together, even for a Thanksgiving dinner. We've got trees to cut, the yard display to set up, the signs to paint, and it all has to be done by the end of tomorrow."

"But I've bought all the food! Surely you can spare half an hour to eat!"

"I'm sorry, but we have to be ready," he said. "If you still feel like cooking, maybe you can invite somebody to your house."

If he'd been in the room with her, Maggie would have been tempted to punch him. True, maybe she should have asked before she'd bought food and made plans. But what kind of man would turn down a lovingly prepared Thanksgiving dinner because he was too busy to sit down and eat it?

A mule-headed, stubborn man. That was the answer to her question. But she could be stubborn, too.

"I'll be cooking dinner and bringing it," she said. "If you and your friends don't want any, I'll share it with the dog!" With that, she ended the call before he could argue.

She got up early the next morning to stuff and roast the twelve-pound turkey and make the other preparations. But knowing her efforts might not be appreciated, or even welcomed, turned what might have been a pleasure to plain old drudgery.

By 2:00 PM, everything was cooked, covered, and loaded into the back of her car. Apprehension tightened a knot in the pit of her stomach as she backed out of the driveway. Maybe she shouldn't have insisted on bringing dinner. Maybe she should have just left well enough alone.

Chapter 11

As she pulled up to the ranch gate, Maggie could see the changes in the front yard. A small fire pit had been dug and lined with stones. Wooden posts had been set up to hold strings of Christmas lights. Two racks, connected by long ropes, supported a row of cut Christmas trees, which Conner was unloading from a two-wheeled cart. They were beautiful trees, lush and green and fresh. Their fragrance stirred memories of childhood Christmases, when the pine aroma would fill the house.

Conner saw her, waved, and grinned. "Hi, Maggie! What brings you out this way?"

She walked around the car and opened the trunk. "I brought Thanksgiving dinner for you all. Didn't Travis tell you I was coming?"

"Not a word. But it's a hell of a nice surprise. Why wouldn't he have said something?"

"He told me the three of you would be too busy to eat."

"That sounds like Travis, all right. But he can damn well speak for himself," Conner said. "I'm starved!" He leaned the tree he was holding against the rope stand and came toward the car. "Hang on, I'll help you carry everything into the house. I could eat it all myself, but I guess I'd better call Rush and Travis. They're out cutting more trees."

"Tell Travis he doesn't have to come if he's too busy."

Conner grinned. "We'll see about that." He took out his cell phone and made a quick call. Then he picked up the heavy covered pan with the roasted turkey in it and set off for the front porch.

Maggie followed, balancing the rolls and salad. Why couldn't she have fallen for Conner? He was so easy to like, so upbeat and charmingly irreverent. And she could tell he liked her.

But her heart had made its choice. Travis, with his troubled past and driven nature, could be a challenge. But his other qualities—tenderness, loyalty, and concern for others—more than made up for his darker side. He was a man who'd been deeply hurt, a man who was still struggling against the pain. If his pride would let her, she wanted to be there for him.

By the time she and Conner had brought everything inside, set the table, and carved the turkey, they heard the ATV roaring into the yard. At least somebody else was coming.

Travis and Rush, the new partner she had yet to meet, stomped the sawdust and pine needles off their boots and left their coats and gloves on the porch. As they came inside to wash, Travis gave Maggie a repentant look. "Smells great," he said.

"Of course, if you're too busy, you don't have to eat any of it," Maggie teased. His answering wink told her everything was all right between them. Her heart slipped back into its happy rhythm.

As the men took their places at the table, she got her first good look at Dr. J. T. Rushford. Tall, with dark hair and brown eyes, he was the handsomest of the three—or maybe he just had the best haircut. Travis had told her he'd be starting his mobile veterinary service after the holidays. Meanwhile, he was helping Travis and Conner with the trees.

Rush had brought another badly needed element to the venture—solid credit. He'd had no trouble getting a bank loan to set up his veterinary practice, with enough money left over to save the Christmas tree project. Maggie knew that Travis was worried about paying back his share after the season. But that was Travis. He worried about everything—just as she did.

Maggie was about to start passing the food around the table when Conner spoke up. "Whoa. It's Thanksgiving—a special day. We should say grace."

"I never knew you to be a praying man, Conner," Travis said.

"Are you kidding?" Conner said. "Back in Oklahoma, my mom took us kids to church every Sunday, rain or shine. And in the arena, every time I settled onto one of those killer bulls, I did it with a little prayer."

"Did that include the bull that stomped you?" Travis asked.

"Yes, but the Man Upstairs had other plans for me that day," Conner said. "Still, you can bet your boots, I'm a praying man."

"Then you're welcome to say grace for us," Travis said.

Conner's prayer was brief but heartfelt. He expressed thanks for the food and for Maggie, who'd prepared it. He prayed for the success of their venture, and last of all, he prayed for snow.

After a hearty *Amen* chorus, the three hungry, tired men made short work of the meal. There wasn't much small talk at the table, but Maggie understood that they were pressed for time and needed to get back to work. For now, the appreciation in Travis's eyes was thanks enough.

She had gathered up the dinner plates and was standing at the counter to cut and serve the pies when the sound of a car pulling in the gate reached her ears, followed by a sharp rapping on the front door.

Travis had started to get up when she stopped him. "No need," she said. "Stay put. I'll get it."

Wiping her hands on a dish towel, she hurried to the door. As she opened it, her heart seemed to drop into the pit of her stomach.

Hank stood in the doorway. His face was flushed with anger. His fist clutched a half-crumpled page from the Cottonwood Springs newspaper. When he spoke, his voice was flat with sarcasm.

"As Caesar would have put it, 'You, too, Maggie?'"

* * *

Travis shot to his feet, almost upending his chair. Three long strides carried him from the kitchen to the front door. "Maggie isn't part of this," he said in a level voice. "If you've got something to say, you can say it to me."

Frigid air rushed in through the door. When Hank stepped across the threshold, Maggie closed it behind him. "Have a seat, Hank," she said. "Would you like some pie?"

She might as well have been a feather in the wind.

Father and son faced each other in cold defiance. It was Hank who spoke first.

"I waited for you when you got out of prison," he said. "If you had come to me, I would have welcomed you with open arms. I would have taken you into my home, made you a partner in my business, helped pave the way to anything you'd set your mind to accomplish.

"When I realized you were still bitter about the past, and that you wanted nothing to do with me, I willed myself to accept that. I was proud to see you standing on your own two feet and working this run-down ranch like a man. But this—" He thrust the page with the newspaper ad into Travis's face. "This is too much! This is a betrayal!"

Travis's stony expression betrayed no emotion. "This isn't a betrayal," he said. "It's business. The trees are growing on ranch property. We have every right to sell them. We know you've owned the Christmas tree market in this town. But there's no law against a little healthy competition. If you don't like it, that's your problem."

"But you could've told me. We could've worked together and both done better than you'll do alone."

"If you're talking about any kind of partnership, forget it. Years ago, I came here looking for my father. I found a foul-mouthed drunk who cursed me and said he never wanted to see me again. I wrote you off that night, with no regrets. So far, that hasn't changed."

"What was I supposed to do, you young fool? I couldn't keep a boy, the way I was living—especially when I'd signed away parental rights for your own good. Your folks could've had me arrested. The only right thing I could do was send you home and make sure you didn't come back. But what about the letters I wrote you in prison—telling you there was a place for you here and inviting you to come?"

"Whatever was in those letters, I never opened them. I told the guard to send them back. He probably just threw them in the trash."

Watching Hank, Maggie saw the fight go out of him. He slumped as if he'd been punched in the gut, but then he squared his shoulders again.

"Have it your way," he said. "But this isn't over. If you want a fight on your hands, by God, you're going to get one." Flinging the crumpled newspaper ad at Travis's feet, he turned away, opened the door, and limped back to his truck.

Knowing better than to speak, Maggie gazed at Travis in dismay. Conner and Rush sat at the table, looking stunned. Surely Travis had told them about his past. But even if they'd known, the confrontation with his father would have been shocking to watch.

It was Conner who spoke. "Man, that was brutal."

Travis exhaled slowly, as if trying to bring himself under control. "We'd better get back to work," he said. "Thanks for dinner, Maggie. If you don't mind leaving it, we'll have that pie later."

Rush and Conner rose and, after murmuring their thanks to Maggie, followed him outside, leaving her alone. She'd been given her walking papers by Travis. It was time to clean up and leave.

She gripped the chair, a sick, sour ball of anxiety forming in her stomach. It wasn't being dismissed and left alone that bothered her—that had been pretty much expected. It was that she'd just seen a new side of the man she was falling in love with—a side that was hard, bitter, and unforgiving.

Still shaken, she recalled every word of the exchange she'd heard. Hank had made the only possible choice in sending his son away. But years later, when he was doing better and Travis was in prison, he'd tried to make amends. He would have helped Travis with the Christmas tree project and probably taught him a lot about the business. But Travis would have none of it.

Hank had been in the right all along. It was Travis who'd been wrong. Today's words to his father had been cruel, aimed to wound where they'd hurt the most.

How could she let herself love such a man?

But deep down, she knew the answer to that question. Travis was lashing out because he was in pain. And it wasn't in her power to take that pain away. Only forgiveness could do that.

Wiping away a tear, she began storing the leftovers, rinsing the dishes, and loading them in the dishwasher. From outside, she could hear the men unloading the trees, followed by the sound of the ATV driving away with the trailer for more. Then the yard was silent.

She wiped off the table and countertop and started the dishwasher. Maybe today had been a mistake. Maybe she should have stayed clear of Travis until the holiday season was over. He had so many worries on his mind, and her presence was just one more distraction.

Something soft and damp nudged her hand. Bucket was standing close to her legs, looking up with heart-melting caramel eyes. She gave him a smile. "You old beggar! At least somebody's in a good mood today."

Opening the fridge, she pulled a sliver of turkey meat from the covered platter. Bucket wolfed it down in a single gulp and begged for more, eyes bright, tail wagging.

"Here you go, just one more." She fed him another piece. Rush had warned her that too much turkey wasn't good for dogs. But after years of living on Abner's farm, eating whatever he came across, Bucket probably had a cast-iron stomach.

"That's enough. Go bother somebody else." She closed the fridge and shooed the dog out the back door. She was just gathering up her things to leave when her phone rang. The caller was Francine. She sounded worried.

"Maggie, have you seen Hank? He was supposed to be here for dinner at three. He didn't show up, and he isn't answering his cell phone.

This isn't like him. I'm afraid something might've happened."

Maggie hesitated, wondering how much she should tell Francine. But the secret was out now, and her worried friend deserved to know everything.

"I'm at Travis's ranch now," she said. "Hank was here about half an hour ago. He'd found out that Travis and his friends are going to sell Christmas trees. They had an argument, and Hank left."

There was a gasp on the other end of the call. "Christmas trees? And you knew all this? Why didn't you tell me, Maggie?"

"They wanted to keep it a secret till they opened. I only found out by accident. I'm sorry, Francine. I wasn't free to tell anybody, not even you."

Francine sighed. "Well, I guess that's water under the bridge. The important thing now is to find Hank and make sure he's all right."

"Have you checked the hardware store?"

"No, I'm still at my daughter's."

"Then let's meet at the store," Maggie said. "I'm on my way. I'll see you there."

Fifteen minutes later, Maggie swung her car into a parking spot in front of Hank's Hardware. Francine's big, red Buick was already there. So was Hank's truck. Both vehicles were empty. The two must have found each other and gone inside.

It would be easy enough to take the coward's way out and leave them to resolve this mess on their own. But Maggie knew she owed them both an explanation. If she didn't make this right, any misunderstandings would only fester and grow.

As she climbed out of her car, she saw Francine and Hank in the Christmas tree lot. They looked up as she came through the gate. Neither of them looked happy.

She cleared her throat. "I'm sorry for this. If there's anything I can do—"

"I thought you were my friend, Maggie." Hank faced her, a scowl on his usually good-natured face. "You know that Christmas tree sales make the difference between net profit and loss for my business. But you let these upstarts cut into my customer base without so much as a word to me. You were even there, having dinner, when I went to give them a piece of my mind. There are ugly words for what you are. One of them is traitor."

The word struck Maggie like a slap. No one had ever called her such a thing before. She felt the sting of tears.

Francine laid a gentle hand on his arm. "You can't blame Maggie for this, Hank. Her telling you wouldn't have made any difference. Besides, she and your son, Travis, are friends." She met Maggie's eyes with a knowing expression. "I'd say, more than friends."

"I don't care a lick about that!" Hank sputtered. "I would've helped my son if he'd so much as given me the time of day. But you heard him. He doesn't want anything to do with his old man."

"Listen to me, Hank." Maggie kept her voice low and calm. "I heard what you and Travis said to each other today. For what it's worth, you were right, and he was wrong. He's the one who needs to learn—and to forgive."

"Well, I'm not expecting that to happen any-time soon." Hank pulled a handkerchief out of his pocket and blew his nose. "Meanwhile, I've got to deal with things as they are—a son who hates me and wants to run me out of business. So if you ladies will excuse me, I need some time to work out a plan."

He motioned them toward the exit of the Christmas tree lot and closed the gate behind them. The two women walked together to their cars.

"I'm so sorry, Francine," Maggie said. "Hank is the nicest man I know. I wouldn't hurt him for the world."

"Like I told him, honey, it's not your fault." Francine patted her shoulder. "We're dealing with two mule-headed men. All you and I can do is wait and hope they'll work things out. Call me if there's any news, and I'll do the same for you."

Maggie watched her drive away. Francine was a good person. So was Hank, and so was Travis. How could well-meaning people get themselves into such a mess?

Walk away, she told herself. *There's nothing you can do.* But Maggie knew better than to think she'd take her own advice. She cared about these people, and she wouldn't rest until she found a way to help them.

Slowly she walked to her car and drove home.

"You didn't introduce us to your father, Travis." Rush lifted the last tree onto the loaded cart.

"He's my biological father. My real father was

the man who married my mother and raised me.
How was I supposed to explain that in an intro-
duction?"

"He didn't seem like a bad sort," Rush said. "Just
angry and hurt. You were pretty rough on him."

"You wouldn't blame me if you knew the whole
story. Come on, let's go."

Travis climbed into the back of the ATV, leaving
the front passenger seat empty for Rush. He checked
the hitch on the loaded cart as Conner started the
engine. This was the last of the trees they'd cut for
sale at the house. Other trees had been trimmed
and left in the ground for folks who, for an extra
$10, wanted to ride out and choose their own.
After some deliberation, they'd decided to sell all
the trees for the same $30 price, with free pine
boughs left over from the trimming.

By the time they reached the house, it was getting dark. In the east, a full moon was rising over
the low hills. Clouds, smelling of moisture, were
rolling in from the west.

All three men were dragging, but there was
more work to be done before they could rest—unloading the last trees, putting up signs along the
highway and in town, setting up the refreshment
table for hot chocolate, and laying logs in the fire
pit for marshmallow roasting.

"Thank heaven for Maggie and that food she
brought!" Conner said. "Otherwise, we'd be half-
dead of starvation. Travis, if you ever decide you
don't want that woman, I get dibs on the next place
in line."

Travis shook his head. "After today, Maggie

might not want me anymore. I sounded like a real horse's ass, didn't I?"

"That you did, old friend." Conner said. "What do you say we wrap this up? I'll volunteer to unload the trees and set them up. Rush, you can put up the lights and tables. Travis, since you know the town best, why don't you take the Jeep and put up the signs?"

"Fine with me." Travis took the half dozen signs they'd made earlier, some heavy tape, a hammer and a box of tacks, loaded them in the Jeep, and headed for town. A stiff breeze had sprung up. He would need to fasten the signs securely in place to keep them from blowing away.

Driving into town, he passed Hank's Hardware. Except for the outside security lights, mounted on poles, the place was dark and deserted. Rows of Christmas trees cast jagged shadows on the bare ground.

What if he'd been friendlier to Hank—maybe invited him to sit down and try to resolve their differences.

But that wouldn't have changed a thing. If they hadn't been enemies before, they would be tomorrow when their trees went up for sale against each other.

The signs were painted on white Masonite, sturdy enough to hold up to wind and weather. Travis put up one big sign outside the entrance to the Shop Mart parking lot and a smaller sign next to the park on Main Street. Two larger signs, mounted on sturdy poles, went next to the highway at the north and south ends of town, where anyone driving into Branding Iron would see them.

The stenciled text read the same on all the signs:

FRESH CUT CHRISTMAS TREES, $30
CUSTOM CUT TREE FROM OUR FARM, $40
FREE HOT CHOCOLATE AND S'MORES BY THE FIRE
SLEIGH RIDES, SNOW PERMITTING
CHRISTMAS TREE RANCH, 400 SOUTH RANCH ROAD

After Travis had put up all the signs but one, he
drove back through town. He should have known
better than to turn down Maggie's street. But he
did it anyway and drove slowly past her house. The
living room drapes were closed, but the dim light
behind them told Travis she was still up.

The urge to stop, knock on her door, and take
her in his arms was eating him alive. But he and
Maggie had parted on uncertain terms today. He
could tell she'd been dismayed by the way he'd
spoken to Hank and then gone back to work with
barely a thank-you for the dinner she'd brought. If
she was still upset with him, stopping by to see her
could only make matters worse. Besides, he needed
to get back to the ranch to make sure everything
was ready for tomorrow. Bracing his resolve, he
kept driving.

He made it all the way to the next corner before
he turned around and went back. He wouldn't stay
long, he promised himself. But he couldn't go
home without seeing her.

The storm front was blowing in. A staggering
wind whipped his hair and blew his coat against
his body as he mounted the porch and rang the
doorbell.

Maggie answered. She was wearing her black

leggings and an oversized plaid flannel shirt that might have been her father's. Travis liked the way she dressed for work. But at home, like this, she looked so natural, so vulnerable and sexy, that it made his throat ache.

She stood gazing up at him without a word.

"May I come in?" he asked after an awkward pause.

She nodded, stepped back, and opened the door for him to step inside. He closed it behind him, shoving against the wind.

Only then did she speak.

"Today I saw a man I didn't even know. And I still don't know what to make of him."

"If you're waiting for an apology, Maggie—"

"No. An apology just to please me wouldn't be real. All I want is to understand how the man I know to be so kind and gentle can hate his father so much."

"You weren't there."

"No, I wasn't. But I know that it was a long time ago. And I know that Hank was in no condition to take in a young boy and keep him. The best thing—the only thing—he could have done was send you home to your family and make sure you didn't try to come back."

"That didn't excuse the things he said."

"Didn't it? What about the letters he sent you in prison? He was offering his support, but you didn't even open them. Your father said some harsh things a long time ago, Travis. You need to forgive him. If you don't, that anger will poison your soul forever. And as for you and me, there'll be no chance for us. I can't fight that kind of negativity. I won't."

He reached toward her, needing to heal in her arms, but she stepped back. "Get through Christmastime, Travis. When you've finished with the tree season and found a way to make peace with your father, come back to me. Until then, we both need some distance."

"And the sleigh? What if you still need it?"

"If I do, I'll ask Conner."

Will you wait for me?

Travis knew better than to ask that question. Maggie was a free woman, and it was too soon for promises. If he wanted the right to love her, he would have to earn it.

He said a subdued good night, left her, and drove out of town, toward the ranch. Howling wind battered the Jeep. The sound only deepened his melancholy. Maggie was right—he wouldn't be fit company until he got his life together. But the thought of not seeing her, not being able to hear her voice or hold her in his arms, was like slow starvation.

The biggest sign of all was to go up where the ranch road turned off the highway. In addition to the text, an arrow pointed the way to Christmas Tree Ranch. Travis had saved it for last, to put up on the way home.

Finding the spot he'd chosen earlier, he pulled off the road and got the sign out of the back. The big square of Masonite caught the wind like a sail. It was all Travis could do to hang on to it and wrestle it into place. Bracing it with his body and one hand, he used the hammer he'd brought to pound the long stake into the earth. The first few blows glanced off, but then he felt the point of the stake catch and sink into the earth. A dozen more blows and the sign was securely in place.

Sweating under his coat, Travis leaned back against the Jeep to catch his breath. Overhead, the sky churned with black clouds that hid the stars and the moon. As he looked up, he felt something cold and wet brush his face. One flake, then more, then millions swirled down around him in a cascade of white.

Hallelujah, it was snowing!

Chapter 12

Maggie always looked forward to the day after Thanksgiving. For her it was a magical time, when Branding Iron awakened to the Christmas season.

Years ago, when her father was mayor, the towns-people had passed a resolution urging that no Christmas decorations be put up on the streets, in shops, or even in houses and yards, until after Thanksgiving had been properly celebrated. The tradition was cherished and honored—except by Shop Mart, which was just outside the city limits and followed its own rules.

This morning, as she drove up Main Street, Maggie could see the town workers putting up the tree in the square, and hanging strings of tinsel and colored lights between the lampposts. The Nativity scene was going up in front of the church, and the PA system in the park was playing Christmas songs.

But the crowning touch of the morning was the first real snowfall of the season. So far, the snow was only two or three inches deep. But that was enough to cloak the town and surrounding countryside in glistening white. And more snow was in the forecast—a line of storms, sweeping out of the Northwest in the days ahead, more than enough to give Branding Iron the hope of a white Christmas.

Maggie was passing the park when she saw the sign advertising Christmas Tree Ranch. Her pulse skipped. Travis and his friends had done what they'd set out to. They were open for business.

She'd been headed to her office to catch up on work while the building was closed to the public. But she had plenty of time, and she was curious. The hour was too early for many customers, but it wouldn't hurt to cruise past the place and see how they'd set up. She wouldn't stop—that would be awkward after last night's encounter with Travis. If they noticed her, she would just give them a friendly wave and keep driving.

She turned around at the far end of Main Street and headed south, out of town. There was another sign at the city limits and one more at the entrance to the Shop Mart parking lot. Stopping nearby, she brushed the windblown snow from the red-stenciled text. She could only hope people would notice the signs and be curious enough to drive out and investigate. If their Christmas tree venture failed, she would be heartsick for Travis and his friends.

Maggie drove on south. She was approaching Hank's Hardware, on the far side of the highway, when she saw the big sign on the Christmas tree lot. She slowed down for a closer look. Her heart sank as she read the hastily painted letters.

TODAY ONLY! ALL TREES HALF PRICE!

Groaning out loud, she pulled off the highway and read the sign again. Everyone driving south to Christmas Tree Ranch would have to pass that sign. Three cars had already stopped outside Hank's lot to look at his trees, and Hank was waiting to welcome them at the gate. Nobody who bought a tree here would bother to drive on and look for another one.

Branding Iron was not a wealthy community. Many families struggled to provide a nice Christmas for their children. A tree at half price, even if it wasn't the freshest, would mean a few more gifts on Christmas morning. How many folks would pass that up?

Maggie knew enough about the tree business to estimate Hank's profit margin. He would be losing money on every tree he sold at half price. But that wouldn't matter to him, as long as he was taking business away from his son.

A Christmas tree war had begun. And Maggie was caught in the crossfire.

What now? It was too late to go in and try to reason with Hank. And calling in Francine, whose first loyalty was to her old friend, would only make matters worse.

She could drive out to the ranch and tell the

partners what Hank was up to. But that would only fan the flames of the conflict—especially if Travis were to come flying into town to confront his father. Sooner or later, he would find out what Hank had done. But as a friend to both men, she couldn't be the one to carry the news.

With a weary sigh, she backed her car to turn around. Just then a sleek white Cadillac cruised past her and headed on down the highway. Maggie didn't recognize the expensive car, but she could see children in the back. She cheered silently as, almost out of sight, the car slowed and made a left turn toward the ranch. The family must have seen the ad in the Cottonwood Springs paper. With luck, the notice would bring more customers seeking fresh trees and a good time.

For now, all she could do was go back to work and put her mind on other things—like the pile of contracts she had to read, the checks she had to sign, and the Christmas Santa she had yet to find.

Taking care on the snow-slicked shoulder of the road, she swung her car around and headed back to town.

By noon, just four families had shown up at Christmas Tree Ranch. The first three had been from Cottonwood Springs. Two of them had bought trees off the lot while their children toasted marshmallows and made s'mores. Conner had driven the third family over the road in the ATV to cut their own tree and haul it back. All of them had enjoyed a wonderful time, and Travis had invited them back for sleigh rides when the snow got deeper. He could only hope they'd pass the word to their neighbors and bring him more customers. If business didn't pick up in the days ahead, this venture would barely make expenses.

After the third family left, Travis had given the two teenage helpers their pay and sent them home for the day. There hadn't been enough work to keep them busy.

The fourth customer was Travis's neighbor, Jubal McFarland, who'd come over with his ten-year-old daughter, Gracie, leaving his wife and their toddler at home. They'd had a good time choosing a tree, making s'mores, and drinking hot chocolate. Gracie threw sticks for Bucket while her father conversed with Travis.

"You've got a nice setup here, Travis," he said. "I hope it works out well for you and your partners."

"Believe me, so do I," Travis said. "But I'm getting worried. We were hoping to start out with a bang, but except for you, the only customers have come from Cottonwood Springs. We can't figure why we haven't seen more locals."

"You don't know?" Jubal looked startled for an instant, then shook his head. "My wife went to town earlier, and she told me when she came home. I'm sorry. I assumed you'd know by now."

"Know what?" Travis felt a sick premonition.

"It's Hank. He's selling all his trees for half price today. Ellie said the place was mobbed when she drove by."

"What the hell?" Conner rose from where he'd been tending the fire. "Did I just hear what I think I heard?"

Rush came down off the porch, where he'd

been tallying the payments—not that there was much to tally. "That's unbelievable. The old boy will lose money on every tree he sells."

"I'm guessing he doesn't care as long as he hurts us—or mainly, hurts me," Travis said. "Besides, he's probably got enough cash socked away to take the hit."

"At least it's only for today," Rush said. "We'll be back on even footing tomorrow."

"Except that a lot of people will have bought their trees by now," Travis said. "They won't be coming out to buy again. And for half price, they won't care if the needles are falling off the tree by Christmas."

Conner's string of curses ended when he realized Gracie was listening. He murmured a quick apology, then turned back to Travis. "I don't care if he is your father. This is a dirty trick. We need to get him back—and get him good."

"With another dirty trick?" Travis shook his head. "Why bother? All it'll do is waste our time and add more poison to the well. We're better off figuring out how to get more people out here and sell more trees."

"So let's put our heads together," Rush said. "What could we do that we haven't done?"

"I have an idea!" Gracie's childish voice spoke up. "How about flyers? You could leave them on all the doors."

"Now that's a thought," Travis said. "Not everyone has seen our signs. And not everyone will have bought Hank's trees. But how would we make them?"

"I can make you one," Gracie said. "It'll have

trees and the fire and the s'mores on it, and it'll say everything that's on your sign."

"She really is a good artist." Jubal glowed with fatherly pride. "The school and office supply shop on Main Street has a copy machine you could use. It might cost a little—"

"If it gets people out, it'll be worth it," Travis said. "Go for it, Gracie. I know you'll come up with a great flyer. We can make copies as soon as you're finished, and pay our teenagers and their friends to deliver them. We'll pay you, too, Gracie."

Gracie shook her head and laughed. "No, you don't have to pay me! It'll be fun!"

"Then how about a free sleigh ride and all the s'mores your family can eat?" Conner asked.

"Yes!" Gracie grabbed her father's hand and tugged him toward their truck, which already had their tree loaded in the back. "Come on, Daddy! Time for me to get to work!"

Conner laughed as the truck drove away. "You know, I wouldn't mind having a kid if I knew she'd turn out like that one!"

Rush turned away as if to hide his expression. Travis remembered his mentioning a daughter, but he never talked about her. Was he hiding a secret sorrow? Travis respected his new friend's privacy too much to ask. Still, he wondered.

But there was no time to think about that now. Another out-of-town customer was coming up the road—and it was starting to snow again.

By the next morning the snow was deep enough to shovel. As the day bloomed under a clear, azure

sky, children romped in the snow, made snow an-
gels, and staged snowball wars. Cars crawled along
white-packed streets or waited for Branding Iron's
only snowplow to come and clear the way.

When Maggie came outside to shovel, she found
a flyer under her door, with fresh sneaker tracks
leading up and down the front walk. Picking up
the flyer, she smiled. Travis and his partners were
doing their best to hold their own against Hank.

The older man, she knew, had sold a lot of trees
yesterday. Driving home from her office late in the
day, she'd spotted more than a few trees on porches
or in windows. But today, unless he extended the
sale, he would be back to his regular prices. And
Christmas Tree Ranch had fresh trees for about
the same average cost, along with treats and fun
for the families who came. The flyers, once people
read them, should give the ranch more business.

After Maggie had shoveled the walk and driveway, she got her purse, backed out of the garage,
and drove down Main Street. Saturday shoppers,
enjoying the sunshine after the storm, strolled up
and down the sidewalks looking at the Christmas
displays in the shop windows. The snow was barely
six inches deep on the lawns, less on the walks and
roads. More than twice that depth would be needed
for the sleigh. But if the ranch could offer sleigh
rides, even the families who'd already bought trees
from Hank would want to visit.

Maggie glanced up at the clear blue sky and offered a silent prayer for more storms.

The Shop Mart parking lot was full. Maggie
knew the aisles would be crowded and the check-

out lines tediously long, but she needed groceries, and there was no place else to get them.

At the bakery counter, she stopped to chat with Katy. The young woman was glowing. Having Down syndrome was clearly no barrier to being head over heels in love.

"Look what Daniel gave me!" She slipped off one vinyl glove and held out her hand to show Maggie a dainty silver ring adorned with a little blue stone. "He says it's a friendship ring. It means we really like each other."

"It's lovely, Katy." Maggie ordered two loaves of sliced whole-grain bread. She could see Daniel at one of the check-out stands, chatting with an old woman as he wheeled her loaded cart toward the exit. He seemed like a nice boy. For Katy's sake, Maggie hoped so.

The checkout lines were long and slow. Maggie took her place in the nearest one and willed herself to be patient. She was tapping her foot and humming along with the Christmas music on the speaker when she heard a pleasant voice.

"Maggie, goodness, that's you! I've been behind you for five minutes, but my mind's been on other things or I would've said hello sooner."

Even before she turned around, Maggie recognized the speaker. Connie Parker, Katy's mother, was behind her in the line with a loaded cart. A thin, graying woman, she was married to Silas Parker, who owned the garage. God had never made two better people than Connie and Silas—at least that's what Maggie thought.

"Hi, Connie." She gave the woman a smile. "I was just talking to your daughter. You must be proud of her, getting a job, meeting new people, and learning new skills."

"Oh, I am. But—" Connie dabbed at a tear. "This is such a hard adjustment. I've always assumed Silas and I would have Katy with us all our lives. Now, suddenly, she's got a job, she's got her own money, making her own decisions—she's even got a boyfriend!"

The conversation had become personal, but between the crowds and the music, nobody appeared to be paying attention. And Maggie could tell that Connie needed to talk. "I know you're worried. Any mother would be," she said. "But I've met him and talked with him. He seems like a nice boy, hardworking, responsible, and well-mannered. And he really seems to care for Katy. Maybe you should get to know him and his family. His father teaches at the elementary school."

"Oh, I'm sure they're fine," Connie said. "It's just taking that step, welcoming him into the family. She's so innocent, Maggie. I can't stand the thought that she could be hurt."

"I understand," Maggie agreed. "This is a whole new world for her. I can imagine what it must be like for her, being different all your life and then finding someone who's the same as you are."

"Oh, I know." Connie sighed. "Katy has the right to her own happiness. She has the right to be in love. But what if they want to get married, Maggie? What if she gets pregnant?"

"Everything I know about Katy tells me she'd be a loving mother," Maggie said. "But I understand you have reason to worry. I'm out of my depth here. You need to talk to an expert on Down syndrome, most likely a doctor. If you want, I can check with the state social service registry. They should have connections to somebody who can counsel you and answer your questions. Would you like me to do that?"

"Oh, could you?" Connie's face shone with relief. "I want what's best for Katy, but I haven't known where to turn. I've been feeling so helpless—" She blinked back tears. "Thank you, Maggie. I've been praying for guidance, and I think perhaps meeting you today was my answer."

"I'll find somebody and get back to you. They might not be available till next week, but at least you'll have a name and a number. If you want, I'll even call them for you and ask for an appointment."

"That would be great. I'm not sure I'd know what to say."

"No problem." Maggie squeezed Connie's arm and moved ahead to the checkout stand. The most satisfying part of her job was helping people get what they needed. Finding an expert on Down syndrome for Connie shouldn't be too difficult. If only it were that easy to reconcile Travis and his father, and to find her beloved town its Santa before the parade.

Francine hadn't called since Thanksgiving. Maybe because she was loyal to Hank, who believed Maggie had gone over to the enemy. What a mess.

Even Maggie's idea of having Hank play Santa from the back of a convertible was out the window now. The man was barely speaking to her. She'd always considered him one of the nicest people she knew, but this Christmas tree war had brought out his dark side. In his present frame of mind, he wouldn't throw her a life preserver if she was drowning.

She paid for her groceries and wheeled her cart out into the parking lot. Lost in thought, she didn't see Conner until she'd almost run into him.

"Whoa there, Maggie!" He laughed as he dodged the cart. "I'd say it was a pleasure running into you, but it appears more like the other way around." He studied her with a thoughtful frown. "You look a little down at the mouth. Is everything okay?"

She shrugged, checking the urge to cry on his shoulder. "Everything's fine," she lied. "Just the usual worries. How's it going at the ranch?"

"Not too bad. It's early in the day, but we're hoping the flyers will bring us more local business. We had a few customers yesterday, but not many, thanks to Hank's half-price sale."

"Is he still selling half-price trees today?" Maggie asked.

"The sign wasn't up when I drove past the place. But that dirty trick really hurt us. I was all for carrying out some kind of payback, but Travis wouldn't hear of it."

"He wouldn't?"

"Nope. He said it would only waste time and poison the well. That surprised me, seeing how things stand between him and his old man."

"It surprises me, too," Maggie said, "especially after that big scene on Thanksgiving Day. But I guess we should give Travis credit for taking the high road."

Conner nodded. "I've known Travis since we were kids. He's always had this idealistic streak. I think that's maybe why he became a cop. I thought sure prison would change him. But it appears I was wrong. Come on, I'll walk you to your car before I go back and load up on chocolate, marshmallows, and graham crackers."

He took her cart and wheeled it toward the far side of the lot. "Any luck finding your Santa?" he asked.

"Are you volunteering? I've got plenty of pillows to fatten you up."

He laughed. "Not me. I said I'd handle the sleigh, but that's the limit. I take it Hank's out of the running."

Maggie sighed. "I'm afraid so. I thought we were friends, but the last time we spoke, he called me a traitor."

"You're kidding!"

"Would I kid about that?"

They'd reached Maggie's car. She opened the trunk, and Conner began unloading her groceries from the cart. He'd nearly finished when a man on a three-wheeled motorbike drove into the lot and made a turn down the row where Maggie was parked. Slight of build, with a sharp, narrow face, he was wearing a helmet and a brown leather coat with an official-looking badge on it. A light-duty pistol was strapped to his hip. Reaching Maggie's car, he slowed down and pulled to a stop. She stifled a groan as she recognized Stanley Feather-stone.

"Are you all right, Mayor? Is this man giving you any trouble?" he demanded.

Maggie forced a smile. "Everything's fine, Stanley. This is Conner Branch. He's helping me with my groceries. You have a nice day, hear?"

Stanley touched his helmet in what might pass for a military salute. The motorbike roared as he drove off.

Conner shook his head. "Who the hell is that little weasel?"

"He's the town constable," Maggie said. "He writes parking tickets, rounds up stray animals, serves papers for the court, catches truants—that sort of thing. I can't say he's well-liked. But he's conscientious, and he keeps getting reelected because nobody else wants his job."

Conner grinned. "Well, he seemed mighty protective of you, Mayor Maggie."

"Don't even go there. I only put up with him because we work together."

"Well, I'll be damned," Conner teased. "Guess I'd better let Travis know he's got a rival for your heart."

"Don't, Conner. It isn't funny," Maggie said. "Believe me, I have no interest in that annoying little man. And right now, things aren't so great with Travis."

"What? I thought you two had something solid going."

Maggie hadn't meant to unload on Conner, but it felt good to talk. "Travis and I have agreed to back off until Christmas. Frankly, if he can't settle this thing with his father, it might be longer than that. I was pretty upset with the way he talked to Hank on Thanksgiving."

Conner shook his head. "Damn, this is enough

to crush my faith in true love. Is there anything I can do?"

"I'm afraid not. But thanks for your help. It's always good to see you. Give my best to your partners."

"Will do. Come visit us again."

"Thanks, but that might not be anytime soon." Maggie said.

"You never know. See you around." Ever cheerful, Conner wheeled Maggie's empty cart back toward the store and vanished inside.

Maggie closed the trunk. For a moment, her gaze followed the motorbike as it cruised down the row of cars and suddenly halted. Featherstone bent down from the seat and peeled a green paper off the snow-slicked asphalt. He wiped it dry on his pants leg and tucked it in his pocket. As she realized what it was, Maggie felt an unexpected chill.

It was one of the flyers from the Christmas Tree Ranch.

By early afternoon, business was picking up, and most of the customers were local. The pre-cut trees were going so fast that Conner and Rush had needed to make a run before dark to cut and haul back a fresh supply. The flyers appeared to have made a difference.

Now that it was evening, more people were coming in the gate, choosing trees, making s'mores at the fire pit, drinking chocolate, and asking about sleigh rides. Rush had surprised him by bringing a guitar out of the Hummer and serenading the customers with Christmas songs in an untrained but mellow voice.

A gaggle of high school girls had discovered Conner. After one of them recognized him, they tagged after him like rock star groupies. "Not to worry, I'm not into babysitting—or jail time," he muttered to Travis as they passed him in the yard. Still, Travis could tell his friend was enjoying himself. Everyone here seemed to be. Looking around the yard, he found himself thinking that this was what he'd imagined when he and his partners had started this project. The only thing missing was having Maggie here to share it with him.

Yesterday the check from Rush's insurance company had come in the mail. The payment had been just five thousand dollars for the loss of Travis's old truck. It wasn't much, but it would be enough to buy another beater truck like it. Travis had resisted the urge to go shopping. For now, he was managing all right without the truck. And the money would be better put aside in case the tree venture failed and the ranch needed help. On a more cheerful note, if they made good money on the trees, he'd be able to buy an even better truck at the end of the season.

He was checking his watch to see how much time remained before 9:00 closing time when a pickup truck with the Branding Iron city logo on the cab door pulled up outside the fence. Travis's pulse leaped at the thought that it might be Maggie. But he should have known better. The driver, who climbed out and walked through the gate, was a wiry little man with a long, rat-like face. Something about his stride, in high-heeled cowboy boots, the badge on his leather jacket, and the clipboard in his hand told Travis the man wasn't here to buy a tree.

He drew himself up to his full, undersized height and squared his shoulders. "Which one of you is Travis Morgan?" he demanded.

"I am." Travis stepped forward. "Is there something I can do for you, Officer?"

"If you want to put it that way, yes. You can accept this citation for littering. Those flyers your people passed out are scattered all over town. I picked up two hundred and twenty-nine of them today. Since the fine for littering is five dollars for each piece, I calculate you owe Branding Iron one thousand, one hundred forty-five dollars."

"Now just a blamed minute!" Travis had resolved to be calm and courteous. But what he'd just heard left him reeling with shock. "Is this some kind of joke? Did somebody put you up to it?"

People turned around to stare. Rush and Conner moved to Travis's side as the man answered. "I was just doing my job. And the charge is quite serious. As evidence, I have a large bag of your flyers in my truck. You're welcome to count them."

"But they're not all litter." One of the teenage girls in Conner's new fan club stepped forward. "You came to our house this morning, Mr. Featherstone. You asked my mom for our flyer, and she gave it to you. You took it, went next door, and got another one from the neighbors."

"That's right. You came to our house, too," her friend put in.

Featherstone's Adam's apple bobbed as he swallowed. "Maybe so. But it doesn't matter. Any of those flyers could have become litter, and you'd be responsible."

"Somebody put you up to this, didn't they?" Conner said. "Who was it?"

"A concerned citizen filed a complaint."

"Who?" Conner demanded.

"I'm not at liberty to say. Here's the citation, Mr. Morgan. You can pay the fine or dispute it in court." He handed Travis a pink ticket. Travis reined back the urge to crumple it and fling it in Featherstone's face. The last thing he needed was more trouble, and surely this travesty wouldn't hold up in court.

"I hope we're done here." Rush, who was well over six feet tall, loomed over the small man.

"Not quite." Featherstone shuffled the papers on his clipboard. "There's also a charge of posting signs without a permit and posting on public property." He handed Travis another ticket. "I left the signs you put up outside Shop Mart and next to the highway because they're outside the city limits. The other signs have been taken down and seized as evidence." He gave Travis a nervous look. "You can read the charges and fines for yourself."

"Same concerned citizen?" Conner's words dripped sarcasm.

"I'm not at liberty to say." Featherstone's voice shook slightly. "I've done my duty. I'll be going now."

He backed off as if expecting to be attacked by three large, angry men. At a safe distance, he wheeled and almost ran for his truck.

Travis and his partners watched the red taillights vanish down the road. By now it was almost 9:00, and Featherstone's visit had put a damper on the merriment. People were gathering their families and heading out with the trees they'd bought. The two high school boys who were helping left, too. Tomorrow would be Sunday, a day the partners had agreed to close, in accordance with Branding Iron custom.

Conner swore out loud. "Concerned citizen, my rear end! You know who's behind this, don't you, Travis."

Travis did. It could only be Hank. Hank with his missing leg, his estranged son, and the business he'd struggled half a lifetime to build. What kind of desperation would drive him to pull a trick like this one?

Good Lord, was he actually feeling sorry for his father? Travis shook off the thought.

"That little weasel must've spent the whole day gathering those flyers," Rush said. "I hope we're not going to pay that fine."

"No way in hell," Travis said. "Thanks to Conner's little fan club and the folks who heard what they said, no judge would rule against us."

"Let's hope not," Rush said. "But remember, this is Branding Iron."

"Maybe Maggie would pull some strings for us," Conner said. "At least it wouldn't hurt to ask."

"No!" The protest exploded out of Travis. "Don't even think about it! We're not going to involve Maggie in this!"

Conner raised his eyebrows. "Copy that," was all he said.

Rush glanced at the sky. "Come on, let's get this place cleaned up. Looks like there might be another storm blowing in."

As they began dousing the fire, cleaning up the mess from the s'mores and chocolate, and getting the tables under the cover of the porch, snow began drifting down around them in soft, white flakes.

Chapter 13

Travis was startled from sleep by a solid weight thumping onto his bed. Warm dog breath and sloppy tongue-licks brought him fully awake. He groaned.

"Damn it, Bucket, this better be important." He pushed the dog off his chest and sat up. The murky light seeping through the bedroom window told him it was barely dawn outside.

Tail wagging, Bucket jumped off the bed, ran to the bedroom door and then back to the bed. The dog didn't appear alarmed or worried, just happy.

Happy—at five freaking o'clock in the morning! The silly beast could've awakened Rush or Conner. But no, it seemed that Bucket had chosen Travis as his pack leader.

Travis swung his legs off the bed. The linoleum floor was icy on his bare feet. It was too early to go out and feed the horses, but it might be a good idea to light the fire he'd laid last night in the old coal stove to warm the house before stumbling back to bed.

Bucket raced ahead of him to the kitchen door. Still muzzy, Travis opened it to let the dog out. A wonderland of white met his eyes. Snow, well over a foot deep and still falling, blanketed everything in sight, coating trees and fences and forming high mounds where vehicles stood. Even the stillness was breathtaking. But it didn't last.

With a joyful *yip*, Bucket rocketed off the porch and went bounding through the fluffy snow, romping, tunneling, and leaping like a crazed rabbit.

Fool dog. Travis shook his head and closed the door, leaving it slightly ajar in case Bucket wanted to come back in and get warm.

By the time he'd lit the fire, he was wide awake. Too bad because, until Bucket had come flying onto his bed, he'd been deep in an erotic dream about Maggie. The chance of picking up that dream where he'd left off would have lured him back to bed. But dreams didn't work that way. Neither, it seemed, did real life.

Travis had lain awake half the night thinking about Featherstone and having to go to court to fight those two bogus tickets. The thought had stirred memories of his last court appearance, which had ended in a nightmare. Then there was Hank and his dirty tricks—and there was Maggie, who seemed on the verge of giving up on him. He should have known that there'd be no chance of anything lasting with such a classy woman.

Damn it, he needed a break. But there was no break to be had from the black cloud of worry hanging over him this morning.

Still in his thermal long johns, he was making coffee when Conner came half-stumbling down the hall carrying his clothes and boots. "What the devil are you doing up so early?" he muttered.

"Ask that damn fool dog," Travis said. "He's the one who wanted to go out and play in the snow."

"Snow?" Conner dropped his clothes, strode to the window, and peered through the frosted panes. "Hallelujah! Will you look at that? Do you know what this means?"

"I'd say it means lots of shoveling." Travis filled two mugs with coffee and put one on the table for Conner. "We haven't even started, and my back can feel it already."

"No, man!" Conner picked up his jeans and pulled them on. "I mean, yes, we'll have to shovel. But think. Think sleigh rides!"

"I'm thinking." Travis sipped his coffee, letting the heat seep into his limbs. Of the three partners, only Conner knew how to hitch and drive a team of horses. If the sleigh rides were to become part of their Christmas tree operation, that would have to change.

Conner seemed to read his mind. "How does this sound?" he asked. "First, we shovel the snow. Then, we take a few hours to teach you and Rush the ropes of sleigh hitching and driving."

"Fine," Travis agreed. "The sooner we get started, the better."

"In that case, we'd better wake Rush," Conner said. "You know how he likes to sleep in."

"Be my guest," Travis said. "If Rush bites your head off, that's your problem."

Just then a black nose pushed open the back door. Covered in snow, tongue lolling and tail wagging, Bucket pattered into the kitchen. When he shook his fur, wet snow flew in all directions.

Conner looked at the dripping dog and grinned. "Sure, I'll wake Rush. No problem. Come on, Bucket."

He led the dog back up the hallway to Rush's room and cracked open the door. Travis could hear the sound of Rush's snoring all the way to the kitchen.

Conner opened the door wider and glanced down at Bucket. His grin widened as he pointed to Rush's sleeping form in the bed. "Go get 'im, boy!" he commanded.

For all the weight of his worries, Travis couldn't remember the last time he'd laughed so hard.

Maggie took advantage of the Sunday storm to sleep late. It was almost 8:00 when she roused herself, slipped on her robe, and pattered into the kitchen to make tea and toast. When she opened her front door to get the morning paper off the porch, she was greeted by sunshine, blue sky, and a wonderland of glistening snow. A helpful neighbor with a snow blower had already cleared her walk, and the city snowplow was just coming down her street. There'd be no shoveling for her today.

This was her idea of a perfect morning—calm, sunlit, and beautiful. There was only one person she wanted to share it with. But that wasn't going to happen. Given the tension between herself and Travis, they were better off staying apart, at least until the end of the pre-holiday season.

As she picked up the paper, she caught sight of her neighbor, a retired teacher who lived next door with his wife. He was blowing snow from the sidewalks farther down the block. Maggie gave him a wave of thanks. But the good man deserved more than a wave for the hard work he'd saved her. As long as she had time this morning, she would make some oatmeal raisin cookies for him and his wife.

After she'd dressed and eaten, she gathered her ingredients and went to work. She had plenty of everything she needed for the cookies. Making a double batch wouldn't be much more work than a single one. She could always freeze the leftovers for when she needed them.

An hour later, she had about four dozen chewy, fragrant, warm cookies ready. She sampled a couple, then arranged half of the rest in a pretty paper bowl, wrapped them in plastic, added a bow, and took them next door. By then, her neighbors had gone to church, but she knew the cookies would be safe on their covered porch.

Coming home again, she stood in the kitchen and pondered what to do with the rest of the cookies. Freezing them seemed like a waste when they were so good fresh and warm. Maybe she could take them out to Christmas Tree Ranch for Travis and his friends. But no—her presence would only be a distraction, and a gift of cookies would only send a confusing message.

But there was something she could do with

them. In her time as mayor, Maggie had made it a point not to hold any grudges or remain at odds with any citizen of Branding Iron—no exceptions. That included the man who'd called her a traitor the last time they'd met.

Resolute now, she boxed the rest of the cookies, put on her coat and boots, and went out to her car. For better or for worse, it was time to make peace with Hank Miller.

She drove slowly on the snow-packed road. Hank lived alone in a small pre-fab house on the south side of town. Maggie could be fairly sure of finding him at home. Hank wasn't a churchgoer, and Francine, his only close friend, would be busy with weekend guests at the B and B. With so much snow on the roads, it wasn't likely he'd be out driving. Still, part of her couldn't help hoping to find him gone when she pulled up to his house.

No such luck. Turning onto Hank's street, she could see his truck in the carport. Bracing for an unpleasant welcome, she parked at the curb, took the cookies, and waded through the snow to the concrete slab that served as a front porch.

She was still stomping the snow off her boots when Hank answered the bell.

"Maggie." There was no warmth in his voice and little more than suspicion in his gaze. "What do you want?"

"Just to talk. May I come in?"

He stepped aside without a word, opening the door to let her come in. The living room reminded Maggie of an economy-priced motel unit—neat and orderly but with no personal touches and no family photos. The older TV in one corner was broadcasting a Sunday news program. Hank walked over to the set and switched it off. He didn't offer to take her coat.

"I did some baking. These are for you." Maggie thrust the box of cookies toward him.

"Trying to sweeten me up, are you?" Still unsmiling, he took the box and put it on the coffee table.

"No comment." Maggie's attempt at humor fell flat.

"Sit down." He motioned her to a chair. Maggie took a seat. He sat on the sofa, facing her. "So," he said, "since you came to talk, go ahead and talk."

He wasn't making this easy. But the man had been wounded by his son's rejection, Maggie reminded herself. And he believed she'd taken Travis's side against him. Of course, his defenses would be up.

"You and I have been friends for a long time, Hank," she said.

"We have." His look was guarded.

"I value that friendship too much to let anything spoil it," Maggie said. "I'm hoping we can get to the bottom of what's happened so we can move on."

Hank's jaw tightened. "If you're still wanting me to play Santa Claus, forget it. You can take your cookies and go."

"That's not what this is about," Maggie said. "I know what happened between you and your son all those years ago. He was hurt when you sent him home. But you did the right thing back then, Hank. You've done the right thing all along. It's

Travis who needs to admit he was wrong and ask for forgiveness."

Her words seemed to touch Hank. His defensive expression softened. His gaze dropped to his hands. "You heard what Travis said to me. I don't think my son is capable of asking for forgiveness— or forgiving."

"But you could be wrong. Listen—this is something I know from a good source. When you put your trees on sale for half price and cut into his opening day of business, Travis's friend Conner wanted to do something to get back at you. Travis refused. He wouldn't act against you. Doesn't that mean something?"

Hank didn't reply.

"Travis didn't go into the tree business to spite you," Maggie said. "He did it because the trees were growing on his property. It was a gift—a way to make the money he needed to run the ranch."

"But he could have come to me. If he had, I'd have helped him learn the business. I might have even given him some start-up money," Hank said. "Now it's too late."

"I refuse to believe that. It's never too late."

He gave her a dejected look. "Hasn't Travis told you what I did?"

"I haven't talked to Travis since Saturday morning. Is there something I don't know?"

"If you don't, you'll find out soon enough. Saturday, when I saw those flyers on the doors, I went to Featherstone and complained about the littering and about the signs Travis had put up."

Maggie remembered the constable in the Shop

Mart parking lot, stopping to collect a flyer off the pavement. She'd assumed he was just picking up trash. Now his action held a different meaning.

"I did something even worse, Maggie," Hank said. "I know for a fact that little rat, Featherstone, is sweet on you. I wanted to make sure he did his job. So I told him that you and Travis were seeing each other. That set him off just the way I wanted. Last night, he called and told me he'd ticketed Travis for more than eleven hundred dollars in fines—and that he'd handed out the tickets right in front of his customers."

"Oh, Hank." Sick with dismay, Maggie shook her head. "You're a good man. What possessed you to do such a thing?"

"I lay awake all night asking myself the same question. I guess I figured that since Travis had hurt me, I had the right to hurt him back. It was a dirty trick, and I'm sorry now. But it's too late to mend fences. Travis will know it was me, and he won't be in a mood to forgive. I'm afraid I've made an enemy for life."

The glimmer of unshed tears in Hank's eyes told Maggie he was genuinely sorry. But why should Travis believe that?

Hank slid the box of cookies across the coffee table toward Maggie. "These cookies smell mighty good," he said. "I know you brought them in the spirit of making peace. But after what I've done, I don't deserve them. Maybe you'd better give them to somebody else."

"Oh, no, you don't." Maggie shoved the box back toward him. "I'm not giving up on you, Hank

Miller. And I'm not giving up on Travis, either. I won't rest until the two of you can shake hands and talk like friends, at least, if not father and son."

Hank leaned back into the couch, his expression sad and knowing. "Do you love my boy, Maggie?"

The question hit Maggie hard. It was the question she'd asked herself again and again—the question she had yet to answer. But she couldn't refuse to answer Hank. And she knew better than to lie.

She took a deep breath. "Yes, I guess I do. And something tells me you love him, too. So what are we going to do about it?"

"I can't answer that question for myself," Hank said. "Travis is a proud man, and he's nursing a lot of hurt. After what I've done to him, I don't know if I'll ever be able to reach him. But maybe you can."

"I can try." Maggie rose. "Are we good?"

"We're good, and I'll keep the cookies. Thanks." Hank stood with her. "Is it okay if I talk to Francine about this?"

"Of course. We're good friends. Tell her as much as you want to."

"If there's anything you can do . . ." Hank's words trailed off, but Maggie knew what he meant. He was hoping she could work a miracle with Travis.

"I'll do my best," she said, squeezing his hand. "And I'll be in touch."

Torn by a storm of emotions, Maggie drove

home. She'd made peace with Hank, but at what cost? If she truly loved Travis, shouldn't she side with him, and not with his father?

After what Hank had done with the signs and flyers, Travis was bound to be furious. And she would be caught right between them.

At home, Maggie busied herself cleaning the messy kitchen, doing laundry, and organizing the papers that had piled up on her desk. She tried to focus on each task, but her thoughts were ricocheting from Travis to Hank to the Branding Iron Christmas celebration and the Santa Claus she had yet to find.

With the parade just short weeks away, it was time she gave up on Hank and found somebody else. Stanley Featherstone would probably do the job if she sweet-talked him into it. But the constable, who scared some children, would make a lousy Santa, and she didn't want to owe the little weasel any favors. There was nothing left to do except milk the city budget for a professional. But she would think about that tomorrow at work.

She was at her desk, paying bills, when her phone rang. The name on the caller ID was Conner Branch.

She pressed the answer button, worry chewing at her. What if something had happened to Travis?

"Conner, is everything all right?" she asked.

He laughed. "Everything's fine, Maggie. Why? Were you worried about something?"

"No, just being me," she fibbed. "What's going on?"

"Well . . ."

She could picture him grinning.

"How would you like the honor of taking our very first sleigh ride?"

"You're kidding!" Her dark mood was instantly gone. "You've got the sleigh out?"

"Yup. And I've been giving lessons to these two city slickers. Now they can hitch and drive that team like old Santa himself. All we need now is somebody to take for a ride—like our favorite lady mayor."

"Can I get there? I know your road won't be plowed."

"Rush has been running the Hummer up and down the road to flatten the snow. You should be fine. If you get stuck, call, and we'll come to your rescue."

"I'll be there as soon as I can."

This was just what she needed, Maggie thought as she layered a thick sweater under her parka and pulled on woolen socks to wear under her boots. She'd spent the whole day dealing with problems, and tomorrow was bound to be even worse. Just for a little while, she wanted to have a good time in the snow.

But her worries came back to roost, like black-birds in an orchard, as she drove down the plowed highway. It was Conner, not Travis, who'd invited her to the ranch, she reminded herself. Did Travis even know she was coming? With so much tension between them, how would he feel when she showed up for a sleigh ride?

Should she tell him she'd just spoken with Hank? But surely that could wait for a better time. And she wasn't even supposed to know what Hank had done about the flyers and signs. Maybe the wisest thing would be to play dumb and keep it to herself.

Heaven help her, it was just as she'd feared—Travis and his father were battling it out, and she was caught right between them.

Inviting Maggie for a sleigh ride had been Conner's idea. But Travis was glad she'd agreed to come. They'd put their relationship on hold—a wise move given the tension between them. But at the time, he hadn't realized how much he would miss her. Amid the stress and worry of getting the tree business off the ground, Maggie—even on the worst days—was like an island of calm sunshine.

But did she feel the same way about him? After his clash with Hank, and the way she'd reacted to it, that was a serious question. Whatever the answer was, he knew better than to push his luck today. He just wanted to feast his eyes on her and hear her voice.

He stood on the porch, watching as she pulled through the gate and parked her car in the spot he'd cleared for her. As she climbed out of her car, the wind rippled her hair and heightened the color in her cheeks. She was so beautiful that even seeing her from a distance made his throat ache.

Bucket came bounding around the house to greet her, scattering snow with his thrashing tail. Maggie laughed and scratched his ears. When she looked up, her gaze met Travis's. He gave her a smile and a casual wave.

Conner came around the house, where he and

Rush had been checking the sleigh and the horses. "Hey, Maggie!" he said. "Are you ready for the season's first sleigh ride?"

"That's what I came for." She took a knit cap out of her pocket and pulled it over her hair and ears. "Will you be driving the sleigh?"

"Nope," Conner said. "I'm leaving that job to my friend Travis, here. He's been training with the team all morning and not doing bad at all. Taking you for a ride will be his graduation." He looked toward the porch with a mischievous grin. "Come on, Travis, she's all yours!"

Travis hadn't seen this coming. He was barely competent with the horses, and right now, being alone with Maggie could be awkward. But Conner had flung down the challenge, and there was no way he could refuse.

He came down off the porch. Passing him on the way, Conner stopped him and leaned close to his ear.

"This is your last chance," he muttered. "Either you put your brand on that woman today, or I'm declaring open season and going after her myself!"

By the time the words sank in, Conner had mounted the porch. His friend was right, Travis realized as he walked toward Maggie. He'd stalled and made excuses, afraid he wouldn't be good enough for this magnificent woman until he'd proven himself worthy. But if he wasn't man enough to lay his heart on the line and make her his now, he didn't deserve her and never would.

"Let's go," he said, offering his arm to steady

her on the snowy ground. She took it, her hand resting on the sleeve of his jacket. He felt the pride of walking with her as they went around the house to the backyard, where the sleigh was waiting. "Are you sure you trust me to drive this thing?" he asked her. "I only just learned today."

"You'll be fine." She squeezed his arm, but he detected an edge in her voice. Was she nervous about going in the sleigh with him? Or was something going on that he wasn't aware of?

The confidence he'd felt a moment before began to fade.

Rush was waiting to steady the horses while they climbed into the sleigh. He gave Maggie a smile. "You're a brave woman," he joked. To Travis he simply said, "Good luck."

But luck was only the beginning of what Travis was going to need.

Maggie settled herself on the driver's bench and pulled on her gloves. When she'd accepted Conner's invitation, she hadn't expected to be riding alone with Travis. But here he was, sitting beside her with the reins in his hands. Had this been his idea all along, or had his partners pulled a fast one to get them together?

Judging from his unease, she guessed that Travis was as surprised as she was.

He nodded to Rush, who stepped away from the big Percherons. A flick of the reins and they were off at a cautious pace, headed west, away from the ranch house.

They hadn't gone fifty yards when a black and white fur ball came rocketing alongside them. Bucket leaped into the sleigh, panting and shaking off snow as he hopped onto the backseat.

Maggie laughed. "Bucket always rode next to Abner in the parade, wearing a Santa hat. You'll never convince him that he doesn't belong here."

"That's okay with me," Travis said. "And the hat's not a bad idea. We should get him one."

"Where are we headed?" Maggie asked, making small talk.

"This road leads out to where the trees are. We've been working to get it ready for the sleigh."

"But can't you go dashing through the snow with jingling bells, like in the song?"

"Not on this road. Anyway, this is a *two*-horse open sleigh."

"I've got a good idea," Maggie said. "Why not get some bells for the kids to jingle on the ride? They could even sing 'Jingle Bells.'"

"Now that's a thought," Travis said. "Maybe next year."

"I'm sure I could find some online. I could have them here for you in a couple of days."

"Please don't bother, Maggie. You've got more important things to do."

He went quiet, and so did Maggie as they passed beyond the fenced hayfields and into the wild part of the ranch. Snow lay over the land like a vast white blanket, broken here and there by clumps of cedar. A red-tailed hawk circled overhead, scanning the whiteness for signs of prey. The sure-footed old horses needed little in the way of urging or guidance. They plodded steadily over the packed snow of the road. The sky was clear blue overhead, the breeze crisp but gentle.

The day was almost perfect. But something was wrong, and Maggie sensed what it was. She was alone with the man she loved, in a perfect setting to open up and be honest with each other. Instead, they were filling the silence with useless bits of small talk, both of them avoiding the things that needed to be said if they were to move on.

She'd come here with the idea of playing it safe and keeping her secrets to herself. But that would only preserve the distance between them. She had to risk her heart. She had to tell the truth.

Chapter 14

Maggie steeled her resolve, knowing what had to be said.

"Travis, I went to see your father this morning."

She heard the catch in his throat. His hands tightened on the reins.

"It's a free country, I guess," he said.

"We had a long talk."

"I don't even want to hear about it. Do you have any idea what that man did to me yesterday?"

"Yes. He told me."

"Did he tell you that he complained to Featherstone about the flyers and the signs? Did he tell you about the tickets that little rat-faced punk gave me, and what it'll cost if I can't convince the judge it was a setup?"

"He did. And he said he made sure it would be personal. He knew that Featherstone would be jealous of you."

"Jealous?" Travis gave her a puzzled glance. "Why? Featherstone didn't even know me until he came out here with the tickets."

"He was jealous because Hank told him you and I were seeing each other. And don't you dare go jumping to conclusions. I only put up with that annoying little man because I have to work with him. Conner knew that. Didn't he tell you?"

"We haven't had much time to talk." Travis nudged the horses from an amble to a walk. "I'm surprised Hank would confess to his guilt. What did you do, twist his arm?"

"Actually, I bribed him with cookies. Or maybe he just needed to talk, and I showed up at the right time."

"Did he tell you anything else?"

"He said he was sorry. Truly sorry. He meant it, Travis. I could tell."

"It's a little late for sorry." Travis stared at the horizon for a long, silent moment. "Why are you taking his side?"

"I'm not taking anybody's side. I see two good men, bound by blood, who can't seem to stop hurting each other. I just want them to quit feuding and make peace."

"Stop wasting your time, Maggie. This isn't your fight. Why should it even matter to you?"

"Because Hank is my good friend. And because you—" She broke off, knowing what had to come next.

"Because what, Maggie?" He turned to face her. "What about me?"

"Because I love you, you mule-headed man!"

She flung the words at him like missiles. "Is that reason enough?"

The sudden change in his expression was like the sun coming out. "Then why in hell's name are we arguing? Don't you know that I love you, too?"

Maggie felt a surge of tenderness as she laid a gloved hand on his knee. What she was about to say would hurt, but it needed saying. "I was hoping you loved me. I've wanted you to. But how can we give each other what we need when you're so full of anger? Let it go. Walk away and move on. That's the only way we can make this work between us."

"Oh, Maggie, you don't know what you're asking!" He stopped the horses on the rise, with a view of the trees spread out like a green carpet in the hollow. "When I was in prison those three years, anger was the only thing that kept me sane and alive—anger at those fool girls who lied about the kidnapping, anger at that idiot boy who drove away and caused me to shoot him, and the judge who let the boy's parents push him into sending me to prison for a damned misunderstanding. And there was anger at the other prisoners, too. Nobody gets ganged up on and tormented in prison the way an ex-cop does. Without the anger to fight back, I wouldn't have survived. That anger's been pounded and punched and kicked into every part of my body. It's who I am."

"But your father wrote to you in prison. He would've helped you if you'd let him."

"I guess my memory was too good. I didn't want anything to do with that mean old drunk."

"He wasn't a mean old drunk when he wrote to

you. He'd sobered up and become one of the kindest men I know."

"So why has he tried to sabotage me at every turn?" Travis demanded.

"Because he thought you'd deliberately set out to ruin his business. But he knows better now. I set him right today."

He sighed. "I want to do what you ask, Maggie. But after what I've been through, forgiving isn't as easy as you make it sound."

"But it's not impossible. The people who hurt you in the past don't matter. You'll never see them again. But Hank is your father, your only living relative. When you have children, he'll be their grandfather. Think about that."

"Come here, you amazing, meddlesome woman." He circled her with his free arm and pulled her close. "You know I'll try. I'll try because I love you and because it's what you want. But it's going to take some time. And right now, I'm so crazy busy that it's all I can do to deal with what's right in front of me."

Maggie nodded, knowing it was all she could ask of him. "So for now, we're back where we started."

"Not quite." He tilted her chin and captured her mouth in a long, deep, heartfelt kiss that she never wanted to end. "I want you for keeps, Maggie," he said. "And whatever it takes, I'm going to make sure that can happen. I promise. Do you understand?"

The kiss she returned was meant to be brief, but it warmed and lingered, leaving them both breathless. "I understand. And I'll wait. But not too long. I'm not a patient woman."

"I can tell." He might have kissed her again, but at that instant Bucket, not wanting to be left out, jumped off the backseat and pushed his way between them. Laughing, they rumpled his ears, turned the sleigh around, and headed back to the ranch house.

On Monday morning, Maggie was back at her desk. Outside her window, a powdery snow was falling. The morning was frigid, the sky the color of old spoons. From somewhere in the rear of the building, Christmas songs were playing over a speaker.

Yesterday, she and Travis had parted on loving terms. But once again they'd agreed to put off their romance until the busy season was behind them. Maggie was already looking forward to the time when they could spend long evenings snuggling by the fire.

But right now, she had work to do.

At the top of her list was a call to a counselor who worked for social services and specialized in Down syndrome. The woman worked out of Amarillo, but she spent one day a week in Cottonwood Springs. She said she'd be happy to spend some time addressing Connie's concerns. She'd also be willing to talk to Katy if and when the right time came. Maggie thanked her, then made another call to pass her contact information on to Connie.

That done, it was on to the next item—checking on a professional Santa Claus. Maggie sighed as the list she'd googled came up. Who'd have guessed that Santas had agencies? For all she knew, they had a union, too.

The nearest Santa agency was in Amarillo. When she clicked on their site, she discovered that they also handled party clowns, Elvis impersonators, and strippers. They probably charged a lot more than she could squeeze out of the city budget, but she was getting desperate. She made the call.

"I'm sorry, but all our Santas are booked for the date you need," the woman on the other end of the phone told her. "We have an Elvis who plays Santa, but he only does it as Elvis, without the white beard. If you'd be interested—"

"Thanks, but we really need a traditional Santa," Maggie said. "As long as we're on the phone, can you tell me how much your Santas charge?"

"It varies," the woman said. "The top ones, who do the malls, get the most, though I'm not at liberty to say how much. A Santa for your little parade would probably cost you between five hundred and a thousand dollars, including travel time, plus expenses."

"Uh . . . thanks," Maggie gulped, ending the call. Maybe she should have asked about the Elvis Santa. But never mind. Given the cost, hiring a professional was out of the question.

Maybe she should seriously consider wearing the red suit herself. Everybody would recognize her, of course. For the adults and teens, that would be a great joke. But the little kids who still believed would be devastated. That would never do.

Maggie rested her head between her hands, fingers furrowing her hair. She was running out of options.

"Hello, Maggie. Are you all right?"

Constable Stanley Featherstone stood right in front of her desk. She jerked upright with a startled gasp.

"I'm sorry," he said. "Did I scare you?"

"You did. You should've knocked. Where's the receptionist?"

"She went to the restroom, so I just came in. I'll ask again. Are you all right?"

"I'm fine." Maggie took a deep breath. "What is it you need, Stanley?"

"It's not what I need. I just wanted to warn you about that man I saw you with at Shop Mart on Saturday. He and his friends could be dangerous."

"Nonsense," Maggie said.

"That's what you think. One of them is an ex-convict. He did time for killing a man."

"And the other two?"

"I'm still checking on them. But you know what they say. Birds of a feather flock together."

"If this is a joke, Stanley, I'm not laughing. And since they live outside the city limits, checking on them is the sheriff's job, and he already knows about them. So you can stop wasting my time."

She looked down at the papers on her desk, hoping Stanley would leave, but he didn't budge.

"You've been seen going out to their place. The one man, the convicted killer, has even been reported coming out of your house at night."

"Reported by whom?" Maggie kept her tone casual and friendly. Inside she was seething.

"By, uh . . . a concerned citizen."

"Concerned? About what?"

"About your safety—and your reputation."

"I see." Maggie knew who the "concerned citizen" was, and this time it wasn't Hank. Stanley Featherstone had been getting on her nerves for as long as she'd known him, but this time he'd crossed the line.

Good heavens, had the little creep been spying on her? The thought made her skin crawl.

With teeth-grinding effort, she kept her self-control. "Thank you for letting me know, Stanley," she said. "I'll consider myself warned, but I don't want to hear another word about this. And if it gets back to me that your 'concerned citizen' is spreading tales, the consequences won't be pretty. Do I make myself clear?"

He hesitated; then his mouth spread in a slow grin. "Clear enough," he said. "I just wanted to warn you, that's all. Didn't mean any harm by it."

"That's fine. Now if you'll excuse me, I'm busy."

"I was hoping we could get some coffee in the break room."

"I've had my coffee, and I've got work to do. So have you. Can you show yourself out, or should I call the receptionist?"

"I'll be going." He moseyed out the door while Maggie took deep breaths to calm her nerves.

Maybe she should let Travis know about this encounter. She was reaching for the phone when she changed her mind. Travis would only worry, and he already had enough on his mind. If Stanley Featherstone made any more trouble, she could deal with him herself. After all, even though she couldn't fire an elected official, she was technically his boss.

Shuffling the papers on her desk, she went back to wrestling with the Santa problem.

Travis stood on the front porch, shading his eyes against the glare of sunlight on snow. Ten days had passed since Stanley Featherstone had ticketed him for the flyers and signs. Today was the scheduled court date. Since the tickets had been written to Christmas Tree Ranch and not to Travis personally, Rush had volunteered to go to town and appear before the judge.

Travis had argued against it at first, but Conner had taken Rush's side. "You're on edge, Travis," he'd said. "Featherstone will be expecting that, and he'll try to get to you. Rush will throw him off his game."

Travis had finally agreed. Rush tended to play his cards close to his vest. Cool and soft-spoken, he would be their safest bet in court.

Travis glanced at his watch. It was almost noon, past time for Rush to return from town. Had something gone wrong?

They could pay the fine if they had to, he told himself. Business had been good. On weekdays when kids were in school, the flow of customers slowed to a trickle. But in the evenings and on Saturdays, they had plenty of activity. They were selling as many trees as they could cut and haul. And the sleigh rides—which could continue for as long as the snow lasted—were catching on as well. Still, an eleven-hundred-dollar fine was a lot of money when the ranch had so many needs.

Relief washed over him as he spotted the Hummer coming up the road. For better or worse, he would soon know what the judge had ruled.

The Hummer pulled through the gate and into its usual parking spot. Travis came down off the porch, and Conner came around from the back of the house as the door opened. Rush climbed out carrying a pizza box and a six pack of beer. His face wore a broad grin.

Travis took the pizza box out of his hand. "I hope this means good news," he said.

"Good enough," Rush said. "The judge dropped the charges for the flyers and fined me twenty-five dollars for the illegal signs. I think she liked me."

"*She?*" Conner whooped with laughter. "So what did she look like?"

"About thirty-five, I'd say. Long, blond hair, up in some kind of twist. All business, mind you, but a real looker. No wedding ring. I'm hoping Maggie can get me her phone number."

"You dirty dog, you!" Conner teased.

"Hey, the pizza's getting cold," Travis said. "Come on, let's go inside and eat."

With Bucket at their heels, they trooped into the kitchen, opened the pizza, and tore into it with the appetites of hungry men. As they sat around the table laughing, talking, and eating, Travis couldn't help thinking what a difference these friends had made in his life. Weeks ago, he'd been here alone, lonesome and bitter, living from day to day. Now his life was richer by two horses, two partners, a beautiful woman, and a goofy dog. He felt blessed, or maybe just damned lucky.

Not that he'd ever admit to a word of this out loud.

A week before the Christmas parade, a desperate Maggie made a call to Francine at the B and B. "We need to talk," she said. "If you can come to my house, I'll have fresh coffee and cinnamon rolls for us."

"I'm still cleaning up after our Saturday buffet," Francine said. "I can be there in half an hour. But don't worry about the cinnamon rolls. If I don't cut down on sweets, I'll never fit into my costume for the Cowboy Christmas Ball."

Maggie was tidying up the living room when her phone rang again. Her first thought was that Francine might be calling to say she couldn't make it over. But the caller wasn't Francine. It was Connie Parker.

"Is everything all right, Connie?" Maggie asked, bracing for more worries.

"Everything's fine, so far," Connie said. "I just wanted to thank you for putting me in touch with that doctor. I spent half an hour with her, and we had a very frank discussion about Katy and Daniel. Some of my questions were hard to ask, but I needed to know the answers. She told me that Down syndrome couples do get married and mostly do just fine. Some of them even live on their own."

"And what about children? I know you were concerned about that."

"She said that the chance of a couple with Down syndrome conceiving a child is less than one in a hundred. But just to be safe, if they decide to get married, they should be checked to see whether they'll need birth control. She offered to counsel them. So at least that's in place. And at least I know what we're dealing with."

"So are you and Silas handling this any better?"

Connie chuckled nervously. "We're crossing our fingers that they'll just stay friends. But at least we'll be prepared for whatever happens. We've invited Daniel to supper tonight. Let's hope it's a step in the right direction."

"I'll be hoping with you," Maggie said. "The one thing we all want is Katy's happiness."

True to her word, Francine showed up a few minutes after Connie ended the call. By then Maggie's sense of desperation over the Santa search had returned. "Oh, honey!" She enfolded Maggie in a warm hug. "You look like you haven't slept in days! I'm sorry I haven't been here for you. It's just been a busy time, decorating the B and B, and hosting Christmas parties there. I take it you haven't found your Santa Claus yet."

"Give me your coat and have a seat." Maggie indicated a cushy armchair with a footstool, close to the fire. "I'll bring you some coffee."

Francine sank into it with a sigh. "Oh, this is heaven. I've been on my feet for four solid hours!"

Maggie brought her the coffee on a tray, which she placed on a side table. "Go ahead, take off your shoes. I won't mind a bit," she said. "I don't know how you manage to work in heels."

"Long habit, honey." Francine slipped off her red pumps and let them drop to the floor. "But this isn't about me. It's about you and your troubles. Hank told me you went to see him a while back."

"Yes, we had a good talk. But he and Travis still haven't made peace. And I couldn't talk him into playing Santa Claus. I was hoping you could talk to him again."

"I could try," Francine said. "But Hank's a proud, stubborn man. When he digs in his heels, it's like moving a mountain." She added a dollop of cream and two cubes of sugar to her coffee and took a sip. "What about the sleigh? Have you got that lined up?"

"Conner's said all along that he'd be willing to drive the sleigh and handle the horses. But he doesn't want to be Santa, and even if he'd do it, he wouldn't look the part."

"He's the rodeo cowboy, right? I've seen him in Shop Mart. My stars and garters!" Francine cooled herself with an imaginary fan. "I wanted to wrap him up with a big red bow and take him home. And that other man—the tall, dark, quiet one. He looks like a young George Clooney! I tell you, the female hormone level in this town has skyrocketed since those three took over the ranch."

Maggie had to smile. "I know what you mean. But we're talking about finding a Santa for the kids, not the women. That's why we need Hank. With the suit and beard, he'd look like the real deal. And I've watched him pass out treats when the families come in for trees. I can tell he likes kids. Couldn't we use that angle—that he should do it for the little ones?"

"I already tried that, honey. At first, I thought it might work, but in the end, he just dug in his heels again."

"Oh dear." Maggie's shoulders drooped. "But there's got to be a way to change his mind. If Conner drives the sleigh, maybe Hank would—"

"It's not enough. He's waiting for Travis."

"So am I. I've told Travis that we can't move on together until he settles this. But Travis isn't ready. In a way, I understand. It's not so much a question of making peace with his father; his real struggle is making peace with himself." Maggie sighed. "I guess we've hit a dead end, haven't we?"

Francine sank deeper into her chair. "Too bad we can't get old Abner back. He was such a great Santa. I can still picture him in that sleigh, laughing and waving at the kids, with that cute black and white dog sitting next to him, wearing its own Santa hat. The kids loved that."

"Abner's dog is at the ranch now," Maggie said. "His name is Bucket, and he's super smart. Travis says he even herds the horses in and out of the pasture. He's—"

Maggie broke off as a new idea struck her.

"What is it?" Francine asked her. "I can almost see the wheels turning in your head."

"You're going to think I'm crazy."

"Try me, honey."

"Think last-ditch, back-to-the-wall Plan B. If we can't get anybody else, Bucket could be our Santa."

"How's that again?"

"Think about it. If we give the kids a fake-looking Santa, they won't be happy. But most of them already know Bucket. He's been in the parade almost every year of their lives, and they love him. He wouldn't be Santa Claus, but he'd be like . . . like the spirit of Santa." She gazed at Francine, who still looked skeptical. "What do you think?"

Francine gave a shake of her Dolly Parton curls. "It's one crazy idea. But I agree with you that a dog Santa would be better than a human Santa who didn't look the part. And having Abner's dog there would be like a tribute to the old man. Do you think Bucket would stay on the seat and behave?"

"Abner did a great job of training him. I'm sure he'd stay, especially if someone he knew was in the driver's seat."

"I could make him a little red cape to wear, with a furry collar and bells around the edge." Francine was getting into the idea.

"Of course, it would still be best if Hank would play Santa," Maggie said. "Bucket could wear the costume and ride with him."

"I'll keep working on him, honey, but don't count on it. Meanwhile, you'd better make sure you can count on the sleigh and the dog."

"I'll go this afternoon," Maggie said. "The guys will be busy at the ranch, but I'll only need a few minutes to talk to them."

"Well, in that case, I'll be on my way home to make roast beef dinner for my man." Francine rose and crammed her swollen feet into her pumps, put on her coat, and tottered out to her car.

Maggie put on fresh jeans and a dark green sweater, touched up her makeup, and brushed her hair before she went out to the garage. The past couple of days had been above freezing, and the snow had begun to melt—good for the roads and sidewalks, but not for the sleigh ride business or the upcoming parade. As she backed out of the garage, she sent up a silent prayer for more snow.

On Main Street, mounds of shoveled snow were thawing and running into the gutters. Shoppers bustled in and out of stores, getting their errands done while the weather was fair. "The Little Drummer Boy" boomed over the speakers in the park.

Maggie passed the crowded Shop Mart parking lot and drove onto the highway. There were vehicles outside Hank's Hardware and people looking at his Christmas trees. In spite of the tricks he'd played, he'd lost business to the Christmas Tree Ranch. By this time last year, he had all but sold out. This year a third of his trees were left, and their boughs were getting dry. More and more customers were passing them up for a fresh tree from the ranch.

She couldn't help feeling sorry for Hank. He was a good man, and he'd done his best with the cruel cards life had dealt him. He deserved a relationship with his son, and Travis deserved to have his father in his life. If only she knew how to make that happen.

At the ranch, she counted nine cars and trucks parked along the road. People who'd put off buying their trees until late in the season were getting them now. But the snow was already too far gone for sleigh rides. The unhitched sleigh was parked in the shed, the horses enjoying the sunshine in the pasture.

Maggie parked across the road and walked through the gate. Bucket, dozing on the porch, came bounding down the steps to meet her. She rubbed his ears as she looked around. The teenage boy and girl they'd hired were tending the fire, the s'mores, and the chocolate machine. Rush was helping a family pick out a tree, and Conner was lashing another tree onto the top of a car. In the distance, she could hear the sound of the chain saw. Travis, she assumed, was cutting a tree from the farm for a customer.

As Conner turned away from loading the tree, she waved at him. He trotted over to where she stood. "Hi, Maggie." He greeted her with a grin. "If you're looking for Travis, he should be back here in a few minutes. You're welcome to go inside and wait."

"Actually, it's you I wanted to talk to," she said. "I hope your offer to drive the sleigh in the parade next Saturday is still good."

"Sure, no problem. It'll be good PR for the ranch. But you'll need to brief me on when and where."

"I've got a page with a map and instructions on it in my office. I'll make sure you get it."

"So, did Hank finally agree to play Santa?"

"No, but I've got a plan B. Right here." She patted Bucket's eager head. "Meet our backup Santa."

"You're kidding!" Conner looked startled.

"Why not? Bucket's been riding shotgun in the sleigh for years. He'll look adorable in the doggy Santa outfit Francine is making him. Better a first-rate dog Santa than a second-rate human."

"You're right! Why not?" Conner burst out laughing. "Some folks might be disappointed, but at least they'll get a kick out of him."

"I haven't given up on Hank. But I'm hoping I can at least count on you and Bucket."

"We'll be there with bells on! Let's hope for snow. It won't be the same if we have to pull the sled on the flatbed."

"I'm afraid it won't be the first time." Maggie's ears caught the sound of the ATV, coming from the direction of the trees.

"That would be Travis," Conner said. "He'll be here in the next few minutes. If you two want some time together, I can check out his customers and load their tree."

"Thanks, I know you're busy. I won't keep him long." Only now, as she was about to see Travis again, did Maggie realize how much she'd missed him. What had possessed her to think she could be apart from him for so long? She couldn't wait to feel his arms around her. But she didn't want to greet him with a yard full of people looking on.

"Tell him I'll be out back," she said, and walked around the house.

Moments later Travis drove into the yard with a young family in the back of the ATV and a freshly cut tree loaded on the trailer. Maggie stepped around the back corner of the house to watch as he stopped and climbed out of the vehicle.

Conner crossed the yard, touched his shoulder, and said something Maggie couldn't hear. Travis turned and saw her standing just in his sight at the corner of the house. The surprise that flashed across his face warmed into a smile. Almost running, he strode around the house to where Maggie waited and caught her in his arms.

Driven by raw emotion, their kiss was long and hard and sweet. When they finally drew apart, she looked up into his face. The weary lines and shadows there told of exhausting days and sleepless, worry-filled nights.

"Damn, but it's good to see you, Maggie," he said. "I don't think I could've lasted till Christmas."

"Conner knows my excuse for coming," she said. "But I had to see you, too."

"If you're wondering about my father, nothing's changed," he said. "I told you it was going to take time."

"It's all right. I understand." Her arms tightened around him, holding on as if she never wanted to let him go. He'd be working hard right up until Christmas, but Maggie knew she couldn't wait to be with him again. They'd already been apart too long.

"We need some quiet time," she said. "Can you come by tomorrow night? It's Sunday. You won't be open for business."

His lips brushed her forehead. "It might be late. We'll have a lot of trees to trim and cut for the week ahead. But don't worry, I'll be there."

"I'll be waiting. Now, you need to get back to work."

He walked her to her car. She smiled up at him as she slid into the driver's seat. "See you tomorrow night," she said.

"I'll be there, come hell or high water," he said.

She could see him in her rearview mirror, standing by the gate to watch her drive away. Everything was good, Maggie told herself. The Christmas tree business was growing; she had a solid backup plan for the parade; and there was reason to hope that Travis and his father might reconcile. Tomorrow night, she and Travis would get some serious time to snuggle and talk.

She had every reason to be over the moon. So why did she have this sense of a looming shadow that was about to change everything?

Chapter 15

On Sunday, Travis and his partners worked all day, trimming new trees, cutting most of them, and hauling them to the front yard for the late buyers. After darkness put a stop to their work, they sat around the kitchen table and took stock of their earnings.

So far, they'd sold 135 trees. At $30 each for most of them and $40 for the custom cuts, plus the money from the sleigh rides, the total, minus expenses, was only a few thousand dollars, far short of the rosy picture they'd imagined when they'd started.

"Well, at least we won't starve," Conner said.

"And I'll know better than to buy a fancy truck," Travis added. "But there must be some way we can make more money."

"The season isn't over." Conner drained the last of his beer. "We should have another good week, at least, especially with the trees in Hank's lot getting dry. But we can't run the sleigh without snow. That'll cut down our profits. Didn't you say you have an old hay wagon, Travis?"

Travis nodded. "It's out behind the barn. But the wagon's too wide for that back road to the trees. If we did hayrides, we'd need someplace to go. But it's a thought. Let's keep it in mind. Meanwhile, with enough snow, we could keep doing sleigh rides all through the holidays. What we really need is another big storm."

"What *I* need right now is a good night's sleep." Rush stood up and yawned. "I'll see you two in the morning." He tossed his beer can in the recycle bin and wandered off down the hall.

"Guess I'll turn in, too," Conner said. "It's early yet, but I'm beat."

"Then I hope you won't mind if I take your Jeep to town," Travis said.

Conner grinned. "So I guess you and Maggie are back on good terms. Sure. Take the Jeep, and don't you dare hurry back."

Travis whistled a tune as he washed the sawdust out of his hair and buttoned on a clean flannel shirt. He wouldn't make it to Maggie's until well after 9:00. Since they both had to work tomorrow, he wouldn't plan to stay more than an hour or two. But even the thought of holding Maggie in his arms in front of a cheerful fire was enough to warm his chilled bones.

In high spirits, he put on his coat, let Bucket inside for the night, and went out to the Jeep.

The night was clear, the stars like pinpoints of ice against a black sky. The road was bumpy with frozen slush, but the highway was dry. Coming up on his right was Hank's Hardware. Strings of Christmas lights still glowed around the tree lot, but there were no cars outside the wire fence.

Slowing down, Travis caught sight of Hank walking alone between the rows. With his head down, his leg dragging wearily, he appeared to be counting his unsold trees.

He looked so lonely and forlorn that Travis was almost tempted to pull off the road, get out of the Jeep, and go to his father. But no, he'd only start another quarrel, he told himself. Besides, he and Maggie had set aside this time to be together, and he'd already kept her waiting long enough. Eyes on the road, he kept on driving, past the Shop Mart and on into town.

Maggie's porch light was on, and there was a faint glow in her living room window. He parked on the street and strode up the walk to the front door. Not wanting to startle her, he gave a light tap instead of ringing the bell.

As if she'd been waiting right there, she opened the door at once, pulled him inside, and melted into his arms. "I was afraid you weren't coming," she murmured between kisses.

"Nothing could have kept me away." He breathed her in, filled his senses with her sweet fragrance. "It's been a long day. I'm dead on my feet. What do you say we sit down?"

She took his coat and led him to the sofa. He sank into the soft cushions with Maggie nestled against his side. The fire in the fireplace had burned down to glowing coals, but the warmth was still inviting. There were snacks on the table—chips and dip, cheese and crackers. But he was too tired to eat them. All he wanted was to hold her.

They talked for a while, small talk interspersed with kisses. Little by little, his mind began to blur. His eyelids grew heavy, and he drifted off in her arms.

"Hey, sleepyhead." She woke him with kisses. "It's after eleven. We need to get you on the road."

Travis groaned and opened his eyes. The fire was out, the room dark and cooling. "Sorry," he muttered. "I didn't come here to fall asleep."

"It's all right. I know you're tired."

"This has happened before, as I remember."

"Yes, it has. But as I remember, *I* was the one who fell asleep. Now we're even."

He put on his coat and kissed her good night. Maybe the time would come when he could kiss her good morning and make her breakfast in bed. He'd have to do it right—one didn't just shack up with a woman like Maggie. But what was he thinking? It would be a long time before he was in a position to marry any woman, let alone the classy mayor of Branding Iron.

At this hour, on a Sunday night, the streets were all but deserted. But as he pulled away from the curb, he noticed a vehicle partway down the block, leaving the curb at the same time. The strange thing was that, in the dead of night, the headlights weren't on.

As a patrolman, his first response would have

been to warn the driver. But as an ex-con, he'd lived in the shadows long enough to know better. All his prickling instincts told him he was being tailed.

Just to make sure, he drove around the block. The vehicle, which appeared to be a dark, older-model sedan, followed a half block behind him.

Nerves quivering, he turned down Main Street, hoping the street lights would give him a look at the driver. But the sedan hung back, widening the distance. All Travis could make out was a single driver with a face hidden by the lowered visor.

What did the bastard want? If he was looking for a confrontation, he was taking his time. Was the driver someone who knew him, maybe an enemy from prison? Was he armed?

Travis had never thought to ask if Conner carried a gun in his Jeep. Steering with his left hand, he opened the glove box and felt inside. Nothing. And nothing under the driver's seat.

By now he was headed out of town. He passed the Shop Mart, then Hank's Hardware, dark now except for the security lights mounted below the roof of the store. Another half mile and the car was still behind him. He thought about making a run for it on the highway. But the rugged Jeep wasn't built for speed, and the sedan could easily have a souped-up engine.

Should he cut across the fields, where the low-slung sedan would probably get stuck? He was weighing that option, looking for a gap in the road-side fence, when he realized that the sedan was no longer following him. Slowing the Jeep, he made a U-turn on the empty highway and switched the headlights on high beam. As he moved back toward town, a pair of red taillights vanished into the dark. There was no other vehicle in sight. The sedan was gone. It was almost as if he'd imagined seeing it.

He was about to shrug off the incident and drive on home when a new thought struck him. His heart slammed.

Maggie!

What if the mysterious driver had tailed him to make sure he was headed out of town, so he could go after Maggie?

Pulse galloping, he pulled off the road, yanked his phone out of his pocket, and called her number.

Maggie was getting ready for bed when her cell phone rang. When she saw Travis's name on the caller ID, her first thought was that he'd been in another late-night accident. Heart pounding, she took the call. "Are you all right?" she asked.

"Yes. Listen to me," he said. "If your doors and windows aren't locked, do it now. If the doorbell rings, don't answer it. I think you might be in danger."

"Everything's locked now. But what are you talking about, Travis? This is Branding Iron, for heaven's sake."

"Listen to me. When I left your place, a car followed me with its lights off. After I got to the highway, it was gone. I think whoever it was might have been waiting to catch you alone. I'm coming back. Stay put, and I'll be right there."

"No, wait—it's all right. I know who it is, and he's harmless." There was only one person who would be waiting outside her house in a car. Stanley Featherstone was beginning to give her the creeps, but Maggie couldn't imagine he would actually harm her.

"Who is it, Maggie? I need to have words with him."

She thought fast. The last thing she wanted was a showdown between Travis and the constable. "It's nobody you know," she lied. "Just an overprotective neighbor. I'll be fine, Travis. Now go home and get some sleep."

He hesitated. "You're sure?"

"Yes. The sheriff lives two blocks from me. If there's any trouble, all I have to do is call him. Now stop worrying and go on home. I'll see you soon."

"If you're sure. Sleep tight. Call if you need me. I love you."

Maggie laid her phone on the nightstand. She had been about to undress and get ready for bed when the call came. Now she was too agitated to sleep. Stanley had crossed one line too many. Tomorrow at work, she would give him a good dressing down and threaten to have him arrested for stalking if he didn't stop spying on her. Knowing Stanley, he would whine and play the victim. But she wouldn't buy his act. She would let him know she meant business.

Right now, if she didn't get some sleep, she'd be a wreck in the morning. Her nerves were jangling like the strings of a badly tuned banjo. Maybe a mug of warm milk and a few minutes of late-night talk show would help her unwind.

She had just taken the mug out of the microwave and settled herself in front of the TV when she heard the fire siren.

Setting the mug on the table, she jumped up, jammed her bare feet into her sneakers, and raced outside. From the front porch, she could see the column of smoke and flame blazing upward. It was coming from the south end of town, from the direction of Hank's Hardware.

With the sickness of certainty, she hurried back inside, grabbed her coat, purse, and keys, and ran for her car. Branding Iron's firefighters were all volunteer citizens. One of them roared past her in his pickup as she backed out of the driveway. More would be converging on the fire station to ride the engine to the blaze. As mayor, she wasn't required to be there, but nothing could have kept her away.

Hank's Christmas tree lot was on fire, the dry trees going up like tinder. Every time a new tree caught, the flames shot up like a Roman candle on the Fourth of July. Burning together, they made a roaring spectacle of fire, smoke, and blistering heat.

With the trees beyond saving, the firemen battled to save the store. They trained their single hose on the south wall that faced the tree lot. The vinyl siding had already begun to melt and buckle from the heat, but if they could keep the fire from spreading into the building, they would count it as a victory.

Maggie parked her car at a safe distance and walked closer, to join the people who were watching. She saw Hank, standing alone at the edge of the crowd. She moved next to him and put a comforting hand on his shoulder. "I'm so sorry, Hank," she said.

When he turned to look at her, his cheeks were wet with tears. "You know my son, Maggie," he said. "Would he do this?"

"Oh, no!" she gasped, horrified that he would even suggest such a thing. "There's no way Travis would ever stoop to this!"

Hank didn't reply. But the look he gave her told Maggie that he still had his doubts.

Travis was nowhere to be seen. Surely if he'd known about the fire, he would have come back. But the ranch was five miles out of town. If he'd driven on home after calling her, he might not have heard the siren or noticed the fire from that distance. She thought of calling him—but she knew he was tired, and there was no need. He would find out about the fire soon enough by tomorrow.

The firemen were winning the battle. By now, most of the trees had burned to ashes, and the rest were smoldering. The wall of the store, with its glass side entrance, was damaged but intact. The stock inside the store was safe.

"Will you be all right?" Maggie asked Hank as the firemen hosed everything down one last time and began to pack up their equipment.

He shrugged. "The building's insured. But not the trees. That's the way it goes, I guess." He walked away, toward his parked truck.

The sheriff was standing nearby, his hand in the pocket of his thick leather jacket. Maggie caught his attention. "Do you have any idea how this started, Ben?" she asked him.

"I won't know until the place cools down enough for me to look around. It could've been some kind of electrical short in the lights. But that's a stretch. I'd lay odds that somebody started it. It wouldn't take much. Just tossing a match or a lighted cigarette into one of those trees would be enough. A kid could've done it."

"Who called in the alarm?"

"The nine-one-one dispatcher got an anonymous tip and triggered the alarm. It must've happened right after the fire started. Otherwise, the whole store could've gone up."

"So maybe a kid, or somebody, is fooling around, starts the fire, calls for help, and runs off."

"At this point, we're all second-guessing, Maggie. I'll know more when I check it out in the morning."

Somebody called the sheriff's name, and he hurried off. People were dispersing now. Hank had already gone, and the firemen were loading the engine. Maggie glanced around for Stanley Featherstone. She didn't see him, but the fire had drawn a crowd. He could easily have come and gone without her noticing.

She wondered again whether she should call Travis. But by now he was probably asleep. He could just as well rest easily until morning to learn about the fire.

The fire engine headed back to the station.

Maggie watched the red taillights disappear up Main Street. Then she walked back to her car, drove home, and went to bed.

Travis and his partners were up early the next morning. With the students out of school for Christmas vacation, families who'd put off buying a Christmas tree were apt to do it today. Too bad the snow wasn't deep enough for sleigh rides. But at least everything else was ready.

They had just opened for business when the county sheriff's big, tan SUV pulled up to the gate and stopped. Travis's heart dropped as two men climbed out. He recognized the tall man as Sheriff Ben Marsden. The other one was Constable Stanley Featherstone. Both of them were armed.

One thing was certain. They hadn't come to buy a Christmas tree. Good Lord, what if something had happened to Maggie?

Sick with apprehension, Travis walked out to meet them.

"Sheriff," he said, ignoring Featherstone, "is something wrong?"

"You might say that." Marsden was soft-spoken, but his presence was intimidating enough. "Mr. Morgan, can you tell us where you were between eleven and eleven-thirty last night?"

Travis knew the drill, and he knew better than to ask his own questions until he'd answered the sheriff's. "I was with Maggie until after eleven— she can verify that. Then I left and drove straight home. My partners heard me come in."

Dread slammed into him. What if something had happened to Maggie after their phone call? Why hadn't he gone back instead of letting her talk him into going home? "Is Maggie all right?" he managed to ask.

At the mention of Maggie's name, Featherstone's face went florid. He appeared to be on the verge of an outburst, but he held himself in check, most likely because the sheriff had ordered him to.

"Maggie is fine," Marsden said. Travis began to breathe again until the sheriff continued. "This isn't about her. The Christmas tree lot at Hank's Hardware was burned down last night. The firemen were barely able to save the store. We have a very reliable witness who claims to have seen you set the blaze."

The cold fear that struck Travis went clear to the bone, but he knew he couldn't show it. "Then your so-called reliable witness is lying," he said. "I drove by the place about that time on my way home. There was no fire. I didn't see anybody there, and I didn't stop."

"Is there any way you can prove that?" Marsden was only doing his job, Travis told himself. It was Featherstone who would do anything to take him out.

"I was tailed by a dark sedan, from the time I left Maggie's until after I passed the hardware store. I'm guessing your so-called witness was the one driving it. Nobody else saw me. But my first thought was that somebody who meant to harm Maggie was following me to make sure I was gone. I called to warn her. But she insisted she was all right."

"Of course, she was. That was me driving!"

Featherstone spoke up in spite of the sheriff's warning look. "I was patrolling the streets, looking for kids out past curfew. When I spotted you, I wanted to make sure you weren't up to something. So yes, I followed you. And I saw you light the fire."

The bottom seemed to drop out of Travis's world. The little bastard was lying through his teeth and might have even started the fire himself. But there wasn't a shred of proof against his story. It was the word of a sworn law officer against the word of an ex-convict.

Travis could almost hear the cell door clanging shut behind him. Lord help him, he didn't have a prayer. But if he was going down, he would go down fighting.

"For the record, Sheriff, I didn't do it. The fire started *after* I passed the hardware store. Why don't you ask the constable, here, how he knew it was me? It was dark, and I was driving my partner's Jeep."

"That's an interesting question, Constable," Marsden said. "How did you know?"

Featherstone glanced at his boots. "Because his Jeep was parked outside Maggie's house. When he came outside to leave, the porch light was on. I saw him plain as day."

The sheriff's eyes narrowed. "So you were watching Maggie's house? Why?"

"To protect her. I'd warned her that this man was trouble, but she wouldn't listen. I wanted to make sure she was all right."

"But you said you were looking for curfew violators when you saw him," the sheriff said.

Featherstone blanched, but then recovered.

"Sorry for the fib. I thought it best not to bring Maggie's name into this, given her position as mayor and all."

"But I'd already mentioned Maggie," Travis said. "I mentioned her before you lied about where you saw me. You say you saw me start the fire, Featherstone. How did I start it?"

"Uh . . . with matches. You threw them through the fence, at the nearest trees. When they started to burn, you tossed the rest of the matches into the fire and drove away. That was when I called nine one one. And it's a good thing I did, or the whole store would've gone up in smoke."

At that point, Travis was about ninety percent sure Featherstone had started the fire. But so far, there was no proof against him—only the vague shadow of the lie he'd told.

"We'll get to the bottom of this later, after I've investigated the alleged crime scene," the sheriff said. "Meanwhile, Morgan, I'll be taking you in for questioning."

"Am I under arrest?" Travis had gone cold inside.

"Not yet. But I'd advise you to come back to the station with me."

"What the hell's going on?" Conner, with Rush, had come up to stand behind Travis. "This man hasn't done anything wrong. You don't have the right to take him."

"It's all right, Conner." Travis knew better than to resist. "This is just a misunderstanding. Go ahead and open for business. I'll be back as soon as I can."

But as the sheriff ushered him toward the SUV,

Travis knew that he was the leading suspect in a case of malicious arson. He had means, motive, opportunity, and no alibi. He was in trouble over his head.

As he was about to climb into the rear seat, he turned back to face his partners. "One thing," he said. "Whatever you do, for God's sake, don't tell Maggie."

Maggie was in her office, debating whether to go home for lunch or grab a snack out of the vending machine when the receptionist relayed word that the sheriff was outside. She welcomed him in. "You're looking far too serious today. Did you learn any more about the fire?"

"Some. For now, I'd like to keep the details to myself, but I did find evidence that it had been deliberately set."

Maggie felt a chill of premonition. She masked it with a smile. "Please sit down, Ben," she said. "You're making me nervous, looming over my desk like that."

"Sorry." He sank onto the edge of the chair opposite her desk. "I have what might be some embarrassing questions to ask you," he said.

"Go ahead." Her pulse clicked into a canter.

He cleared his throat. "Were you aware that Stanley Featherstone might have been spying on you?"

"Wow, where did that come from?" she joked.

"Were you, Maggie?"

"I suspected it. He's asked me out a few times. I always shrugged it off. I have no interest in him.

But when he came in here to warn me about Travis, saying that a concerned citizen had seen him coming out of my house . . . that gave me the creeps."

"So you are seeing Travis Morgan?"

The weight of the premonition deepened. "Yes. It's no secret. What's all this about, Ben?"

"Has Travis ever mentioned wanting to get even with his father for trying to harm his business?"

"No." Now Maggie was getting scared. "In fact, Conner once told me that Travis had refused to retaliate against Hank. He'd said it would only poison the well. Ben, what is this? What's going on?"

"Was Travis with you last night?"

"Yes. He dropped by after work and was so tired that he fell asleep on the sofa. I woke him around eleven, and he left. But he did call me on the way home to say that somebody was following him. He said they turned around after he passed the hardware store. And he didn't mention that the place was on fire."

"Did you notice any other vehicle nearby when he left? One that didn't belong in the neighborhood?"

"I didn't even look!" Maggie rose out of her chair, trembling. "For the love of heaven, Ben, I've always thought we were friends! Tell me what's going on!"

"All right. Sit down." He paused while she took her seat again. "Stanley Featherstone is claiming he followed Travis from your house last night and saw him set the fire."

Maggie gasped. Her head swam with disbelief.

"No! Stanley's lying! He's out to get Travis because of me!"

"That's one theory. Right now, we've got no proof either way. But we brought Travis in for questioning this morning. Stanley's story did sound fishy in spots. But Travis had means, motive, and opportunity. And whether he started the fire or not, the fact that he called you could've been a ploy to set up an alibi."

"Well, now that you've talked to me, you know that Stanley had means, motive, and opportunity as well. Ben, Travis didn't do this thing! He wouldn't! He has too much to lose. Locking him up again would kill him—and Stanley knows that."

"Travis is locked up now, in holding, until we sort this out," the sheriff said. "Arson is a serious crime, and I'm sworn to do my job. I'm sorry, Maggie, but if the guilty finger points to him, he'll be placed under arrest."

"Can I see him?"

"Travis gave specific orders that you not be allowed to see him. Sorry."

Maggie's head sagged. She fought back tears. "This is a nightmare. I love him, Ben. He would never risk what we have for a stupid act of revenge, especially if someone else was close enough to see him do it."

Ben rose and laid a gentle hand on her arm. "I'll keep that in mind, Maggie. The truth is out there somewhere, and I won't stop looking until I've found it."

Just then the receptionist buzzed Maggie's desk phone. "Hank Miller is here. Can I show him in?"

Maggie gave Ben a questioning glance. Ben nodded. He would stay.

The door opened, and Hank stumbled in, rumpled and breathless, his face the picture of distress. "I was on my way to your office, Ben, but then I saw you come in here. I hope you don't mind, Maggie. This concerns you, too."

"Sit down, Hank." Ben held out the chair where he'd been sitting. Hank shook his head.

"Thanks, I'd rather stand. Stanley Featherstone phoned me a few minutes ago. He said my boy had been arrested for burning my Christmas tree lot."

"Not arrested, just held for questioning. What else did Stanley tell you?"

"That he saw Travis set the fire last night, lighting matches and pushing them through the fence. But that's why I'm here, Ben. Stanley's lying. Travis didn't start that fire. I did!"

Chapter 16

Maggie and the sheriff stared at Hank. "So you started the fire?" Ben asked. "Tell us what happened, and you'd better sit down. You look ready to collapse."

Hank sank onto the chair, his face pale. "It was an accident," he said. "I have one of those outdoor space heaters for cold nights. When I closed shop, I forgot to turn it off. In the middle of the night, the breeze carried some dry needles into the heating element. They caught fire, blew around, and the fire spread."

Ben looked skeptical. "Did you see that happen, Hank?"

"No. But when I saw the fire, I figured it out. It may not have happened exactly like that, but I do know for sure it wasn't Travis who started it."

"Well, you'll have to come up with something better than that," Ben said. "I did an inspection of the fire scene this morning. If a metal space heater had started the fire, it would still have been there, in the ashes. It wasn't."

Hank looked frustrated. "Well, maybe you're right. One thing I do know, it wasn't Travis. If that little weasel says it was, he's lying."

Ben's eyes drilled into the old man so sternly that Maggie wanted to tell the sheriff to back off. But she knew better than to interrupt.

"How do you really know it wasn't Travis?" he demanded. "Are you sure, or do you just want it to be true?"

Hank looked ready to cry. "All right, I guess there's no other way but to tell you the truth. The store's been losing money. I hoped to make it up with the trees, like I usually do. But with the way the competition from the Christmas Tree Ranch cut into me, I knew if I didn't do something I'd lose it all. So I decided to burn the place down for the insurance. I figured if I started with the trees, it would spread to the store and take it all. But some fool came along and called the fire department. I headed out through the back of the store and joined the crowd in front."

"That's a pretty plausible story," Ben said. "So how did you start the fire?"

"I set a couple of Ready Lite charcoal briquettes next to the trees and fired them up. I figured that way, before the trees caught, I'd have time to get out of the way. Then I cut out through the store."

"And what time was that?"

"Can't say I checked. Eleven-fifteen, maybe."

"And you didn't see anybody? Any vehicles?"

"No."

It was all Maggie could do to keep from stepping in. The upright lawman she'd known and respected since childhood was destroying this harmless, kindhearted man, and she didn't understand why. She was about to speak up when Ben did something unexpected. Turning away from Hank, he found a piece of notepaper, scrawled something on it, and passed it across Maggie's desk. Puzzled, she read just two words.

Trust me.

Trust him? Did she have a choice?

"Stand up and turn around, Hank," Ben said. "I'm placing you under arrest for arson with intent to commit insurance fraud." As he recited the Miranda rights, he unhooked the handcuffs from his belt and placed them around Hank's wrists. A tear ran down Hank's cheek, but he held his head high as Ben led him out of the room and back toward the jail, leaving Maggie in a state of shock.

Travis had been in the holding cell less than two hours, but his nerves were crawling. His body was clammy with sweat. Those three years he'd spent behind bars had been the worst hell of his life, and now he was facing them again—this time for a crime he hadn't committed. As a convicted felon charged with a second offense, nobody would believe his story, and he would get no mercy from any judge or jury.

And everything he would lose—his friends, his ranch, his new business, and a woman he could love forever—even the thought was enough to break his heart.

Flanked by a deputy, Stanley Featherstone walked up to the bars. His narrow rat face wore a self-satisfied smirk. "The sheriff wants you brought to the interrogation room. I'm guessing it's time for you to be charged and booked. Good luck, Morgan."

"Shut up, Featherstone," Travis growled as the deputy unlocked the cell door. "I may have to be here, but I sure as hell don't have to listen to you."

The deputy escorted Travis and the constable down the hall to the interrogation room and opened the door. Travis stepped inside, looked across the table, and gasped as if he'd been kicked in the gut. Sitting next to the sheriff was Hank—his father—in handcuffs.

"Come in and sit down, Morgan," the sheriff said. "You, too, Constable. You're part of this. Deputy, please take the constable's weapon. Then you may go and close the door."

Hank kept his gaze lowered. He didn't look up as Travis sat down across from him, still stunned by the sight of his handcuffed father. Featherstone, who'd surrendered his pistol without protest, sat at the foot of the table, looking uncomfortable.

The sheriff cleared his throat and spoke. "Hank Miller has confessed to setting the fire that burned his own tree lot and damaged his store. He's been arrested and charged with arson, with intent to commit insurance fraud."

"I'll be damned!" The constable chuckled out loud. Travis caught his breath, reeling as the implications struck him. His father's confession would clear him of all charges. But this wasn't making sense. If Hank had started the fire, why would

Featherstone bother to lie about it? And Hank? Had he actually done this crazy thing, or was he lying, too?

Why would he lie about committing such a serious crime?

The only possible answer to that question sent a dagger through Travis's heart.

He couldn't let this stand. The only way to resolve the situation was to find the truth. "Sheriff, something's wrong here," he said. "My father wouldn't do this."

"Hold your horses. I'm not finished," the sheriff said. "There's just one problem with Hank's so-called confession. The evidence I found when I went through the crime scene tells me he's lying. The fire was started using an accelerant—most likely gasoline. It was splashed through the front of the locked fence, from the outside and trailed on the ground, where it was lit. Hank claimed he was inside the fence when he started the fire, and that he used charcoal to get the blaze going."

The sheriff took his key and unlocked Hank's handcuffs. "Good story, Hank. Now let's get to the truth."

Hank was shaking, still unable to raise his eyes. Travis stared at his father, a lump rising in his throat. There was only one reason Hank would make a false confession about starting the fire—to save his son from a second prison term. The gesture was so rich in love that Travis felt a rush of tears. The sheriff didn't stop him when he reached across the table and clasped his father's hand.

"We're not finished here," the sheriff said. "There are two versions of our story left, and only one of them is true. Travis Morgan here claims he drove past the store before the fire started and didn't notice anything except that somebody was following him.

"The constable claims to have seen Morgan start the fire. But what I'm wondering is, why would Morgan get out of his vehicle and start a fire if he knew that somebody was watching—especially if that somebody was close enough to see him lighting matches, as Featherstone claimed? And why wouldn't the constable, as an officer of the law, have honked or yelled—tried to stop him in some way—instead of waiting till the fire was blazing to call nine one one?"

He turned toward Featherstone where he sat at the end of the table. "Maybe you can answer those questions, Constable. And maybe you can tell us what my deputy will find when he gets a warrant to search your car."

Stanley Featherstone's cocky expression crumpled. He made a move as if to jump out of his chair and flee, but he had no place to go. He had been trapped by his own ill-thought-out lies.

The sheriff summoned his deputy in to cuff Featherstone and take him out. In a way, it was hard not to feel sorry for the little man, who had so many strikes against him. But Travis figured he'd manage.

"You two are free to go, with all charges dismissed," the sheriff told Travis and Hank. "You can pick up your personal effects at the front counter."

Travis and his father faced each other in the hallway. Their handshake dissolved into an awkward but heartfelt hug. They had some distance to go on their way to a comfortable father and son relationship. But they'd taken the first step.

They came out through the sliding glass doors into the parking lot—and into the joyous arms of Maggie and Francine, who'd gotten word of what was happening. With everybody talking at once, the story slowly came out.

"This is a real Christmas miracle!" Francine exclaimed. "You've got a helper to run the store for now, Hank, so you won't need to get right back. I say we all go celebrate with a meal at that great steak house on the way to Cottonwood Springs. My treat!"

"Great, but I'll be a minute or two," Travis said. "I need to make a phone call."

"And I want to talk to the sheriff," Maggie said. "It won't take long."

"We'll be in my car," Francine said.

Travis stepped away from the others and made a call to his partners. They would be waiting for news—it was good, thank heaven. But Travis also had an idea. He could only hope they would agree and help him carry it out.

Maggie caught Ben outside his office. "I had a feeling you'd be looking for me," he said. "Come on in."

He ushered her into his office and offered her the chair opposite his desk. "I think you know what I'm going to ask you," she said.

"Ask me anyway." His smile showed an appealing dimple.

"How did you work this? And why did you arrest

Hank if you knew up front that he was innocent? I want the whole story."

"Luck played a part in it," he said. "At first, I thought Travis was a legitimate suspect. He and Hank were competing for business, they'd had words, and Travis was in the vicinity that night, with no alibi. That was why I brought him in.

"But the more I thought about Stanley's story, the fishier it sounded. Like, why didn't he try to stop Travis from setting a fire? And the part about him spying on your house—that tipped me off that something wasn't right."

"I know. That was creepy. I still get shivers when I think about it," Maggie said. "But what about Hank?"

Ben chuckled. "Pure, dumb luck! I was planning to sit down with Travis and Stanley face to face and compare their stories. Then Hank walked into your office and confessed. He was the wild card I couldn't resist playing."

"But if you knew he was innocent, why did you arrest him?"

"It gets a little personal here. You know I'm married to Francine's daughter, so I was aware of the relationship between Hank and his son, and that Hank wanted to reconcile, but Travis would have none of it. I knew what it took for Hank to make that false confession to save his son, and I wanted to make sure Travis knew it. There was no risk involved. By then I knew Travis wasn't guilty. And I would never have tried to prosecute Hank."

"Which was why you wrote me that note. I really could trust you."

"Yup." He grinned.

Maggie rose from the chair. "Thanks for sharing. I've got to go now, but one more thing, Ben."

"What?"

Maggie laughed. "Remind me never to play poker with you."

"And I've got one more thing for you," Ben said.

"Oh? What's that?"

"You've got a damned good man there. You might want to think about keeping him."

She did have a good man, Maggie reflected as she rode next to Travis in the cushy backseat of Francine's big, red Buick. His arm was around her shoulders, his hand clasping hers as if he never wanted to let go. She didn't have to think about keeping him. She'd already made up her mind.

The four of them were in a festive mood as they drove to the restaurant. Christmas music was playing on the radio. Francine and Hank were singing along—Hank in a mellow baritone that sounded almost professional. He would make such a wonderful Santa, Maggie thought. Maybe he would say yes the next time she asked him. Maybe he would even offer. It might not hurt to wait a day or two before asking, in case he wanted to volunteer. Or maybe she should ask Francine to give him a nudge.

After feasting on the best prime rib in the county and pie that was almost as good as Buckaroo's, they drove home. "I can drop you off at your office, Maggie," Francine said. "I'll drive you out to your ranch, too, Travis. I've been wanting to see what you and your partners have done with the place."

"That would be great, thanks," Travis said. "But can you wait and let Maggie off on your way back? There's something I want her to see."

"Sure," Francine said. "Is that all right with you, Maggie?"

"No problem. I've got a two-thirty meeting, but there's plenty of time. Besides, I feel like a teenager on a date back here."

Francine giggled. "Hey, you can even go ahead and neck. I won't mind."

"That can wait." Maggie gave Travis a playful wink. "What is it you want me to see?"

Travis answered her in a whisper. "It'll be a surprise—a good one, I hope, especially for Hank. But I won't know for sure until we get there."

They were coming into the north end of town on the highway. As they drove down Main Street, Maggie could sense Travis's restless tension. Whatever he was waiting for, it must matter a great deal to him.

They passed Shop Mart on the way out of town. Now they were coming up on the hardware store. Travis leaned forward and touched Francine's shoulder. "Stop here," he said.

Francine pulled the Buick off the highway in front of the store. Maggie heard Hank gasp.

The burned-out Christmas tree lot had been swept clean. Rush and Conner were busy stocking it with the lush, green Christmas trees they'd brought with the Jeep and trailer. They grinned and waved as the car stopped, then went back to work.

Hank climbed out of the car. He seemed to have

something in his eye. "What is this?" he demanded in a shaky voice. "You know I can't pay you for these trees."

Travis came over to stand beside him. "That's not the idea. We're not selling you these trees. We're offering you a partnership—fifty cents on the dollar for every tree you sell out of this lot."

"A partnership?" Hank blinked in disbelief.

"For as long as you want it. No more paying for trees off a truck. You can sell ours and split the profits with us. Everybody wins, including the customers."

"And you can pass out a coupon for a free sleigh ride with every tree—to use when it snows." Conner had come over to shake Hank's hand.

Rush did the same. "*If* it snows," he added.

They looked up at the cheerless winter sky and shook their heads. The snow from the last storm had melted. The ground was bare, the sky unpromising.

Maggie shared their disappointment. White Christmases were magical in Branding Iron. But they were all too rare. Most years the townspeople had to make do with brown earth, yellow grass, bare trees, and Santa's sleigh on a flatbed. It appeared that this year would be no different.

She glanced at her watch. It was almost 2:30. "I need to get back for my meeting," she said. "Do you mind taking me now, Francine?"

"Go ahead, Francine," Travis said. "I'll be staying here to help set up."

Maggie blew him a kiss and followed Francine to her car. Both women were in high spirits as they drove back into town. "I had a feeling everything would work out all right," Francine said. "It just took a little time and patience."

"And some help from your very smart son-in-law," Maggie added. "Ben was unbelievable. But we still don't have our Santa for the parade this weekend—unless we just want to go with Bucket."

Francine laughed. "You leave that to me, honey. I can be *very* persuasive when I put my mind to it."

Maggie's meeting, a line-item budget review for the next year, which was just like last year's, seemed to drag on forever. She tried not to remind herself that she was only here as a courtesy. All she really needed to do was sign the budget when it came across her desk.

Now it was almost 4:30. They had at least half an hour to go, and Maggie wasn't the only one stifling a yawn.

The plate glass window of the conference room looked out on Main Street. As the budget chairman's voice droned on, she gazed out at the bare trees and darkening sky.

Christmas lights, strung between the lampposts, swayed and danced in the wind. Was a storm moving in? Or was it just another dry cold front that would pass before the night was over, leaving nothing behind?

A single, fluffy speck of white drifted past the window. Maggie held her breath, wishing like a child, as another, then another, then more swirled against the glass like the flakes in a snow globe—a beautiful snow globe as big as the sky.

"Earth to Maggie." The budget chairman's teasing voice caught her attention. She blinked herself back to the present.

"Maggie, it's been moved and seconded that we adjourn until tomorrow, so we can get home ahead of the storm. All in favor say 'aye.'"

"Aye!" Maggie was on her feet, dashing back to her office to grab her coat and purse. Right now, there was only one place she wanted to be.

Snowflakes caught in her hair as she flew down the sidewalk to her car and flung herself inside. The big Lincoln was solid on the road, with good tires. Still, eager as she was, she willed herself not to speed. Last month, when she'd slammed into Travis's gatepost, the icy slip had changed her life. But she didn't want to change anybody else's life on the highway.

When she pulled up to the hardware store, people were already stopping to buy the fresh trees. Christmas music was playing, and the hot chocolate table had been set up next to the building. Hank was hanging a hastily lettered sign next to the gate. The sign read:

CHRISTMAS TREE RANCH
FRESH TREES $30
FREE HOT CHOCOLATE

It took Maggie a moment to spot Travis. He was on the far side of the lot, mounting the last few yards of six-inch wire mesh between the metal posts to replace the old fire-damaged fence.

She climbed out of the car and ran around the outside of the fence to where he stood. Snow swirled around him as he dropped his tools and caught her close, swinging her off the ground before he set her down again. She filled her gaze with him. The cold wind had reddened his cheeks. Snow coated his hair, brows, and lashes. "What is it?" he asked her. "What are you looking at?"

"I'm looking at the man I love and thinking that I could never get enough of seeing you like this," she said.

"And I feel the same way about you, Mayor Maggie." He bent down and kissed her. Snow swirled around them as they held each other tight.

"Hey, look at them!" a childish voice piped from somewhere inside the fence.

Flushed and breathless, they broke apart. Travis laughed as he handed her some pliers and a handful of metal clips. "Here," he said. "Make yourself useful."

In Branding Iron, the last Saturday before Christmas was the biggest day of the year. No matter what the weather, the celebration started at 10:00 AM sharp with the Christmas parade down Main Street. It ended that night in the high school gym with the Cowboy Christmas Ball.

In recent years, the celebration had grown. The two big high schools in Cottonwood Springs now sent their marching bands to join Branding Iron High's small group. Businesses contributed floats and antique cars for celebrities and politicians. Local riding clubs came with their horses. The Badger Hollow Boys, who furnished the music for the ball, always rode in the back of a 1937 Ford pickup. But the star of the parade was always Branding Iron's own Santa in his beautiful sleigh.

For every year in recent memory, that Santa had been Abner Jenkins. This year there would be someone new.

Today's weather was perfect for a Christmas parade. The storm, which had left nearly a foot of snow, had passed two days ago, giving work crews time to clear the roads and sidewalks. The sky was clear, the sunlight dazzling on the diamond-bright snow.

The crowds began gathering nearly an hour ahead of time, everyone hoping to get a good spot for parade viewing. In the past, Maggie had usually ridden in one of the antique cars with the visiting dignitaries. This year she had begged off. She wanted to watch her beloved parade from the sidelines, with Travis.

Travis, too, had bowed out of the parade. He'd left the sleigh driving to Conner, the only one with the skill to handle the big Percherons amid the crowds and noise. Rush would sit next to him on the driver's bench to troubleshoot and toss treats to the kids.

Happy to the bone, Maggie clasped Travis's hand as they strolled along the crowded sidewalk. Everywhere she looked, she saw folks she knew. Ben was there with his wife, accompanied by Francine, who was holding her little granddaughter, Violet. Travis's neighbor, Jubal, gave her a friendly wave as he ushered his wife, Ellie, and their two children through the crowd. Now she caught sight of Katy and Daniel, holding hands. Silas and Connie walked behind them, trying not to hover too closely. And there were so many others—her people, her town, and her man. She was on top of the world.

The parade was flowing past them now. Because they were both tall, Maggie and Travis moved back to let the children and shorter folks stand in front of them. The cars, floats, horses, and bands made a festive sight, but Maggie could sense the anticipation as the grand procession neared its end.

"Where's Santa Claus?" A little girl in front of them tugged at her mother's hand.

"He's coming soon," her mother said. "Just wait."

"Will he be the real Santa?" the little girl asked. "The one in the mall was fake. I could tell. He didn't look one bit jolly. He just looked tired."

"I'll tell you what," her mother said. "When Santa's sleigh comes by, you take a really good look and let me know if he's real."

"Okay!" The little girl jumped up and down, trying to see if the sleigh was coming.

Travis nudged Maggie. "We've got an expert here," he whispered. "I can't wait to hear what she has to say."

"I just hope she won't be disappointed." Maggie's heart skipped as the sleigh came into sight, gliding like magic on its runners behind the majestic Percherons. Brass bells jingled on their harnesses as they walked along at an easy clip over the packed snow.

The little girl was still jumping up and down. "I see him! There he is! Look—he's got a funny dog with him—a dog in a Santa suit!"

"But is he the real Santa?" her mother asked.

The little girl paused, but only for an instant. "Yes! Look at him! He's so happy! He's the real Santa! I can tell!"

She waved her hands. Hank waved back at her. At that moment he was, as the little girl had said, the real Santa, perfect in every detail. Bucket sat next to him in his costume, head up, tail wagging, loving the attention.

Travis glanced down at Maggie. "Good Lord, woman, you're crying! Are you all right?"

Maggie smiled and wiped her eyes. "I'm sorry. This happens to me every year. You'll just have to get used to it."

His arm tightened around her. "Yes," he said. "I plan to."

The Cowboy Christmas Ball that night was as grand and festive as it had ever been. The tree in the high school gym glowed with its traditional lights and ornaments. The buffet table groaned under the weight of donated hams, casseroles, breads, salads, and dazzling desserts. A crystal fountain, resplendent on its own table, poured cascading streams of sparkling red punch.

The Badger Hollow Boys were in fine form, the dancers and merrymakers looking like something out of an Old West movie in their party finery. This was a magical night—a night to celebrate the blessings of friends and family, a night of feasting, fun, and Christmas spirit.

For Maggie, the most magical thing of all was being on the dance floor, in Travis's arms. She could feel his possessive pride and see the love in his eyes as he held her. She didn't mind a bit that people were looking at them. She could imagine them saying, *Well, it looks like Maggie's finally caught herself a man. It's about time!*

Francine and Hank sat on the sidelines, holding hands. Hank didn't dance. But Maggie knew that Francine would be itching to get out on that dance floor and that Hank would enjoy watching her. She gave Travis a smile. "I need to play mayor and do some meeting and greeting. Would you be a sweetheart and ask Francine to dance? She'll enjoy it, and so will you. Maybe your friends can give her a few twirls around the dance floor, too. I warn you, she's one hot dancer!"

"I already figured that." He gave her a wink and a grin as she slipped out of his arms. Then he turned and strode over to where Francine sat, fresh from the beauty shop and looking spectacular in her red satin saloon-girl dress.

At the edge of the dance floor, Maggie paused to catch her breath and look around. Conner was surrounded by a clutch of high school girls who were teaching him fancy dance steps. Rush was alone. He was gazing around the gym as if searching for someone he couldn't find. But the looks that some of the women were giving him told Maggie he wouldn't be alone for long.

From where she stood, she could see Katy and Daniel on the dance floor, lost in each other's eyes. Katy looked adorable, wearing a dress that matched her blue eyes and a dreamy smile that seemed to light up the whole gym. The little friendship ring sparkled like a diamond on her finger.

Daniel made a handsome and gallant cowboy in jeans, boots, and a leather vest.

Connie and Silas stood nearby, as if keeping a protective eye on their daughter. Maggie moved to their side. "Can I take it that your supper went all right?" she asked.

Connie gave her a tentative smile. "He's a nice boy. And his family is nice, too. They're as concerned as we are. But what can we do?"

"I haven't met Daniel's family," Maggie said. "Are they here?"

"No," Connie said. "His mother is in a wheelchair from a car accident years ago. It's hard for her to get out, and her husband doesn't like leaving her except for work. They have an older daughter, too, who's grown up and lives in California."

Maggie watched Katy and Daniel a moment longer. "They really do make a lovely couple," she said.

Connie nodded. "I know. But in this big, uncertain world, I can't help being scared for them."

Maggie squeezed her hand in a gesture of understanding before she moved on to greet other people she knew. She moved from one friend to another, feeling the warmth of community around her. Her people. Her little town.

And now the man she loved was coming through the crowd to claim her again.

Epilogue

New Year's Eve, the same year . . .

Maggie hadn't put up a tree in her house in years. Either she'd been too tired, too busy, or both.

But this year was different.

Travis had come with the tree on Christmas Eve and insisted they decorate it together. He had even climbed up into the cobweb-infested crawl-space under the roof to find her mother's old box of Christmas decorations. What kind of man would do that for his woman?

Now, on New Year's Eve, the tree stood in front of the window, glowing with the lights and ornaments she remembered from her childhood. Snuggled with Travis on the sofa, she watched the old-fashioned lights twinkle on and off. It was almost midnight. Tomorrow, sadly, she would be taking the lights down, boxing the decorations, and putting the tree outside before going back to work the next day.

"I'd forgotten how lovely it could be, having a Christmas tree at home," she said. "Thank you again for bringing it to me and helping decorate. I wish I could leave it up forever—in fact, I wish this whole crazy holiday could last longer."

"It's been crazy all right." His arm tightened around her shoulders. "But we made some good memories. I almost lost it when you took off your coat and walked into the Christmas ball in that gorgeous green western gown. It was like having a queen on my arm. I knew every man in the room must be envious of me."

Maggie laughed. "And I loved the reaction of the single women when Conner and Rush walked in. I guarantee you, those two aren't going to be lonely for long. It's going to be an interesting year."

"And a busy year for both of us." Travis brushed a kiss across her nose. "How are we going to manage this, Mayor Maggie, with me building a ranch and you running a town? I'm already jealous of every minute I can't spend with you."

"We'll find time. We'll find time because we matter, and because what we have is too good to let go." Maggie knew better than to rush things. They both needed time to get to know each other and work out the details of their busy lives. Right now, she only knew that she was head over heels in love with this man, and that wasn't about to change.

"That works for me," he said. "But only for now. This is wonderful, but damn it, it isn't enough."

She lifted her face for his kiss. As their lips met, they could hear the sound of bells, horns, and exploding fireworks outside. It was midnight.

"Happy New Year," she whispered.

Read on for an excerpt from Janet Dailey's next
Tylers of Texas novel, coming soon.

TEXAS FREE

*She's a woman with a burning need to break free
from her past . . .*

Rose Landro is on the run. Seeking refuge at the
Rimrock Ranch, she is finally ready to claim the
land her granddaddy left her and make a fresh
start. But her return is rife with controversy when
cattle begin disappearing—and a handsome
menace named Tanner McCade starts watching
Rose a little too closely. Could the new cowhand
be connected to the men she's hiding from? Or
is there another reason the rugged stranger is
shadowing her every move?

He's a man ready to fight boldly for his future . . .

There's a secret in Rose Landro's eyes, a mystery
that Special Ranger Tanner McCade is
determined to uncover. Even if the beauty isn't
behind the cattle rustling he's investigating, she's
way too skittish, and all too exquisite for Tanner
to just let slide past his piercing gaze. Then he
discovers a vulnerability in Rose that has him
aching to protect her—and longing to
possess her. . . .

The Mexican village slumbered under the light
of a waning crescent moon. In the empty plaza,
windblown shadows flickered over the cobblestones.
The cantina was closed for the night, its outdoor
tables and chairs locked away behind corrugated
metal doors. A bat fluttered from the tower of the
old adobe church and melted into darkness. A
skinny dog foraged for leavings in the deserted
marketplace.

The night was almost peaceful. But the stillness
was heavy with tension—especially in one small
adobe house on a dusty side street. Nothing in Río
Seco was the way it had been before the Cabrera
cartel took over the town. And for Rose Landro,
after tonight, nothing would be the same again.

The click of a boot heel on the tiled patio startled Rose to full alertness. Lying fully dressed in

the dark, she checked the impulse to sit up, fling aside the covers, and bolt out of bed. She was a small woman. Face-to-face, she'd be no match for the burly intruder who was stalking her. Her only chance of survival lay in surprise.

The loaded Smith and Wesson .44 was a cold lump under her pillow. As footsteps clicked across the patio, she closed her hand around the grip, cocked the hammer, and slid to the floor. Her free hand bunched the pillows into a semblance of her sleeping body and covered them with the blanket.

She knew who was coming for her. Lucho Cabrera, younger brother of the local cartel boss, was built like a short pile of bricks. He wore high-heeled cowboy boots to make him appear taller. The sound of those boots, clicking across the kitchen, chilled Rose's blood.

Gripping the heavy pistol, she crawled across the floor and pressed upward to stand against the wall, in the shadows behind the door. Her breath came in shallow gasps. Her pulse hammered in her ears.

The cartel would kill anyone who stood against them. They had already murdered Ramón and María Ortega, who'd taken Rose into their home twelve years ago. Rose would have fled for her life before now, but she could not leave without avenging the couple who'd cared for her like their own daughter.

Honor. The Ortegas had lived by that code. Now it was Rose's turn to carry on the tradition.

The footsteps were coming closer. Would Lucho stand in the doorway and fire at the lump in her bed, or did the sadistic pig plan on raping her first, as he'd done two months earlier when he'd caught her walking home alone after dark?

At the memory of his filthy, sweating body, her finger tightened on the trigger. If ever a man deserved killing, it was Lucho Cabrera. Only his older brother, Refugio, was worse.

The bedroom door creaked open. Rose held her breath as Lucho stepped into the room, his pistol drawn. The faint moonlight, falling through the high, barred window, cast black shadows across his fleshy face. As he neared the bed, he holstered the gun. One hand fumbled with his belt buckle. *Good.* This was almost too easy. She could shoot him now, in the back. But something in her wanted more. She wanted him to see her. When the bullet tore into his body, she wanted him to know who had fired it.

She forgot to breathe. Every muscle was a coiled spring as she waited for the right moment.

"Brujita fea . . ." he muttered. The name, given to Rose because of the birthmark on her face, meant "ugly little witch." Over the years she'd learned to bear it with a measure of pride. Superstitious people tended to fear her, especially some of the men. But that wouldn't stop Lucho. He might even be planning to take a trophy back to his brother—an ear, a hand, or even her head—as proof of his bravery.

Still muttering, he loosened his trousers and jerked back the blanket. That was when he realized he'd been tricked. He spun around, cursing as Rose stepped out of the shadows, the .44 gripped between her hands.

"Muera, pendejo. Die, you bastard," she said, aiming the heavy revolver at his chest.

Lucho had no time to draw his weapon, but in the instant her finger tightened on the trigger, he lunged for her. The pistol roared, but Lucho's move had thrown off her aim. The bullet struck his right shoulder, barely slowing the brute's charge.

Slammed by the recoil, Rose staggered backward. Her feet tangled in the loose rug on the floor. Losing her balance, she went down hard, landing on one arm.

She managed to keep a one-handed grip on the gun, but now he was standing over her, blood streaming down his sleeve. She could hear the hiss of his breath between his teeth as he reached for his holster, then paused, cursing. That was when Rose realized her shot had disabled his shooting arm. The flicker of distraction as he switched to draw with his left hand gave her the only chance she had left.

She cocked the .44 and pulled the trigger.

More from Bestselling Author
JANET DAILEY

Calder Storm	0-8217-7543-X	**$7.99US/$10.99CAN**
Close to You	1-4201-1714-9	**$5.99US/$6.99CAN**
Crazy in Love	1-4201-0303-2	**$4.99US/$5.99CAN**
Dance With Me	1-4201-2213-4	**$5.99US/$6.99CAN**
Everything	1-4201-2214-2	**$5.99US/$6.99CAN**
Forever	1-4201-2215-0	**$5.99US/$6.99CAN**
Green Calder Grass	0-8217-7222-8	**$7.99US/$10.99CAN**
Heiress	1-4201-0002-5	**$6.99US/$7.99CAN**
Lone Calder Star	0-8217-7542-1	**$7.99US/$10.99CAN**
Lover Man	1-4201-0666-X	**$4.99US/$5.99CAN**
Masquerade	1-4201-0005-X	**$6.99US/$8.99CAN**
Mistletoe and Molly	1-4201-0041-6	**$6.99US/$9.99CAN**
Rivals	1-4201-0003-3	**$6.99US/$7.99CAN**
Santa in a Stetson	1-4201-0664-3	**$6.99US/$9.99CAN**
Santa in Montana	1-4201-1474-3	**$7.99US/$9.99CAN**
Searching for Santa	1-4201-0306-7	**$6.99US/$9.99CAN**
Something More	0-8217-7544-8	**$7.99US/$9.99CAN**
Stealing Kisses	1-4201-0304-0	**$4.99US/$5.99CAN**
Tangled Vines	1-4201-0004-1	**$6.99US/$8.99CAN**
Texas Kiss	1-4201-0665-1	**$4.99US/$5.99CAN**
That Loving Feeling	1-4201-1713-0	**$5.99US/$6.99CAN**
To Santa With Love	1-4201-2073-5	**$6.99US/$7.99CAN**
When You Kiss Me	1-4201-0667-8	**$4.99US/$5.99CAN**
Yes, I Do	1-4201-0305-9	**$4.99US/$5.99CAN**

Available Wherever Books Are Sold!

Check out our website at **www.kensingtonbooks.com**.